# Tiny Seedlings

### ... their journey

Book One in the Trilogy
The Trees of Etainia

# Tiny Seedlings

## ... their journey

By
J. A. Fitzsimmons

Cover Design: Jasper Stone Collections © 2009
Book production by Fishead Design Studio & Microgallery, San Antonio, Texas

ISBN-10:  0-615-26568-5
ISBN-:13:  978-0-615-26568-1
Library of Congress Control Number: 2009910269

Printed in the United States of America
First Edition

*T*here is a vast land known as Etainia. It is an Ancient Land made up of different countries, unlike any place that has ever existed. In between great rivers, seashores and lakes, which are miles and miles apart, are cities, towns, and villages. Throughout Etainia are large and small countryside's, forests, hillsides, swamplands and desert lands. Within these lands are mystical creatures living in hidden and undiscovered places. Within these lands are events waiting to happen and mysteries yet to unfold. Within these lands are seasons with magical days and nights, where Time and Colors speak.

You are about to journey into a place where the elements, plants and animals have a voice and where known and unknown creatures roam about. The war between what is good and what is evil exists on many different levels. *The Soil of the Earth and The Sun of Splendor,* work closely together as the Trees in Etainia search for their purpose and identity in life.

One of the lands in Etainia is called Cordaya Valley. Five tiny tree seedlings will be born there. Each seedling will have challenges to face, incredible obstacles to overcome and encounters of strange yet awesome adventures- . . . adventures that will uncover and reveal many hidden truths.

As you travel with the five tiny seedlings, you will be enraptured by their individual personalities. You will walk with them through their experiences as they search for unknown futures, hoping to fulfill their dreams. You will feel their pain and excitement as each one seeks their own unique Destiny and Purpose in life. And somewhere during your journey, you may even see yourself.

# Chapter I

# The Land of Etainia

Throughout the vast and widespread Land of Etainia, The Soil of the Earth waits patiently to feel the tapping of tree roots upon her soil, hoping that some young tree will find its Destiny Land. High in the sky, The Sun of Splendor periodically releases thin vapors of his Amber light, signaling to The Soil of the Earth that he too is waiting and hoping. These two powerful mystical entities wait and work together on behalf of all the trees in Etainia. For this is a land where trees live and trees rule.

Some of the trees choose to remain permanently rooted in the ground where they were born. Those trees will never grow past six feet. Some trees are travelers, desiring to root just about anywhere on their own. Many trees in Etainia are considered outcasts because they are sickly, ugly or deformed - some of the little seedlings are unwanted by their parents. Of course, there are some trees that never root into the soil at all – they are the Wanderers.

Then, there are the trees that believe they have a unique purpose in Etainia. They are the Seekers, those who are searching for their Destiny Land and the community that they are meant to reside in. This is no easy task by any means. While not all of them want to, some of those trees also become Overseer Trees, which are the trees with the most authority, responsibility and power.

The Soil of the Earth and The Sun of Splendor are constantly looking for noble and honorable trees of good character. Once the Seeker trees think they might have found their Destiny Land, they tap on the ground and dig deep. Then they wait to see if The Soil of the Earth will accept their roots. If she doesn't accept them, the trees continue traveling in search of their Destiny Land.

If The Soil of the Earth does accept their roots – the ground that holds her rich soil will burst open and the individual tree will send its roots down. After that, both tree and soil must wait to see if The Sun of Splendor will approve of their union. If he doesn't, the roots must be released and the trees will continue on with their search. If he does approve of the union, his Amber Rays of Light will push through the atmosphere and surround both tree and soil with blankets of life-giving energy – confirming the connection.

Once this happens, the trees are assured that they have found their Destiny Land and place of residence. Usually, within moments of this experience, and sometimes instantly, the trees are allowed to grow past their six-foot limit. As they stretch higher, their roots will dig deeper, attaching themselves into the Soil of the Earth. Her fertile soil will only release their roots in cases of emergency or extremely important circumstances. A few of the Elite Overseer Trees are granted the privilege to move at will and adjust their height when necessary. But this is indeed rare.

## Cedra

Cedra was a young two-year-old Cedar tree seedling. She had come from the East. Her parents sent her off to travel across Etainia to find her Destiny Land. While traveling, Cedra faced many obstacles and battles, but one by one, she overcame them. The scars on her trunk and limbs were evidence of the long treacherous journey she had been on. She had persisted in her search and even attempted to settle in three different lands along the way – but the Soil of the Earth did not allow it. By the time she reached the outskirts of

Cordaya Valley, she stood about five and a half feet tall. Like most trees in Etainia, Cedra was born with two branch arms and hands, two intertwined tree trunk legs and branch feet – and would only grow up to six feet tall until firmly rooted into the soil.

Once Cedra's roots touched the rich, fertile soil in Cordaya Valley, she knew she belonged. As she walked, she noticed a close-knit group of over two hundred Cedar trees that had already settled into the community. She went near them and began searching for just the right spot. She discovered an area with a large amount of space around her and began to unravel her tree trunk legs in order to dig her roots deep, deep into the ground. While digging, she felt the Soil of the Earth break open wide to accept her roots. As earth and roots joined together - the unified connection went even deeper into the soil. They waited. Soon, the Sun of Splendor shone his Amber rays of light upon them, confirming and sealing her Destiny Land. Cedra found her place. Cedra found her future. Now she would allow the environment around her to get used to the idea that she was here to stay. As she settled in, she also knew that one day she would give birth to her own tree seedlings and that they too would travel through many lands to search for their unique Destiny Land.

Within a few weeks, Cedra grew to over twenty-five feet tall. Her branches reached higher and farther out than most of the others. She had long, massive branches that the animals loved. She was a safe dwelling place for many forest creatures. The birds felt secure and safe enough to build their nests within her limbs. The Ladybug families often nestled on her branches, flying in and out during the day, while several deer families visited in the afternoons under the dwelling of her shade. There was a large stream below her where several of the animals gathered after dinnertime. Playful squirrels often scampered throughout her branch limbs; oblivious of the pollen they were carrying on their tiny little feet.

## R.T.

R.T., a strong Cedar tree seedling, had journeyed from the West. After leaving his parents' forest, he focused entirely on finding his Destiny Land. While searching numerous lands to find his connection with the Soil of the Earth, he had walked through many severe experiences and unsightly places- acquiring several gashes on his trunk. He crossed over into Cordaya Valley a few months after Cedra had rooted. Every day he walked and searched to see if this was his Destiny Land. Off and on he would meet a female tree, but it wasn't until he noticed Cedra that he felt a deep stirring in his heart, along with a strong desire to seek out the Soil of the Earth.

Once he saw Cedra, R.T. began to move toward her. But not so close as to cause a disturbance, since she was fast asleep when he arrived. He then began to unravel and dig his roots into the soil and was happy to feel the Soil of the Earth rising up to meet him. Once his roots were secured, he knew it was only a matter of time before Destiny took place. Moments later, The Sun of Splendor sent down his magnificent rays of Amber. Time moved swiftly for R.T. and he instantly grew to his full height of over fifty feet tall.

The noises of the Earth moving and opening up woke Cedra. Feeling the presence of another tree near her, she looked up to see a handsome male cedar tree. She saw the Amber light surrounding him and knew that he was here to stay. Cordaya Valley would now be his Destiny land. As she continued looking up at him, she noticed the deep green color of his foliage and his rich, warm red-toned bark, which was free of knots. R.T. looked down and at that moment they caught the admiring looks in each other's eyes, and smiled. They instantly knew that they had found their Destiny Land with one another. Several nearby female trees began to frantically rustle their branches, trying to catch R.T.'s attention. But it was Cedra who captured his heart.

## Squeegie the Squirrel

Destiny continued to form its unique purpose between Cedra and R.T. It was several weeks later when Squeegie, one of the youngest and most active of all the squirrels in Cordaya Valley, was wandering around in a rich green forest that was far beyond the river, on the other side of the Valley. While running up a hill, he felt a light in his eyes. The Sunclouds were spreading their golden rays over the valley. As they began their timely descent of moving below the horizon, their rays of light turned orange and reminded Squeegie that it was time to return home. He reached Cordaya Valley before dark. Cedra was the home he always came back to. But this time, as he began to run through her fertile branches, he spotted something red on top of the taller male Cedar tree next to her. He raced to the edge of a strong branch and jumped into the taller tree to check it out. As he jumped, the red object, which was a cardinal, flew away. So he ran up through the tall tree, searching for another strong branch to leap from so he could get back to Cedra's branches. In the meantime, he was unmindful of the large amounts of pollen he was collecting on the bottom of his feet. The massive tree he was climbing through was R.T.

While racing through R.T.'s dark, lustrous foliage, Squeegie finally found the perfect branch to leap from. He immediately jumped high and strong, landing back on one of Cedra's long branches. As he continued to scamper playfully up, down and all around, he was unknowingly moving within Destiny, while depositing pollen throughout her foliage.

About a mile away flew a young owl nicknamed Wyo, who also lived in Cordaya Valley. Although he was young, Wyo was known throughout all of the lands within Etainia as being very wise. Some even thought he had Ancient Wisdom that was passed onto him through his grandfather's generation. Others thought his wisdom

and insight were gained from the experiences he had on various jour-
neys throughout the land of Etainia. Several of the elder trees and
grandmother animals of all species, would often share with him
some of their stories of old. Trees would go out of their way to tell
him their stories. They knew he would remember every detail and
pass them on.

Wyo rarely forgot anything. He had the unique ability to
remember the names of every tree, animal, creature, insect or plant
that he had ever met. Once his eyes fell on something or his ears
heard something, it was eternally etched into his mind. This was an
amazing mystery to all who knew him. He was well loved by almost
everyone in the land of Etainia, except for those who had dark evil
secrets.

While Wyo continued enjoying the flying exercises with his
mother Seono, he looked up and noticed the grand cedar trees in the
distance, as puffs of smoke seemed to burn from the tops of their
branches. "Looks like we'll have some new cedar tree seedlings next
spring," he said as he flew next to his mother who had stopped to
rest. "You're right son," she said softly as they both sat on a giant oak
and continued to watch the treetop pollen shoot up into the air like
little puffs of smoke.

## The Birthings

The weeks and months went by as spring gave way to summer.
Cordaya Valley was filled with its usual commotion and activity. The
summer nights were warm and inviting. The tree gossip was ram-
pant, especially when everyone noticed how well Cedra and R.T.
were getting along. He looked after her every need and bathed her
with his attention. She felt calm and complete during those days. As
Time moved on and the days changed to the Cool Season, the rabbit and raccoon families gathered around Cedra's roots at night,

lying in the soft grass to share with one another the events of the day. It was a peaceful time in Cordaya Valley, as everyone waited for the birthing of the soon-coming seedlings.

Time began to move more rapidly as the Cool Season left Cordaya Valley - moving itself into another land. Soon, the trees in the valley began to feel the budding of their branches. It was spring once again and everyone in the forest could feel it through the life-giving soil. The birthing of the seedlings was greatly anticipated. Everyone knew it was just a matter of time.

One evening the rabbit families were visiting with each other near Cedra while R.T. was taking his usual short nap. It seemed like any other typical spring evening until Cedra reached over and gently touched R.T. He knew her touch, even in his deepest sleep. He slowly woke from his slumber and gazed at her through sleepy eyes as she pointed below. He looked down and immediately jolted awake! There they were, five tiny seedlings all planted and growing in the soil between Cedra's roots. He shouted and reached out to Cedra with his long branches and pulled her close to him with a strong hug! Standing in absolute awe, they held onto each other while looking down upon their children. They saw that each seedling was different from the others, yet it was obvious that each one them also carried a unique characteristic of their parents.

News traveled fast as the rabbit family raced over to the raccoon family, and the raccoon family raced over to the squirrel family, to tell them the exciting news! Even before Grinny Green, the boisterous giant tree frog could climb the hill and ring the Cordaya Valley bell - to announce the birthings; the forest had already been alerted. Several trees, bushes, animals and seedlings were racing to come and see the tiny newborn trees. Cedra and R.T. looked down at their seedlings with pride as several animals came to congratulate them.

Wyo was one of the first to come visit. He had a special interest in these five seedlings.

"Hello Wyo" said Cedra. "Thank you so much for coming to see my family."

"Of course," he answered, "I'm delighted to see they are all doing so well! I see you have three female and two male seedlings. Now . . . you haven't named them yet – have you?"

"Oh no, not yet!" echoed R.T and Cedra together. "We're waiting to have the traditional ceremony when they turn one year old. Then, they will be given their names."

"Very good, very good," exclaimed Wyo. "That's the proper way."

Cedra smiled, "Now Wyo, you *will* be at the celebration won't you?"

Wyo jumped off the limb he was on and flew in a circle over the entire family before he took flight. "Of course I will be there and so will the whole forest!"

R.T. and Cedra smiled as they noticed their little seedlings glancing up to see where the strong breeze was coming from as Wyo's wide span of wings sent them a refreshing wind.

"See you next year little seedlings!" shouted Wyo as he left Cordaya Valley – on his way to scout out new lands and hear more ancient stories from the elders.

## The Naming Ceremony

The Colors that lived in the atmosphere changed as Time moved through the seasons. Cedra and R.T. continued to nurture the seedlings, and they grew. The days and months flew by in Cordaya Valley. Soon it was spring once again in a new dimension of Time. Cedra stretched her branches in contentment. She and R.T. were very happy and deeply in love. He was a good companion and father - very attentive and protective of his family. It was almost a year now since Cedra had given birth to the five seedlings. The two male and three female seedlings were growing quite well. The entire valley was excited because the night had finally arrived when they would be able to attend the special *Naming of Trees Ceremony*. Although Cedra was joyfully anticipating the night's events to begin, she was also a little concerned. Earlier she had noticed the thick black clouds in the sky, which were now forming over some hills far away, on higher ground. She glanced over at R. T. and smiled. She had felt his gaze for a while – she felt comforted by his attention, but didn't tell him of her concerns.

The winds began to pick up a bit, but not enough for R.T. to notice anything unusual. He went to talk to the elder trees about the ceremony. All of Cordaya Valley's inhabitants were making excitable noises while preparing for the night's celebration. Everyone was curious to find out what Cedra and R.T. named their little seedlings. The tradition was that after the Naming Ceremony each seedling would receive a rolled up scroll stating their names, their parent's names, the time they were born and the land they were born into. On the bottom of each scroll would be a seal of the insignia of the Ancient Ones of long ago. The Naming of Trees Ceremony was a tradition that had been carried on by several of the tree families for many generations.

Cedra had tucked her custom designed Treasure of Truth Box, with five scrolls inside, into a hole in her trunk. Chops, the youngest member of the Bold Beaver family, had built if for her, carving it out of a strong older Acacia Tree that had passed away. The Acacia Tree had known that he was going to die before the Naming Ceremony. He made it a point to tell Cedra that he would be honored if she used part of his tree trunk to build the Treasure of Truth Box. She assured him that she would.

Chops used Cedra's sap to set in the beautiful Amber Stone that she had given him. It was a stone handed down to her by her parents. Even when the sun wasn't shining, the Amber Stone would reflect a sunlit glow at times. When that happened, a small fire would burn on the inside of it, yet the stone itself was never hot. The fire inside symbolized that *the passion of life, would never burn out* for whoever owned the stone or wore it. Chops then designed a unique etching on the top of the box that read **"Cedra & R.T. - The Birthings."** On the opening of the outside of the box, Chops had carefully carved out a lock-hole that would only fit the left branch of Cedra's lower limb. This was her unique branch print, which made sure that she was the only one who would be able to open the authentic Treasure of Truth Box.

Loud trumpet sounds began to fill the air as four Trumpeter Birds alerted the residents of Cordaya Valley - the Naming Ceremony was about to begin! The Newsybirds then flew around the Valley from tree to tree sharing the events with others who were unable to attend. Four massive eagles began to fly in a circle high above Cedra and R.T. Their presence symbolized 'Strength and Courage' for the young seedlings.

In front of the proud parents was a ten-foot Mound of Colorful Stones that the entire forest had spent a year building just for this occasion. Four large flat pure White Stones, with a word etched into each one, were placed on the ground between Cedra and R.T. and the Mound of Colorful Stones. At the end of the ceremony, each one of the four words would be spoken out loud. Elaborate banquet tables had been designed out of some of the older trees that had fallen down in times past. Those tree tables were brought in and placed in a large circle surrounding R.T. and his family, the Mound of Colorful Stones and the White Stones on the ground. The circle was complete.

Several forest animals were scurrying and running to claim their seats. Lightening Bugs and the Lantern Fly Wing-Flashers, gathered in several sections - lighting the celebration. The Night Moon released an extra glow. Wyo looked down from the top of a nearby cedar tree. The sight of so many different animals and plant species gathering together to celebrate - warmed his heart.

As the Trumpeters' sounds began fading to a gentle whisper, a strikingly beautiful bird known as the Toucan Seer, slowly glided down and settled on top of the Mound of Colorful Stones. He looked up at the four eagles as they continued circling in the sky. Then he quickly flew down to the four White Stones and tapped his beak three times on each one. A hush ran through the crowd. He then flew to the top of the Mound of Colorful Stones. As He looked up at R.T and Cedra - his strong, clear voice rang out,

*"This night I charge R.T. and Cedra, parents of five seedlings, to call out each of their seedlings names, one by one. Let your voices join in unison and echo into the forest and throughout the surrounding lands. When the echoes of your voices subside, I will blow a Breath of Peace unto your seedlings."*

Wyo was well aware of how important the Naming Ceremony was for all the trees in Etainia. He knew the procedure well and what would happen next:

First, R.T. and Cedra would speak out their seedlings names consecutively, starting with the youngest - ending with the eldest. After the names were spoken into the air, the Breath of Peace would be blown unto the seedlings. After that, the youngest seedling was to come forward and face R.T. and Cedra by standing in the middle of the four pure White Stones, which were in front of the Mound of Colorful Stones. The other seedlings would wait their turn to come forward. All guests would be instructed to keep very still - very quiet.

R.T. and Cedra would then speak out the name of the seedling standing before them while presenting their Naming Scroll. The seedling would repeat the new name loudly - so that our of their own voice saying their name would echo and reverberate into the Soil of the Earth, the streams, through other branch trees and over the mountains into the Sun of Splendor. Once that took place, a Misty Vision would appear in the atmosphere in front of the seedling and release a unique musical sound while unveiling a brief colorful glimpse into the future.

With the sounding of their names echoing in the air and the Misty Vision waving before them, each seedling would then seal their name by proclaiming, *"I hear the music. I see the Misty Vision. I have spoken out my name. Now I will journey into my future with honor, truth, courage, kindness and love."* After that, the seedling would be allowed a few moments to observe and memorize the Vision before it rolled up into a giant air-born scroll and dissolved into the air. Shiny brightly colored particles of mist would then fall upon the seedling and dissolve into their bark. It was a profound mystery and awesome moment.

Wyo watched as Cedra looked upon her seedlings with love and admiration as she tucked the Treasure Box tightly into her roots one more time. Then, with soft eyes, she looked at R.T. They both nodded and began to call out their youngest seedlings name in unison:

**"5th born female Seedling . . . your name is Aya."**
**"4th born male seedling . . . your name is . . . ."**

Suddenly a loud deep vibrating noise, along with tremendous winds came through the land. Almost in an instant a thrashing storm was upon the forest, violently ripping at the trees. Things began to fly everywhere! Tree branches were cracking all around them. The animals of the forest scattered frantically in different directions. Some of them fled to their homes only to find them crushed by rolling boulders that had been loosened by the waters.

R.T. immediately looked toward Cedra, wanting to protect her and the seedlings. As he moved his tall branches to cover them, a strong rush of wind blew into him, forcing his branches to go back. Cedra was facing the storm and it hit her first. Instinctively she raised her limbs to shield R.T. and then twisted her body quickly to try and hinder the force of the winds. A huge boulder smashed through the bushes hitting R.T. on the front of his trunk. Even though the Soil of the Earth had immediately released him upon the impact of the boulder, R.T. was unable to pull his roots up from the ground, because the boulder had landed directly on his roots. He felt helpless and unable to cover Cedra because the impact of the fierce winds kept forcing his branches backwards. Then the rains came. Like buckets of water drenching the land they came . . . again and again. Soon several areas of the ground became saturated. Little by little the rushing water soaked and uprooted the smaller bushes and objects, swiftly taking them down into its rushing flow.

The five young tender seedlings were embedded in the dirt between Cedra's roots. But they hadn't had enough time to build their roots strong enough to hold on to hers. They were helpless against the heavy rain pellets and fierce wind. Cedra's branches bent low to the ground as she tried to shield her seedlings. But just then she felt a slashing jolt on her right side as a bolt of lightening struck one of her heaviest limbs, shafting through, splitting her side. Lightening struck her roots again and again, cutting them into pieces, preventing her from uprooting and escaping! The squirrels within her branches jumped around trying to find cover elsewhere, as a large section of Cedra's limb was pulled off – as if it were a single leaf. Fearfully holding on within the roots of that section was the unnamed 1st born male seedling. Cedra's huge limb was carried away into the storm down river, past the other trees. No one noticed the trembling little male seedling that was within Cedra's torn limb, fearfully holding on. No one saw which direction he was blown.

The forest was violently fighting back, desperate to survive. The deer raced alongside the foxes and squirrels – all trying to save their young and move to higher ground. Suddenly the wind turned another direction and just as Cedra reached down to hold onto her, the 2nd born female seedling was whisked away with the wind. She kept flipping over and over in the air, as the wind took her away into another unknown land. Right after she was blown away, the 3rd born female seedling was swiftly rooted out of Cedra's roots by the swirling water. She lay on the ground below her mother, who was now literally split in two, burning on the inside of her trunk - having being hit by a another violent bolt of lightening. Cedra reached for her seedling, but an eerie gushing sound came and the floodwaters swept the little female seedling away.

R.T. was frantically swinging his branches, fighting the strong wind and heavy rain as he was trying to reach his beloved Cedra. He was only able to touch her briefly. As she quickly turned to look at him, she pointed down to one of her larger roots. There next to the Treasure of Truth Box in her tree trunk, were two seedlings, one slightly smaller, clinging to the bigger one. R. T. reached for both, pulling them over to the bottom of his trunk. But just as he did, a large branch came smashing through and tore the smaller 4th born male seedling out of his grasp. This seedling, which was smaller than all the others, became lodged into a section of the branch and rapidly went downstream in full force.

Cedra cried out in pain as she watched yet another seedling swept away from her. Then, as she looked over again at R.T., she saw the 5th born youngest seedling, Aya, holding on to one of his strong roots. Aya was gulping and gasping for breath as her little branches desperately held on to her father's roots. R.T. immediately saw where Cedra was looking and swiftly pulled the youngest seedling closer, tucking her into in a hole within one of his roots - so she would be safe.

As the wind and heavy waters swirled around her, Cedra watched him. During that brief moment, R.T. and Cedra stood there, looking intensely at one another. She knew then that she had served her main purpose in life. She had found the land of her Destiny. She had given birth to five tiny seedlings and the favored male tree of the forest, R.T., was their father. She looked at the little one tucked in his root and saw that Aya was safe. Cedra fixed her gaze intently on R. T. and their eyes locked. Then, she loudly shouted into the wind and into R.T.'s heart, **"They all will live!"** She saw in R.T.'s eyes the affirmation and strength of agreement. With peace in her heart, she released her need to struggle and let go.

At that point, R.T. looked on helplessly. His agonized cry went into the winds as he saw his love release herself. She was then hit with a violent force of destructive jagged rocks. In the next moment he saw her struck down. His heart wrenched as he watched Cedra bend over low and die. Before he could even cry out his deep anguish and tears, he felt a slight movement near one of his roots. He looked down and there was the last tiny seedling, Aya – wobbling, squirming and desperately hanging on to him!

He took one of his lower bushy branches and covered her with his protection. He bent his head low and wept fiercely as he waited out the storm. Then, while he was weeping deeply over his loss, he didn't notice that the little seedling had lost her grip on his root. Another large branch sped through the rushing waters, catching one of her tiny roots and swiftly overtook her. The large branch quickly swept her down into the rushing waters to a land far, far, away.

Chapter II

# The Landings

## Denotoria Forest . . . in the Land of Valorous

The sun was rising slowly over the lush vibrant land called Valorous. Here there were forests, open green lands, crystal clear streams and even a few mountains. One of the forests, named Denotoria, is where Aya, the youngest 5th born female seedling had blown into during the middle of the night. The fierce winds had slammed her into the trunk of a huge willow tree named Willow Weeper, who was rooted near a gently flowing brook. When Willow bent over to see what hit her she saw a tiny seedling laying next to a small owl. Both of them were passed out. She immediately recognized Wyo and knew that the seedlings name was Aya. The news about the Great Storm and the battle at Cordaya Valley had traveled far.

As if she were weeping over Aya's losses, Willow Weeper leaned forward allowing her long full branches to drape over Aya and Wyo, protectively covering them until they woke. At one point during the evening, Aya sat up and briefly rubbed her eyes. She looked around, blinked a few times and then fell back to the ground in exhaustion - entering into a dark, somber sleep.

As dusk began to fall once again and the evening dew was felt all around, Willow leaned over a little more and tightly pulled her long wispy limbs closer together - covering and hiding the two of them from any immediate danger. As it grew darker outside, it was also growing darker in Aya's mind. She was slowly and methodically being lulled into a "seemingly" restful place inside the depth of her fitful slumber. In that place of darkness, Aya heard the words, "Wake up! Wake up!" She tried to open her eyes, but the hypnotic-like darkness kept pulling down, down, down. She continued to drift into darkness. She didn't want to wake up. Her pain was too deep.

As the moments passed, a cool crisp breeze swept across her face. She heard a voice saying, "Wake up Aya". The breeze came again, only stronger this time along with the voice, "Come back Aya!" Slowly Aya began to move her body toward the direction of the air on her face and opened her eyes - just slightly. Through thin slits, she saw light and what appeared to be a huge beige and white object with wings slowly fanning her! *That feels so crisp, so-o-o cool,* she thought. Then as she opened her eyes fully, she saw that it was a huge bird with long wings that were flapping over her.

Frightened, she sat up quickly, asking, "Who are you? Where am I?"

"Don't be afraid!" came a firm yet soothing voice. "I'm Wyo! Remember? . . . from Cordaya Valley? I was swept away with you in the Great Storm." Wyo realized that Aya had gone into shock and wasn't remembering who he was.

She struggled to rise into a sitting position, trying to remember what happened. Her eyes began to droop again, "I just want to sleep," she said.

Wyo continued to watch Aya as he slowly fanned her. He didn't want her to drift away again! "No," said Wyo, "that's not a good idea right now."

Willow moved back some of her branches that were covering Aya, making a path for the soft sunset glow that was trying to peek in and help Aya stay awake. The soft yet powerful light moved across Aya's face. Wyo looked closely into Aya's blue eyes and saw that she was starting to come out of shock. She recognized him! Relieved, he let out a long quiet sigh.

"Wyo – how did we get here? Where are my mother and father?

Where are my brothers and sisters?" Aya felt panic stabbing into her stomach and her heart began to beat rapidly as she tried to get up and look around.

"Slow down, don't get excited Aya!" said Wyo. He continued to watch her as he spoke. "I only remember little bits and pieces of what happened! I was floating on a huge branch and all of a sudden I felt a thud on my left side and there you were - next to me, passed out! I pulled you to the top of the branch so you wouldn't drown. I saw that we were floating down a rushing flood-like river that had formed from all the rain! I must have passed out while clinging to you and the branch. The rains finally stopped and we were swept underneath this huge willow tree named Willow Weeper."

Willow had a little grin on her face, happy to have been some assistance to these two characters. Aya looked at Willow and Wyo. She tried to muster up a smile, even though there was a thick ache in her heart. With tears in her eyes, she lay back down on the ground. Wyo walked over next to her, spread out his right wing to cover her and then he too lay down. Soon they both fell asleep. Willow pulled her thickest branches around them once again, providing a nighttime shield of protection. As the evening breeze blew through her leaves, a slight whistling sound could be heard in the air. Then again, perhaps it was a gentle cry coming from a young owl and a little seedling as they tried to find comfort in one another - under the shelter of her all encompassing branches.

## Wake Up!

Since landing in the forest of Denotoria, Aya slept off and on for almost three days. During that time Wyo discussed with Willow different ideas he had about trying to get back to Cordaya Valley. She gave him several instructions and especially told him about a Healing Field of Flowers that they would eventually come upon.

Now and then Aya would wake up crying - missing her family. Sometimes she would tell Willow about Cordaya Valley and the storm she experienced during Naming Ceremony. But while sharing, she would often begin to cry all over again. Willow knew it was important for Aya to talk things out, so she listened attentively as Wyo stood at Aya's side, encouraging her.

On the fourth day Aya began to take short walks around the forest with Wyo. Although they met a few neighbors, they never strayed too far from Willow. One evening as they were all sitting under the clear sky, watching shooting stars flash through the night clouds, Willow noticed a deep sadness in Aya.

"What is it Aya? Are you remembering the deeper things?"

"Yes I am," Aya replied as she lowered her head.

"Aya, why don't you share what's on your heart?" Willow said. "You can trust me."

Aya looked up at the compassionate face of Willow and exclaimed, "Oh I know Willow. I trust you completely! I know I'm safe here with you. Wyo told me that you are a Nurturer Overseer and that this is your Destiny Land. No wonder I have felt so comforted by you." Willow nodded and smiled as she waited for Aya to continue.

"I watched my mother struggle in the wind and I saw her hit by lightening and start burning!" Aya began to cry. "My mother didn't think of herself, she only thought of saving us, her children! I remember seeing her trying to hold on to one of my brothers and the horrible sound she made when he was swept away. Then suddenly my father pulled me away from her and I clung to his roots." Aya was standing now, walking back and forth crying profusely, waving her branch hands as she spoke. Wyo started to go and comfort her, but Willow's signal stopped him. He nodded in understanding - Aya needed to release the deep sorrow she hadn't shared yet.

"I remember waves and waves of water rushing over me, I kept gulping for air, and it began to fill my lungs! Then I climbed into a crevice within my father's roots and held on tightly. I looked across at my mother whose side was burning, and then I saw a huge jagged rock slash into her! Willow, I saw my mother die!" Loud gulps came out of Aya as she wept. Wyo knew that now he should go to her. He wrapped one of his long soft wings over Aya and pulled her close to him. In between gasps of breath Aya whispered in a hoarse voice, "I heard sounds come out of my father that I had never heard before – it scared me and then I lost my grip!" By now Aya was screaming as she buried her head in Wyo's thick wing. "I lost my grip Wyo. I was pulled away from my father!"

Then Aya let it all go. Tears upon tears fell as she wept and cried for what seemed like hours. Willow quietly stroked Aya with her long healing branches as Wyo laid Aya down, using his right wing as a pillow and covering her with his left. Having emptied herself of some of her deepest painful memories, Aya slept with a semblance of peace. Now and then Wyo would hear her shudder. Then finally, she let out a huge sigh and Wyo knew she had found a bit of peace within her heart.

## Time to Go

A week went by. During that time Willow had several more talks with Aya and Wyo. One morning Willow gently rustled her branches to wake them up so she could speak to them once again. She knew that Aya needed to begin her journey back to her homeland soon. Willow looked down at Aya and thought to herself, *Her mind and heart have been restored since releasing so much of her pain. She's also found some peace under the healing power of my leaves.* Once Wyo and Aya were fully awake, Willow began to speak. "Aya, I know you'll soon be ready to start traveling."

Aya looked up. It was true, she was anxious to get back home.

But she was also a little afraid of what she might find when she got there. Her deepest hope was that her father was alive and that somehow her siblings also found their way home. Willow continued, "I've shared many new thoughts and secrets with you. Hopefully you will remember them in your time of need. I'll be sending you off tomorrow morning, but there are more hidden truths that you should know."

Willow's voice was intense as she spoke. "On your journey use all of your senses when encountering various, creatures, trees and seedlings, so you can perceive who is good and who is evil. There will be unique signs and messages within the environments you travel into and the surrounding atmospheres. Pay attention. Regardless of how frightened you are in some of your situations, evaluate them. Notice how they fit into your past, present or future. Many mystical events that you encounter won't make any sense to you. If you discard things you don't understand, you may be throwing away truths that will play a crucial part in your future. You must try to remember all of this."

"Yes Willow, I will," replied Aya somberly.

Willow turned to face Wyo. "Wyo, you already know many of the things I'm telling you, because of the Wisdom you carry within. Watch out for Aya's safety and impart wisdom and correction to her when necessary. Some of the lands will look familiar to you since you've already traveled through them. Because you perceive many things before they happen, you will be tempted to always warn Aya. Don't do it. You must allow her to learn through some of her experiences. There are some decisions that only she can make on this journey and you'll have to follow."

"I understand Willow. I'm honored to look after Aya."

Willow smiled. "I know. And I'm sure you're anxious to find your mother as well."

Wyo slowly nodded his head in agreement as Aya gently put

one of her branches around him.

"All right then!" Willow said. "Very good! Now let me introduce you to the youngest member of the Hairy-tailed Mole Family, Rusky Runt. He's one of our forest guides and already knows who you are." Under her feet Aya felt a rumble and out popped the head of the most interesting looking mole. His snout was short, pale and pink. His coat was a rich deep brownish black color. He looked at Aya and smiled, causing his already thin slitted eyes to almost look like they were shut.

"Hello Aya. Hello Wyo," he said as he jumped on top of the soil. "I'm ready to be commissioned on your behalf."

"All right," said Willow. "Let's not get too dramatic, we've got business to attend to."

Rusky quickly stood next to Willow waiting for her to continue.

"I'm sending Rusky with you to lead you out of Denotoria Forest. You will still be in the Land of Valorous for a while. Once you are on your way, Rusky will go back under the ground, but he will be available to help you if you ever need him. Here's a small pouch. Hide it in one of your bushy branches. Tie it tightly. When you find certain treasures or keys, put them in there. I have placed a few items in it, including this small branch." Willow held up a thin branch that had three short roots on the end. "When placed into the ground, the mystical roots on this branch will begin to grow downward, alerting some of our Underground helpers. The helpers will then swiftly send a message to Rusky and before you know it, he will be there for you."

Aya began to move her lips to ask 'how' . . . when Willow interrupted, "Aya, the question you're trying to ask me cannot be answered right now. But remember; don't discard something just because you don't understand it. Sometimes trying too hard to understand or find out 'how' something works, will rob you of Time. Be careful - or your moments will be stolen. The mystery of this special branch is one that only the Undergrounders and myself can know about."

Aya was a little embarrassed but responded, "I know what you're saying is important, even if I don't understand it fully. I'm just ready to go home and be with my father and siblings. But I'm also frightened at what I might find when I get there."

Willow smiled, stroking Aya with one of her branches. "I know Aya, I know." The soft light of the setting sun then came down and surrounded all of them. Taking the queue, Aya and Wyo quietly settled in under Willows great branches, to enjoy their last night of rest under her protection.

Before long, the bright rays of the sun shone brightly through Willows long limbs. She woke up quickly and began to fan her branches over Aya and Wyo so they could get an early start. It was a quiet morning as they all prepared for the day; each one engrossed within their own thoughts. As she moved around, Aya felt several drops of water begin to fall upon her leaves. "Oh, it's starting to rain!" she said.

Wyo quietly nudged her and pointed upward. Aya looked up. She then realized - it was Willows' tears that were dropping down.

"Don't mind my tears little one," said Willow. "I've enjoyed this time with you and Wyo. I'm sad you are leaving. But these are also tears of joy, because you survived the storm and now you have an opportunity to journey into your future. That makes me very happy."

Aya reached over and hugged Willow tightly. "Thank you for everything! We wouldn't be going on this journey if it weren't for you!"

"That's right!" echoed Wyo. "We'll never forget you!"

With one swoop of her long branches, Willow embraced them for the last time. "Off with you now," she said, gently nudging them toward Rusky who was waiting to lead them out of the forest. With misty eyes Aya looked back at Willow and smiled before slowly turning back to join Wyo and Rusky. After they had gone, Willow called out to her personal Seeker Bird - Zeno and gave him instructions. Seeker Birds were a small but elite group of multi-colored birds with green eyes that looked like glass. Born in the Land of Valorous, they were assigned to various tasks by some of the Overseer Trees and traveled where needed throughout Etainia.

Several hours had gone by when Rusky finally stopped at the edge of the forest. "This is where I leave you," he said in his raspy voice. "The Land of Valorous is big, but don't worry, I'll be there when you need me!" Then he quickly dove into a small hole in the ground nearby and disappeared. They both grinned at Rusky's quick departure. Wyo flew up and perched himself on Aya's left shoulder as she began to walk. He was proud and honored to be with her. There was mutual respect and tender affection between them. Soon they were crossing some of the open fields. Unbeknownst to them, Zeno was watching over them from a distance. The two slowly trooped down the dusty road toward the horizon. As their silhouettes disappeared over the hill, Zeno quickly took flight to inform Willow that Aya and Wyo were well on their way.

## Rensamor Island

It was a strange and eerie place. After being knocked out for a while, the 4th born seedling finally came to and tried to stand up, but was only able to reach a sitting position. As he sat up, feeling the dampness around him, he smelled an odd, pungent stench in the air. He then heard a loud rumbling noise that kept echoing in his ears. It vibrated and shook the insides of his whole body.

He blinked a few times and rubbed his eyes as they gradually became adjusted to the dark. He began to see faint outlines and silhouettes of curious objects around him. There was a thin beam of light above where he sat. He thought he was on the bottom level of a cave. He wasn't sure where he was. He looked around and saw rubbery-like walls on the sides of this vast, dingy place he was in. He noticed what looked like a long vine or rope, hanging from the ceiling in the very center of wherever he was. Now and then, a big breeze would come through the opening of the cave-like structure.

Dazed and disoriented, he rubbed his eyes again, trying to see more clearly. It didn't help. He tried standing up again. This time he succeeded. While standing, he turned his head to the right. There appeared to be a pond. But the thick watery substance in it looked murky and green. Straight ahead he saw what looked like a black bridge with yellowish white rocks on both sides. Every now and then a light would flash across them. Although he wasn't quite sure where the light was coming from, he wanted to walk toward it. As he began to move, he felt a tug on one of his branch feet – it was caught under a heavy, slippery vine-like object. Frustrated at not being able to move- the seedling started jumping up and down – stomping and pounding around the object to loosen its hold!

Although his arm and hand branches were small – they were very strong. He continued swinging his powerful branches at whatever was holding him down. The more he pounded, the angrier he became, but his foot would not come loose! Suddenly, a flood of sunlight came bursting toward him. He looked up, past the black bridge that he had noticed earlier. The huge opening that led to the outside was growing larger! He strained and looked out from where he stood, catching a glimpse of green grassland. *Wow*, he thought to himself. *There are other trees out there!*

That made him even more anxious to cross the strange bridge and get out of the smelly place! With all of his might, he began to pound on the soft wall near the vine like object holding his foot. It began to loosen. He pulled, yanked, pounded and stomped, until all of a sudden – he heard a loud noise! Shortly after that came even louder grumbling noises! It scared the young seedling and he began to swing his small, but strong fists in the air erratically, hoping to knock out whatever was making that noise! With each loud sound came a strong blast of air with an awful smell!

Finally his foot branch was loosened. At that instant, another massive blast of wind blew, catching him up into the air! Swiftly after that there was a loud roar, along with another huge gust of wind, and he went flying through the air and out the opening of the cave-like structure! The seedling was being tossed and turned in the wind - way, way, up and out toward a swamp. By now he was flying backwards and was terribly frightened! He barely opened his tightly closed eyes, and thought he saw the opening of the cave-like structure he was just in; move!

It all happened so fast! With fists still flying in the air, he looked down thinking; *I hope I don't crash against that huge jagged rock sticking out of the swamp and die!* The instant his thought ended, another strong wind came rushing from the cave-like structure - altering the direction of his fall – whisking him over the grassy land he had seen earlier. He began to spiral downward at rapid speed! He braced himself to be slammed unto the ground. But then . . . when he landed . . . he bounced up and down. He actually bounced up and down, landing on the softest grass he had ever known. It was so tall that it formed a long green wall around him as he sat up in it.

Although he was still in shock from all the bouncing around and everything else that happened, he couldn't help but notice the fresh, clean scent in the air. He breathed it in, over and over again. For a moment, he just sat there. Now, feeling a bit safer and comforted in the tall, soft grass, he tried to get up. But he was too exhausted, feeling extremely weak; having spent most of his energy in the fight for his life. Finally, he let his body slump slightly forward and then he slowly dropped back onto the soft, soft grass, immediately falling into a deep, restful sleep.

## Who are You?

The young seedling slept peacefully though the night. But just before dawn he began to have a profound dream:

*He was high up on a mountain. A cool breeze was blowing. He looked down below and the grass was plush and green. There were valleys with streams of crystal clear water. Now and then flying fish flew out, as if wanting to glimpse the beauty all around, before diving back into the water. His eyes were feasting on the vibrant colors of everything. He took deep breaths of the crisp clean air. The sun's rays fell all over his limbs, gently caressing him. Even the sound of the wind blowing through the other trees and the chirping of the birds was like music to his ears. Then he heard a voice in the wind. It was a soft voice, almost a whisper at first, "Little Seedling, where are you going? Little Seedling, what are you doing?" Then a louder, deeper voice entered into his dream saying, "Little Seedling wake up!"*

Startled, he was immediately pulled out of his dream. Then he heard a sniffing sound. He quickly sat upright and looked around, blinking the sleep from his eyes. He rubbed his sore shoulder branches and saw that the tall green grass surrounded him, except for a small area in front. As he leaned forward, intensely staring ahead, he suddenly saw two pairs of pink eyes staring at him! He jolted back and scrambled to get up, but because of the weakness in his body and stiffness in his legs, he couldn't.

There, sitting only a few feet away, right in front of him - were two large white rabbits with pink eyes – looking at him. A small fox was sitting by their long feet. All three were smiling at him. "How do you feel?" said the slightly smaller rabbit. "My husband and I were sitting on our porch earlier and saw you flying into the air. We alerted a few of our neighbors and came running over here to see what happened. Are you o.k?"

The seedling, now fully awake, was relieved that they were friendly and said, "Well, I'm very stiff and sore. I was in a swampy like cave and my foot branch got caught on something, so I was stuck!"

The smaller rabbit smiled at him and said, "Let me introduce myself and my family. I'm Mrs. Whiskers LongEars. You can call me Whiskers and this is my husband Sniffer and our little fox named Rocky. We live here. You've landed on Rensamor Island."

Sniffer leaned over reaching out his paw to help the seedling to his feet. "Hello young seedling, what's your name?"

As the young seedling stood, he looked up at the rabbit and began to talk rapidly. "I don't know. I'm from Cordaya Valley - we were in the middle of The Naming Ceremony - a huge storm blew through - destroying everything in its path!" He slowed down and took a deep breath as he was remembering. "It all happened before my parents announced my name." He dropped his head down. "I don't even know if my parents or brothers and sisters are alive."

Sniffer put his arm around the seedling. "Well, come home with us, we live just down the road."

Noticing that the seedling had winced a little when she shook his branch hand Whiskers asked, "Did I hurt your branch hand earlier?"

The seedling looked up, grateful for her compassion. "No, you didn't. My branch hands are sore from making a fist and pounding on the vine-like thing that caught my foot. For a moment I felt like a boxer. I kept pounding and pounding. I was determined to get out of there!"

Whiskers looked at him with her kind soft pink eyes, "Well then, since you don't know your name yet, if you don't mind, I think we'll call you Boxer, in honor of your determination to fight to live!"

"Boxer," repeated the seedling. "Yes, I like it!"

As they began to walk together toward the LongEars' home, Sniffer said, "By the way Boxer, you weren't in a cave. You flew out of Geseemo, the Giant Slime Fish that lives in the Swamp! You flew right out of her mouth! We heard her grumblings long before we saw you fly in the air. You're lucky to be alive. That pounding and fighting you did probably kept her from swallowing you!"

Shocked, Boxer stopped suddenly and looked at both of them! Surprised with the knowledge of where he had actually been trapped, he began to reflect out loud. "When I saw the black bridge with yellowish white rocks on each side - I was actually looking at her black tongue. The rocks were really her yellow teeth on each side of her tongue!" The rabbits had never known anyone who survived being in Geseemo's mouth; so they were intensely listening to Boxer describe his experience.

"And that rope like thing hanging down from the ceiling . . . that was attached to her tonsils!! – and the rubbery walls – the slippery floor – it was all part of her slimy mouth!!"

As Boxer came to the full realization of where he had been trapped, he sat down in the middle of the road feeling sick.

"I don't feel so well," he said to them.

And then he starting uttering sounds they had never heard before. "Blagh . . . argh . . . ugh . . . "

Whiskers and Sniffer bent over, patting him on his shoulders. "Boxer, it's O.K., you're out now, there's a spring of fresh water close by our house. You can rinse off there. It will be o.k."

Boxer stood up, a bit embarrassed at all the sickly little noises he had been making. "I'm sorry," he said as his eyes rolled around. He held out his branch hands to look at them, while wrinkling up his nose. "I just got caught up in the gruesome idea of being in a slimy mouth and almost being chewed up!" The rabbits looked at Boxer trying not to laugh at his expressions, but after a few moments, they could hold it in no longer! Both of them burst out laughing! Boxer looked at them and before long he found himself laughing along with them! "Wow, this has been quite a day!" he said as he continued laughing at how funny he must have looked.

"We're sure glad you landed here Boxer," said Sniffer as he tried to control himself.

"Yes, I agree," said Whiskers in between giggles. "Things will really be different now that you're here!"

They walked Boxer down to the nearby spring so he could wash off all of Geseemo's slime. Sniffer patted the seedling and said, "We're going to go back to our house Boxer, so take your time. We'll leave Rocky with you. He'll show you the way to our house. It's not far."

Rocky's ears perked up. He stood next to the young seedling and said, "I'll look after him, don't worry." Boxer shyly shifted his branch feet back and forth as he looked up and smiled, thanking them both.

Whiskers added, "After you clean up we'll all sit on the porch and enjoy a nice quiet evening, while Sniffer and I fill you in on some of the history of Rensamor Island and other happenings here."

"I'd like that," replied Boxer as he happily turned toward the stream, with Rocky leading the way.

---

## Krontia Land

"Get that spider web out of there!!!" The loud screaming voice frightened the 3rd born female seedling. She tried to adjust her eyes to the dimly lit area in order to see where she was.

"I said GET THAT SPIDER WEB OUT OF THERE . . . NOW!" came the loud voice once again. The seedling looked up so see a huge spider web very close to her in a corner on the outside of a building. She looked around and saw large cans full of trash all around her. She realized she was in one of them! She tried to move her trunk, but one of her branch legs was stuck. Suddenly she heard some noises coming from behind. She watched as several skinny weasels come running toward her holding large brooms. It looked as if they were going to beat her with them! She started to duck her treetop, but they didn't even notice her as they rushed by.

They were so focused on taking down the spider web, they didn't bother looking when they bumped the trashcan she was in and it fell over. While they continued racing toward the spider web, she fell out of the can and swiftly rolled into a large tree trunk, with some of the trash still stuck in her treetop. "Oomph . . . o-o-o-h!" she moaned, hoping no one heard her. Her body had bumped over the roots of the tree and she was slammed into a sitting position. Stunned, she shook her head. She looked back up to where she had been and watched as several weasels frantically rushed around, moving some of the other trash cans out of the way and then raced off - leaving only three weasels to finish the job of destroying the spider web.

The three weasels began to beat at the large spider web. Their brooms knocked into each other as they tried to capture pieces of the webbing into the brush part of their brooms. "Get that last piece or she'll get mad!" yelled Klon, one of the larger weasels.

"I'm doing the best I can!" screamed Rig, the weasel with white spots on his brown fur.

"Hey you two, stop arguing! Let's hurry and get it down before she comes to inspect!" shouted Joff, the weasel with no tail. They continued to squabble back and forth while knocking each other's brooms, trying to get the last of the webbing.

"What are you three doing?" bellowed a tall thin tree that had no bark or leaves on it. The three weasels stopped what they were doing and stood straight up, with their brooms at their side.

"Dr. Tearrent, we've gotten most of the spider web," said Joff in a quiet tone.

Dr. Tearrent came up close to Joff. Towering over him she screamed in his face, "Listen you tailless idiot! Most is not good enough! Get some disinfectant and wash that area down!"

Joff ran off to do as he was told. Frustrated she turned and yelled at Rig. "Once he's done with that, straighten up the trash cans and make sure the lids are secure on each one of them!" As she finished her sentence, she looked down in the small yard and saw that a trashcan had rolled over, dumping trash everywhere.

Rig saw where she was looking and quickly ran over to pick up the can and the scattered trash all around it. Dr. Tearrent motioned to Klon to walk with her. She walked past Rig, straight to the large tree that the seedling had crashed into. Noticing that a young seedling was stiffly propped up against the tree, Dr. Tearrent came closer. Once there, she just stood and stared at the seedling. Rubbing her chin with her hand branch, the doctor was thinking to herself, *This one is only about three feet tall. H-m-m, she must be about a year old. I wonder which direction she came from?* She looked down at the seedling and saw that she was very frightened.

Klon stood next to Dr. Tearrent, wisely saying nothing, until he knew for sure what she was going to do.

"Why hello there," she said while leaning over to smile at the young tree. "Let me help you up," she continued as she reached out her large hand branch to hold one of the seedlings small hand branches. Klon took the queue and assisted the seedling into a standing position. The Dr. continued, "And how did you happen to come here to Krontia?"

The little seedling was still trembling and her leg branches were shaking as she spoke. "The last thing I remember was seeing my mother hit by lightening and then I was swirled into the waters and whisked away from my family!"

The seedling began to weep. Dr. Tearrent picked her up and began walking, holding the young tree in her arms. "Don't worry, we'll take care of you here. You must have been in that Great Storm that everyone has been talking about - the one in Cordaya Valley."

"Yes!" replied the seedling, happy that this friendly tree knew about the land where she was born.

*A Friend?*

Dr. Tearrent began walking toward a large square building with no windows in it. Still carrying the seedling in her arms, she asked, "Have you been through your Naming Ceremony yet?"

The seedling looked up, amazed that this tree knew all about that.

"No, my sister Aya was the only seedling that was named - just before the storm hit."

As she got closer to the building Dr. Tearrent made a mental note to remember that name. "Klon, go ahead of me and prepare the examination room so I can make sure that . . . " her voice trailed. She realized that this seedling had no name. She thought for a moment and said, "We'll think up a name for you before the end of the day. Right now we want to make sure nothing is broken and you're in good shape!"

Klon went into the examination room and waited for the next command. The young tree felt the cold table beneath her as Dr. Tearrent set her down. She wasn't used to being in place where she couldn't see other trees or creatures.

"Why aren't there any windows?" she asked innocently.

The doctor acted as if she didn't hear. "Don't be frightened," she said. "We won't be here long. Go ahead and lay down. I just need to examine you. Once I know you're in tip top shape, we'll take you to one of our guest rooms."

The seedling lay back down on the cold table; feeling assured that they would take care of her from this point on.
Dr. Tearrent then sternly instructed Klon, "Remove all the webbing from her branches. Call me when you finish."

Klon hesitated for a moment. "Removing the webbing will take a long time Doctor Tearrent."

The doctor looked at the seedling lying on the steel bed. "Yes, I realize that, but take as long as you need and remove every bit of it. I'll complete the examination when you're done." Her long thin branch feet made a hollow clicking sound as Dr. Tearrent walked toward the door. She grabbed the handle with her gloved hand and looked back at the seedling. "And Klon, we'll call her Webber."

After about an hour, Klon called Dr. Tearrent back to finish the examination. As Webber lay there looking up at the ceiling, she was remembering the night of the Naming Ceremony in Cordaya Valley:

*She was sitting by a brook, (Cedra had reminded her earlier not to wander off too far) hugging her knees and thinking about how excited she was to finally receive her name. While she was sitting there with her arms folded across her knees, Squeegie, the neighborhood squirrel, ran over her branch feet while chasing his younger brother. She playfully called out to him, "Hey Squeegie, you tickled my feet!" He called back to her, "Sorry 'bout that!" and continued running through the forest.*

"All right," said Dr. Tearrent as she finished examining Webbers branch feet. The voice immediately pulled Webber out of her thoughts, into the present. "Looks like you're in good health!"

Webber slowly sat up and swung her branch legs around, dangling them over the edge of the table. While sitting there for a moment, she realized that during the entire examination, she had drifted into her past.

Klon came over to help her down as the Dr. continued, "Klon will take you to your room and tomorrow morning I will show you around my land. There is a lot going on here and I think you might want to be a part of it!"

Webber nodded and stepped down from the table saying, "Thank you so much for all that you've done for me." Dr. Tearrent smiled as she opened the door. Klon led Webber out and they began to walk toward the stairs at the end of the long corridor.

They walked up two flights of stairs, entering into another long corridor on the third floor. As they walked, Webber noticed that the bright white walls were empty and bare. Everything she saw was white, except for the beds and chairs, which were silver. Klon stopped in front of one of the doors and unlocked it.

"Why is the door locked?" she asked. Klon was a stocky weasel and stood about five feet tall. He had a patch over one eye. The other eye was black and his fur was all white. Webber was a little afraid of him.

He looked down at her with his one eye. "The doors are self-locking. The locks are there to keep you safe from any bugs, diseased trees and creatures. This building is very secure, but now and then there have been break-ins."

Webber walked into her room and noticed that instead of a window, there was a painting on the wall of blue clouds and trees with foliage standing near streams of water. She turned to thank Klon, but he had already stepped out. As the door shut, it locked her in the room. As she listened to the clicking sound of the lock, she looked around thinking how strange it was not to be able to see outside. "The picture on the wall is beautiful, but I'd rather be able to look at real trees and creatures," she said out loud. She continued exploring the brightly lit, sterile room. There was a steel bed and chair - nothing else. Feeling sleepy, she lay down on the bed hoping to fall asleep quickly. Soon the bright lights in the room began to dim slowly. It must be late, she thought as her imagination took off again. *Maybe I'm in a dream and I'm going to wake up soon. Maybe I'll hear my mother say, "Are you okay? You've been awfully quiet lately."*

Webber spoke out into the dimly lit room. "She always knew when I was deep in thought or in my little dream world." Webber smiled then, remembering her mother Cedra. Webber closed her eyes and finally began to doze off, reflecting on what she had just spoken about her mother. As she drifted into her world of nighttime imaginings, Webber vaguely heard her own voice as she uttered her thoughts into the night. "But she never once discouraged me from going into the creative world of my mind."

# Barren Land

Barren Land - a place to be feared by many. It was here that the 2nd born seedling landed after the Great Storm. She had been blown briefly, into a large flat mold of hot plastic that hadn't hardened yet. She quickly fell out of the mold unto the ground, but some of the hot plastic was stuck to part of her body. It had splattered on different sections of her left limb, ankle and trunk. One of the giant Armadillo guards of Barren Land heard her agonizing cries and saw her fall on the ground. Using the megaphone he immediately called his master, whose name was 'The Mixer'. His master came swiftly, followed by a second Armadillo guard. The Mixer, a large scaly alligator, sized up the situation and saw that some of the seedlings cedar bark was peeling off as a result of the hot plastic. He also saw that the plastic was beginning to be molded to her. He wasted no time. He walked over to her and began tearing the loose bark off of her left side. She screamed out in pain, but he kicked her leg and yelled at her, "Stop that screaming!"

He hurriedly threw the extra bark into a nearby wheelbarrow and the second Armadillo guard took it directly into the factory. The Mixer looked at the first guard. "Stay here and watch her. The sun will dry up her left side and in a couple of days she'll be ready to work for me." Then he began to walk back up to the factory office to speak to a potential customer. That tree bark will trim at least one hundred idols, he thought to himself. *I'll use that peeling bark on some of the idols I'm making.* In Barren Land, tree bark was extremely scarce and very expensive.

The next morning The Mixer came to check on her. She was still lying on the ground, with a sickly expression on her face. He looked down at her and said, "I'll give you one more day of rest here and you'll be as good as new. I'll call you Plasick, because you are part plastic and you look sick!" He laughed loudly, thinking he was quite clever. "Tomorrow morning the Armadillo Guard will take you to the factory. You're being watched all the time, so don't try to run away!" He turned abruptly and went back up to the hill to eat breakfast with his wife, Messer.

## Mixer & Messer

The Mixer and his wife were both very huge alligators that walked upright on two legs most of the time, but they could also easily lie flat on the ground and go into the water if they chose to. Many years ago they escaped from the Chucalla Swamp. Over time the swamp had become a dark place where some of the strange alligators often attacked each other, looking for babies and eating them out of desperation for food. The couple had secretly fled the swamp during the night; swimming for hundreds of miles to be sure no one followed them. They ended up in a vast and dry land called Barren Land, a place that had been taken over by the Reptiles. There was no Overseer Tree on this land anymore.

The Mixer and Messer fit right in with the Reptile Community on Barren Land. They also made friends with several of the larger Reptiles in the surrounding areas. They discovered that in Barren Land, trees and plants were scarce. After a lot of thought, they came up with the idea of making idols out of tree bark and plastic. They knew they would profit greatly because the value of trees and bark kept going up. Plastic was cheap to make and by adding just a bit of tree bark to each piece, they could charge more.

They designed a plan on how to build the factory. All the Reptiles in the Community liked the industrious idea and helped them to build the factory. They also helped The Mixer to overtake and capture whatever trees; bushes and creatures were left in the land. Eventually most of the stronger and healthier captives were forced to become workers in the factory. The weaker trees, bushes and plants were rooted out, cut up and stored. They would be used at a later time for making idols and other products to sell. Soon there were very few trees or plant-life left growing on Barren Land.

They named their business *The Idol Factory*. Soon, many Reptiles in Barren Land heard about the factory and started to come and buy idols from them. In a very short time *The Idol Factory* became a lucrative business for The Mixer and his wife. They built a huge house for themselves made out of mud, rocks, plastic and trees. It was shaped like a huge dome and built very close to the factory, which was made out of the same materials.

Next, they invented a product called Fur Balls. These were toys with a bit of fur on them. They were used in the Reptile Games. Fur was also a scarcity because before The Mixer and Messer came upon Barren Land, the Reptiles had eaten most of the furry animals and then nonchalantly threw away the skin and fur. The Mixer had ordered some of his workers to search the land to find any and all types of fur and quickly bring it all back to the factory. Then, because of the demand, thousands of Fur Ball Toys were made. The only furry animals that were left on Barren Land were those that went underground and those that hid in various caves. Some even hid in the swamplands. The Mixer issued rewards for the capture of any kind of furry animal. The Fur Ball Toys became a priceless commodity and were available only as a special order.

As time moved on and the Idol factory grew, the couple decided not to have any children. The Mixer told the Reptiles that he and Messer wanted to focus all their attention on the business and helping the Barren Land Community grow. Because of this, the Reptile Community held them in high esteem and built a 100-foot statue on a hill above their home. The statue was constructed out of rare tree bark and plastic. The design was in the image of The Mixer and Messer holding up a broken tree. Yet, the real reason the couple did not want to have children was hidden from everyone. Deep in the back of their minds, was the nightmare of their past and the fear that strange alligators would find this land by night and eat their young. This is the environment that Plasick was blown into.

### General Saguwas

As The Mixer walked away, Plasick's mind briefly wandered back to the time of the Great Storm. The floodwaters had crashed into her mother, ripping Plasick away from her. *What is to become of me in this place?* she thought as she lay in the hot scorching sun. The strong ray's penetrated through her limbs. Still very weak and in great pain, Plasick could barely raise her left branch to shield her eyes.

As she did, she saw her ugly branch with the bark torn off and pieces of plastic stuck to it. She turned her head to the side and began to weep quietly so the guard wouldn't hear. *Was it only yesterday, when my mother was stroking my neck with one of her long thick branches, singing to me and telling me how much she loved me?* Other dreaded thoughts came to her mind. *What happened to my brothers and sisters? Are my parents still alive?* A loud clang of a bell rang from the other side of the huge yard, jolting her back to the reality of the moment. The smell of heavy plastic was thick in the air. From what The Mixer had said, it wouldn't be long before they put her to work. She closed her eyes and tried to get comfortable and get as much rest as she could. For a while she tossed and turned restlessly. Finally out of sheer exhaustion, she slept.

As the smoldering hot sun came up once again, Plasick felt her back being poked. Her body ached as she turned to see the Armadillo guard holding a steel-like rod with a hook on top. She struggled to get up and slowly followed him to the factory. On the way up the hill she saw a flag with a picture of an alligator on it, being raised by a purple land lizard. Several web-toed lizards were lined up, saluting the flag, looking sideways at Plasick through their thin slitted eyes. As she got closer to *The Idol Factory*, General Saguwas, a giant speckled lizard with a long tail, looked at Plasick and stopped her.

"Who is this?" he asked the Armadillo guard.

"This is The Mixer's new worker," replied the guard. "The Mixer said she'll be in the Tearing Section for now."

Plasick stared at the large lizard standing in front of her. He had a huge belly that jiggled when he spoke. He looked like he had five chins, but they were actually just folds of his skin hanging loosely on his neck.

"What are you staring at?" he yelled at Plasick. She put her head down. "Yeh, you better put your head down before I really give you something to be ashamed about." He and the guard laughed loudly as they went through the door of the factory, pushing Plasick in front of them.

As she walked inside, the strong smell of plastic caused her head to reel and she almost fell over. She walked with a limp, because of the crack on the left side of her leg where The Mixer had kicked her. "Come on, come on, get moving!" said General Saguwas as he poked her with a long stick. Plasick was still trying to get used to walking with her hurt leg. The plastic on her body had hardened and was stiff. Although the plastic wasn't heavy, the stiffness of it caused her difficulty in bending over or getting up.

Just then the door flew open and in walked The Mixer and Messer. He acknowledged the guard and looked at General Saguwas who was in charge. "Well, is she going to work out for us?"

The lizard looked Plasick up and down and replied, "Yes Sir! I'll put her in the Tearing Section just as you requested."

He pulled The Mixer and Messer aside and whispered, "I have an idea Sir. Let's not strip off the rest of her bark. It will give the other tree workers false hope - like maybe we're changing our ways!" He began stroking his chins as he continued whispering, "We can milk that idea by taking them aside, one by one, promising them that one day soon, we'll free them and bring in new worker trees as their replacements.

The Mixer and Messer smiled at the idea. "Great!" said The Mixer. "I see your point. We'll get more productivity out of them because they'll have hope. One thing though, take her to the Medic and have him patch her leg up, and then wait only one more day to put her to work."

General Saguwas agreed, saluting The Mixer before going off to his other duties. The Armadillo guard followed orders and took Plasick back outside and up another short hill to the Medic. The Mixer and Messer continued their daily tour through the factory, making sure everything was running smoothly.

Once inside The Medic's office, Plasick was surprised that he too was an alligator - because he was so kind to her. She thought it might just be a trick and was careful about what she said. "My, how did this bad crack in your leg happen?" he said. Plasick just looked up at him and didn't say anything. "Never mind then. You don't need to talk, I do plenty of that myself!" he said as he laughed while helping her to sit on the medical bed. As Plasick sat there, she closed her eyes, trying not to reveal any emotions. This was the first Reptile that showed her any tenderness and it made her want to cry, but she didn't.

The Medic continued to ramble; "The Mixer and Messer did-n't know I was following them when they escaped Chucalla Swamp. I, too, wanted to flee from the strange devouring alligators. I hid for about a week when we got to Barren Land. Then one day Messer spotted me. At first they were very upset because they thought if I followed them here, maybe others would also try to find them! They're a little paranoid about that. But Messer liked me, so they both agreed to let me stay. I learned about medicine by taking care of all of us whenever we got sick or hurt. I experimented a lot - still do. Soon other creatures, mostly Reptiles, found out what I do and they started to bring their family members to me whenever they didn't feel well. I had a lot of subjects to practice on! They started to call me *The Medic* and eventually The Mixer built this clinic for me. The rest is history!"

He helped Plasick stand up and handed her a walking stick that had strange markings on it. "Here," he said. "This is one of my personal walking sticks. I carved it myself so don't loose it!" She looked up at his kind smile and managed to grin back at him. "There now, I knew you could give me a smile before you left! If you ever need to talk or just don't feel well, come on by. They'll give you at least one pass every two weeks or so to visit the clinic."

Plasick took that to heart as he helped her walk to the door. She stood on the porch trembling and listened carefully as he gave instructions to the guard. "Here she is, take her to one of the private rooms where she can rest overnight. You have the key. You can pick her up tomorrow morning, but she must have her walking stick with her at all times." The guard nodded and then took Plastic to a private room around the corner. After walking through the door, because of the pain in her leg, she barely made it to the large bed. Slowly she climbed in and almost instantly fell asleep.

—◦—

# Sand City

It was a breezy day when the eldest 1st born seedling blew into a desolate land known as Sand City. This city was often called *The Land of the Misfits* by outsiders and had a population of about 50,000 seedling trees and creatures of all kinds. Some of them came from broken homes. Many had simply lost their way, wandering into the city by accident. Several of the trees and creatures that had been captured by evildoers in other lands, escaped from various work camps to come to Sand City and start over. Some had run away from home. Others were rejected by their families because of some sort of deformity they had on their bodies. Then again, there were many trees and creatures that came here on their own, searching for wealth and success. From all over the Land of Etainia – they came.

Sand City was a city of many financial opportunities. It was not the biggest city or the smallest, but assuredly it was the most lucrative when it came to corruption and attaining materialistic things quickly. The shrewd got richer in Sand City and pity the fools who didn't play the game right. Some of the occupants existed only to serve those who ruled over them. Often the only rewards were beatings and humiliation.

The young seedling had no idea where he had landed. When he blew onto the beach shore, which was on the outskirts of the city, he crawled far away from the water. In exhaustion he laid his head down on the sand and passed out. Over three days had gone by before he was found by another older, tougher tree named Numby. He reached over and shook the little seedling.

"Hey, wake up"

There was no response. He leaned closer and could hear the seedling still breathing. Numby was a stocky Monkey Puzzle Tree about five feet tall. Sizing up the situation he absent-mindedly scratched the long thin scar on the right side of his face. Thinking out loud he said, " This guy is about three feet tall, so I should be able to carry him to Jentia's apartment. She's my girl so she won't mind." He picked up the little seedlings' limp young body and began to walk. Suddenly he stopped, rethinking the situation. "Nah," he spoke out loud, "I plan on using this little fellow in our street group and Jentia wouldn't like that." Numby quickly turned around and carried the seedling back to his apartment.

Numby's three-story apartment building was located in a bustling upper class neighborhood. His apartment was on the ground level, so he didn't have to carry the seedling far. As Numby placed him on the couch, the seedling woke up. He looked at Numby through hazy eyes.

"Where Am I?" he asked.

"Don't worry little tyke, you're safe here, what's your name?" said Numby in a kind voice.

Feeling groggy, the seedling looked up and mumbled, "I don't know . . . there was lots of rain and . . . I just don't know." He passed out again.

*Hmmm,* Numby thought, *looks like he might have amnesia. He doesn't' even know his name!* Sorting through his mind to figure out how he could use this situation to his advantage, Numby said out loud. "I'll call him Greedo! When he wakes up I'll make up some story, so he thinks that's always been his name. I'll teach him that greed is a great quality and dough is a great commodity! Ha! Greedo! I like it . . . Yeh, that's what I'll do."

## What's My Name?

The sun shone brightly through the window on the little seedlings eyes, waking him up. It took him several minutes to focus. Numby was sleeping in a chair across from the couch. When he heard the seedling stirring, he became fully awake. "Hey Greedo, how do you feel?" The first-born seedling looked over at him and said, "Is that my name?" Where am I?" "Who are you?"

"Hey, hey, not so fast. I'll fill you in soon enough. Let's just make sure you're feeling all right." As Greedo sat up on the bed, there was a knock on the door. Numby called out, "Who is it?" "It's me, Jentia. Remember? You were going to pick me up to go see the movie, Root 'n Toot." With all the new excitement, Numby had forgotten all about it. He opened the door and as she walked in Greedo noticed she was almost as thin as he was. "Come on hon, don't be mad. I want you to meet a friend of mine . . . Greedo." Jentia looked at the skinny seedling on the couch. "Hello Greedo," she said while embracing Numby briefly. He knew she was upset at him for standing her up. Greedo nodded his head in her direction.

"How do you know each other?" she inquired.

Numby quickly responded, "I'm his godfather and he's the son of a distant friend of mine. When my old friend and his wife both passed away at the same time, their relatives sent the seedling to me so I could mentor him. He doesn't remember anything, except that his parents died in a terrible storm. He's feeling pretty sad and depressed."

That explanation seemed to satisfy Jentia so she went to the couch and sat down next to Greedo. Numby leaned up against his favorite chair feeling good about the whole situation and his plan. His girl believed him and now he had a plan to develop Greedo into a young protégée. *This is gonna work out just fine,* he thought to himself as he watched them talk. After a while he said, "Hey you two – why don't we all go to the movie, there should be another showing tonight!" Greedo wobbled a bit as he stood up, still feeling a little fearful in his new environment, yet happy to be included. Jentia stood next to him holding his arm branch.

"Do you feel up to it?" she asked. He timidly smiled and said, "Oh yes! Thank you for inviting me!"

The next morning, after an evening of fun with Numby and Jentia, Greedo woke up feeling much better. Across the room Numby was reading and looked over as he heard Greedo stirring.

"How do you feel today?" he said.

"Gosh Numby, I feel good. Thanks for taking me in!" said Greedo.

"Think nothing of it little fella, I'm glad to do it!"

Greedo then innocently asked Numby how long he had lived in Sand City.

Numby sat back with his branch legs stretched out in front of him. "Oh, I was kicked out of my home when I was barely three feet tall. Actually, they threw me into a large plastic bag and took me to a dump yard. My family was very poor and couldn't afford to keep me. They left me there. It was a windy day. Brutal winds blew all day long, eventually ripping the bag off of me. There I was, curled up on the ground, shaking from the cold. I jumped to my feet, looked around and then I ran and ran and ran. Soon I came upon an old, abandoned farmhouse on the edge of town near some burial grounds. I went into the field and for some unknown reason; the soil let me temporarily root myself. During the rainy season I grew strong. While I was there, I had a lot of time to think. I was all alone, with no other trees or bushes around me. It was during that time, that I swore I would never be poor again. I swore that no one would ever dump me again." The seriousness of Numby's face caused Greedo to stop asking him any more personal questions.

## Around Town

Over the next few weeks, Numby and Jentia took Greedo around the city, introducing him to all of their friends. Jentia agreed that Greedo should live with Numby. Silently she hoped that perhaps Greedo would help Numby become more responsible. She wasn't aware of all the secret things Numby was involved in. Day-by-day Greedo began to bond with Numby. He believed that his name was Greedo because that's what Numby told him. He tried to remember exactly where he came from, but all he could remember was that there was a really bad storm that frightened him.

With no mother or father to guide him, Greedo placed his trust into his mentor - Numby. Over time, he even began to develop some of Numby's personality traits. They went everywhere together.

Greedo quickly took up the life of "ripping off" some of the trees and creatures in Sand City. At first he wasn't sure if they were doing the right thing. But Numby explained to him that they only robbed creatures and trees who were already crooks.

"Don't worry Greedo," he had said. "The ones we rob are those who take advantage of the less fortunate in the city – so we're actually doing the community a favor!" Greedo trusted everything Numby said and was an eager learner. Over time Greedo began to accept this lifestyle as normal.

The weeks moved into months, and often, during some of the escapades, Greedo got in trouble because he didn't go about some of the robberies with the right techniques. One afternoon, while he was sitting on a bench in Sunnyvale Park, Numby approached him from behind and smacked him on the head. Greedo almost fell off the bench. When he tried to stand up again, Numby punched him in the back and he fell forward onto the ground. He tried to stand up but Numby had jumped over the bench and stomped on Greedo's right branch hand. Greedo yelled out in pain and looked up at Numby, stunned that this was happening.

"Listen to me *carefully*," said Numby angrily looking down at Greedo who was sprawled in the dirt. "You cost me a lot of money on your last two fumbled jobs!" He let up on Greedo's branch hand and abruptly walked off, cursing loudly - kicking at anything that got in his way. Greedo sat up holding his hand while watching Numby walk away from him. Tears welled up in his eyes, not just from the pain of the beating, but also the emotional pain of being mis-treated by his friend and mentor.

These incidents became more and more frequent whenever Greedo did the least little thing wrong. Numby always explained the beatings away by saying afterward, "I'm just teaching you a lesson - it's nothing personal." Greedo eventually began to believe that he deserved those beatings. In his mind, if he messed up, Numby had a right to straighten him out. One time the beating was so bad that Greedo cried. Numby laughed hard when he heard Greedo gulping and trying to hold back his tears. All day long, Numby kept making fun of him in front of the other creatures and seedlings of Numby's gang. That day, Greedo promised himself he would never cry again. No matter what happened in his life, no one would ever again see him cry again.

This was the only life Greedo had ever known. As mean as they were to him, Numby and the other seedlings in the gang became his family. Their motto was to stick together and no matter what, never turn each other in. Even if you had to go to the work camps – you did not talk! There was a strange sense of comradeship among the other robbers and cutthroats. Greedo was proud that he had been mentored by one of the best. He became sharp and callous and knew how to work every situation to his advantage. When new seedlings or creatures came to this city – they had no idea of all the darkness that was lurking within. Such was the life in Sand City.

The Five . . .

# After the Landings

# Chapter III

# Mysteries & Discoveries

## Aya & the Learning Times

Aya and Wyo had traveled several miles. It began to get dark so they stopped by a small lake. Nearby was a huge dead tree. They decided to settle in for the night. Aya sat down leaning against the dead tree while watching the orange sunset begin to go down. She was struck by the awesomeness of all the colors she saw. It almost looked like a large campfire, inviting her to come closer. It had been a wonderful, but tiring day. Her mind trailed back again to the worry of what was left in Cordaya Valley. Etania was a vast land and there were many unknown places she was going to have to go through in order to find home. Her mind continued to trail as she tried to remember all of the new trees and creatures she had met in Denotoria Forest with Willow. She looked over at Wyo who was already asleep.

## The Strange Tree

As the evening sun shone down upon Wyo's feathers, they reflected a light golden brown color. She too was also very sleepy. It was a nice warm evening to sleep under the stars. Just as she was beginning to doze off she heard a rustling sound and was startled. She sat straight up and noticed a large figure standing before her! Frightened, she looked at Wyo, but he was fast asleep and snoring heavily. She looked back up at the figure that was at least five times her size. She couldn't make out the face but was able to see its' out-line. It was shaped like a fig tree and had little tiny cakes of figs on some of its' branches. The tree turned away and began to walk toward the lake. Aya stood up and felt compelled to follow.

Once it reached the edge of the lake, the tree turned and faced her. Aya stopped abruptly in her tracks and looked at all the little fig cakes and suddenly wanted to eat one. As she reached out her branch hand to take one, the tree slapped it away. He turned around. With his back toward Aya he pointed his right branch toward the moon. As Aya looked up at the moon, she saw several birds flying toward her and the tree. There were blackbirds, bluebirds, hawks, sparrows, a buzzard and an eagle. Aya watched the birds quickly stop their flight and nestle one by one into the tree. Then, the tree turned slowly around to fully face her once again. It was a very eerie sight for Aya, as she looked up at the tree looming over her, with all of the birds sitting within his branches, just watching.

"My name is Xeraino. There are many friends and enemies where you are traveling. Don't be fooled into thinking all the friend-ly ones are good and all the mean ones are bad." He reached out and touched one of her branches with one of his and it burned her. She looked at her branch and saw smoke coming from it and began to tremble. "Don't be frightened," he said. "When you are not sure if someone is your friend or enemy, try to touch them with that branch. You will feel their sincerity through it. But don't overuse the branch or you will become dependent on it. Learn to have Wisdom in your 'responses' to the experiences you go through. Collect Wisdom like a treasure; hold on to it tightly."

The sight of the tree was almost overpowering for Aya. She was spellbound as she listened to Xeraino's voice speaking to her. "Sometimes you won't be able to touch the object in question and at other times you will be tired and drained, not noticing the slight zap when it is an enemy, so learn to depend on the Wisdom within." All of the birds in the tree were peering at her closely. Some looked friendly and others looked like they wanted to devour her. "Go ahead", he said. "Try it, but first use Wisdom." She looked at a blue bird who was singing a most pleasant tune and thought, *Oh, this one is gentle, such a soft gentle song could not come out of someone who was mean.*

She reached out and touched the bird, only to experience a sharp jolt in her singed branch, which caused her to yank it back quickly. Xeraino looked at her saying, "No, that one is evil, don't be fooled by a pretty song, look at his eyes" As she looked into the blue-birds eyes, she saw a cold darkness within them that startled her. She stepped back, almost stumbling and then felt foolish for not noticing the darkness in the birds' eyes earlier. "Don't worry," said Xeraino. "You'll do better - practice will help. You must exercise your senses if you want to be able to spot evil ahead of time. It will save you much grief and heartache."

She looked back at Wyo who was stirring in his sleep. She turned around to ask Xeraino a question, but he was gone. She closed her eyes tightly and opened them again. *Where did he go?* She looked down and realized that she was now standing next to the dead tree that she had been leaning on earlier! *Was I dreaming?* she thought. *Gosh, it seemed to be so real!* As she reached out one of her branches to sit down, she noticed that the branch was singed on the end of it. Shocked, she pulled it back to look at it. "Oh my . . . " she said out loud. "It really did happen!" Immediately she knew it wasn't just a dream. She then remembered that Willow had told her she would encounter several mysterious and mystical things. *This will help me on my journey,* she thought as she glanced again at her singed branch. *I won't forget.*

### The Ditch

Aya was singing loudly as she and Wyo continued on their journey. It had been several weeks since they left Denotoria Forest. Wyo recognized a few of the hillsides and knew they were still in Valorous. "I'm just not sure how far away Cordaya Valley is from here," he said. "But at least I know this is the direction to take."

Aya began to skip and sing a little tune; happy to hear they were headed the right way. She was looking up and didn't notice the large ditch in front of her. Wyo had looked back at her and saw what was about to happen. He flew back to warn her, but it was too late. She let out a scream as she fell! Once she landed on the bottom of the ditch, she stood up - making sure nothing was hurt and then looked around to see where she was. The ditch was about six feet wide and ten feet deep, much too deep for her to jump out of. She tried to climb up the sides of the dirt walls but she kept falling back down. Try as she might, she couldn't jump out. She screamed and cried and yelled for Wyo to help her, but each time he pulled at her with his beak, he accidentally tore part of her treetop or cut into her limbs. It was going to be difficult for him to get her out.

Several hours had gone by and Aya was tired from trying so many times to get out of the ditch. She didn't like it in there. She felt utterly helpless and out of control and was very frustrated and angry with herself for falling in! Wyo called back down to her, making sure she was all right. Angrily she yelled back, "Yes! I'm all right!" Wyo stood over the ditch wondering how to help her. Aya sat back and closed her eyes in frustration. As she waited for Wyo to figure out what to do, a memory of a conversation with her father began to unfold in her mind:

*I was almost a year old and I remember that it was a cool evening in Cordaya Valley. Mother was looking after the other seedlings when father began to speak to me:*

*"Little one, when you search for something, what do you think the first step should be?"*

*"I think I should know what it is I'm searching for, before I try to find it."*

*"What if that thing you are searching for is in you?"*

*"In me? But father I'm right here with my mother, brothers and sisters and you! Why would I search for something in me when I know where I am?"*

*I remember seeing father's gaze go off into the distance as he spoke outloud. He probably didn't really expect me to answer.*

*"How much of this information will you remember and realize as truth?"*

*Then he quickly looked back down at me and very seriously said:*

*"You know where you are, but you don't know why you are or who you are."*

*I was so confused then, and a little frightened. My father . . . he has such a strong presence, especially when he's so serious! But I remember on that particular day, all of a sudden a tender, gentle look came over his face as he looked down at me and spoke. Gosh, it touched my heart.*

*"Who you are is even more important than the name you will be given. Even though your mother and I will choose your name carefully for the Naming Ceremony, and it will have great significance . . . who you are is even more important. Some day you will understand. Once you find your identity and purpose, don't ever let anyone take it away from you. Always remember, you are more that just a daughter or sister —much more. But you won't really know this until you learn it through some of your experiences."*

It had been a strange conversation. Whenever her father spoke, it carried a lot of weight. She had listened very intently, even though she didn't totally understand. Aya open her eyes, still reflecting on the memory. "Well," she said out loud, "I know I'm here in a ditch, but I sure don't know how this can help me find me. And I sure don't know how any good can come out of this!" The frustration at being delayed in her journey was mounting. *Why did I have to fall into this big ditch and where did it come from anyway?* She had no way of knowing that a tremendous wind was sweeping through that area. A young tree seedling would be no match for it.

She looked over, surprised to see Wyo who had his head tucked beneath his wing. *He must have come in to keep me company when I was in my memory walk,* she thought. All of a sudden she heard a loud noise above the ditch. It sounded like thunder, only louder, deeper and longer. Wyo looked up and quickly flew to the top edge of the ditch. He saw dust flying and coming toward them. He flew back down and yelled, "There's a big wind and heavy dust coming toward us. Duck your head down and I'll cover you with my wings." Wyo spread his wings over her entire body to protect her. From below they could hear branches snapping and see flashes of light coming into the ditch as the noise escalated. The winds blew into the ditch, tossed some of the dirt around them and then went out. Soon it was quiet. Wyo removed his wings from around Aya and slowly flew up to the top of the ditch to look out.

"Oh-h-h-h!" He saw the large tree that he had been standing in front of earlier. It was now broken and stretched across the road. Several other trees had been struck by lightening and were split in two. He looked toward the north and saw a huge grey and black cloud approaching. The heavier rains were coming – he had to get Aya out of that ditch or she would drown in it! He flew back down, warning her of the coming storm.

"Hold onto my claws!" he said while trying to shelter her under his wings. They each felt heavy drops of rain begin to fall harder and harder into the ditch. He wrapped his claws gently around the middle of her trunk as she clung to him. Although he was shorter than Aya, he was extremely strong, with a long wingspan. He felt the pellets of rain coming down swift and hard on his wings. As the rain came down, it brought with it some of the dirt that was on the inside walls of the ditch. A small but potentially dangerous mudslide was beginning to form. Some of the mud fell on his wings and was beginning to close in on them, almost like quicksand. Aya panicked when some of it got in her eyes and mouth. Flashbacks of the Great Storm began to flood her mind. She sputtered and squirmed as fear gripped her.

Sensing her fear, Wyo firmly said. "Aya! Don't panic! Don't kick so much or you'll make me lose my balance. I'll get you out of here if you'll just settle down!" She quickly came to her senses. His tone of voice stilled her squirming. Wyo was deeply concerned, but he didn't let Aya know it. She needed his strength right now. "We haven't come this far for us to give up now!" he shouted loudly as the mud rose up, reaching the bottom of his claws.

Although his wings were soaked, and mud was seeping in between his feathers, he continued to try and flap his wings. Using his right claw and beak he began to dig and pull, dig and pull, inching his way to the top, while holding Aya securely in his left claw. The slight flapping of his wings gave him a little leverage. Slowly, against the elements, he struggled to pull them both out. Although they had come up about four feet, he was getting exhausted. But he knew if he gave up now, they would both go under what was now become a dangerously thick mudslide.

"If anyone is listening out there, we need help!" he screamed into the wind.

"Yes!" echoed Aya. "Someone! Help us!"

## Seven Pieces of Bark

As soon as the words were out of their mouths, a huge gust of wind blew in seven pieces of bark that came from another tree that had died. The seven pieces went down and settled in the mud below them. Wyo looked down and saw that the mud and pouring rain were causing the bark to rise up toward them. Soon he could feel the bark beneath his right claw. The bark was slowly becoming a raft! He set Aya down on the largest piece of bark and sat next to her, watching her intently making sure she was okay. There was fear in her eyes, but she managed to reach over and hold tightly onto his left leg.

He looked around, noticing that the more the rain came in, the higher the mud began to rise - soon bringing them to the top of the ditch! All of a sudden, the makeshift raft was literally pushed out of the ditch by the mud and rain! They were both seated on the largest piece of bark, as it slowly began to float about a half mile down the hill. Once they reached the bottom of the hill - and could float no longer - the rain stopped. Wyo took his wing off from around Aya and she let go of her tight grip on his leg. They both sat there for a moment, amazed at what just happened!

As she looked out at the mountain across the plain, Aya saw a rainbow. The sky was light blue, looking as if it wasn't even aware that there was a storm. Still sitting on the bark, covered in mud, the two of them looked at each other. An incredible bonding took place at that moment. Aya realized that falling into the ditch had saved her life. The monstrous winds would have destroyed her. Yet, when the rains came and it looked as though they would drown, the water formed mud and the bark from another tree that died, had saved them. The very storm that almost took her life also saved it. Aya was in awe at the struggle of life and death that she had just gone through. They had cried out for help, and help came.

Near them was a small puddle of water. Wyo went over to it and began splashing around. Aya came running after, joining him in the moment. Wyo looked at his friend, who was soaked and splattered with mud! Aya looked at Wyo as he flapped his mud-laden wings in the puddle, trying to clean them. All of a sudden they both began to laugh uncontrollably.

Finally they settled down, and looked at each other with tears still in the brims of their eyes. The love they felt for each other at that moment was the deep abiding friendship kind of love. Wyo had risked his life for her; he would have died for her. *What kind of love was this?* She would never forget this day as long as she lived. Reflecting on the memory she had earlier, she now understood some of the things her father had spoken. Through this experience, she learned some things about herself. She realized how angry she was when she didn't get her way. She saw how being impatient didn't help the situation. Most of all, she learned through Wyo's actions, what it means to be a friend.

They came out of the puddle then, shaking themselves off while reaching out to each other. Wyo's wing span tenderly wrapped around Aya's tree trunk. For the first time, since the Great Storm tore her away from her parents, Aya felt secure and loved. *I have a friend for life with Wyo* she thought. *And so does he.*

---

## Boxer & His New Family

Once they arrived at their home, Whiskers and Sniffer sat out on their long porch while waiting for Boxer to finish washing off the slime from Geseemo. Whiskers worriedly looked at her husband. "Do you think he can find his way back to the house?"

"Yes, Rocky knows the way. He'll lead Boxer back here when he's finished cleaning up."

Rocky was their friendly, but mischievous fox who loved to roam the neighborhood. He was about a year old when his parents abruptly left Cordaya Valley and moved to another land. He tried following them for a while, but lost their scent and went down a wrong trail. He had been wandering near the swamp for several days when Whiskers and Sniffer found him. It was love at first sight for all of them. Since that day he became a permanent member of their family.

Before long, Boxer was approaching their porch with Rocky leading the way.

"Wow, do I feel so-o-o much better!" he said while bounding up the stairs and plopping down in a rocker next to the rabbits. Rocky went over to lie down on the floor next to Sniffer. They all began rocking back and forth, simply enjoying the sunset. At one point they were rocking in unison and they looked at each other and chuckled.

Boxer yawned, "Gosh, I guess I'm still kind of tired."

Whiskers smiled over at him. "Of course you are Boxer, it's been quite a day for you. You can relax out here for a while and then you should probably get a good nights' sleep. I've fixed up a bed in our extra room."

Boxer yawned again, nodding his head in agreement.

"You know Sniffer," said Whiskers, "wouldn't it be nice to throw Boxer a little party to celebrate his arrival to our island?"

Sniffer nodded his head, "Yes dear, in due time."

Boxer drifted back into the thoughts of all his experiences over the last few days. He had witnessed the terrible violence of the Great Storm in Cordaya Valley. He had been soaked by the heavy rain and torn away from his parents by a forceful wind. He was tossed and turned within those winds for a long time until he crossed the borders of Rensamor Island. Then the wind stopped and he rapidly fell into the mouth of Geseemo, the giant slime fish who was watching him from the Swamp below. Boxer now realized that the only reason he wasn't immediately eaten was because one of his branch feet had gotten caught on some object in her mouth. That alone had prevented her from swallowing him!

Boxer continued the journey in his mind as he rocked. *When I began to pound and jump - it must have caused Geseemo's saliva to run back down into her throat and that's why she began to cough and choke, eventually spitting me out of her mouth!* He laid his head back on the rocker and closed his eyes. It was comforting as he listened to the soft background sounds of Whiskers and Sniffer talking about the plans for tomorrow.

"Well," said Sniffer, rising out of his rocker and helping Whiskers out of hers, "let's all get some sleep. We've got a big day planned out for you Boxer." Boxer stood up with a big grin and followed them into the house.

## Rabbit Grass

Soon it was early morning once again on Rensamor Island. The sun barely peeked out from beneath the horizon when Sniffer called out to his wife. "Looks like a perfect day for a walk dear." She walked over to him and held his hand as they both looked out the window. Just then Boxer came out of the bedroom, yawning and stretching his long limbs.

"Good Morning Boxer!" Sniffer said. "We're going to take you on a tour of the island today and introduce you to some of our friends and neighbors."

Boxer looked surprised. "I'd like that, but why would you do that just for me?"

Whiskers looked at him tenderly. "We're hoping you will like it here and consider staying."

Boxer hadn't even thought about his future. Things were moving so fast.

"Come on you two," said Sniffer, hopping down the steps. "Let's get moving!"

At the bottom of the stairs they all turned to the right and began walking up and down another long road. After about ten minutes, Boxer noticed they were entering into another area of the island that looked lush and green. Then he saw some of the soft grass that he liked and blurted out, "Hey, this looks like that long soft grass that I bounced in!"

Sniffer was impressed with Boxer's alertness. "Yes, Boxer, it's called Rabbit Grass. The seeds of that grass are extremely precious and are planted in special places. Where the seeds come from, is a generational secret within the lineage of our family. We planted this particular field a few years ago during the planting season." They all walked through some of the grass on the edge of the road as Sniffer continued talking.

"While we were plowing up the soil for the Rabbit Grass seeds in this area, we heard cries coming from the land surrounding Geseemo, so we ran down there to see what was going on."

Boxer looked up then and interrupted, "Weren't you afraid of the that ugly slimy fish?"

"No," replied Whiskers. "For some reason she can't move out of the Swamp. We're not sure why, but she never, ever leaves the Swamp."

Boxer looked relieved as Sniffer continued his story.

"After searching the land and looking over at the quicksand near Geseemo, we saw nothing. Then we heard the cries come again and looked up in the air to discover that it was only the Neoflight Messenger birds making loud sounds to each other as they flew east."

"Who are the Neoflight Messenger birds?" asked Boxer.

"Honestly I don't know where they originally came from or who sends them," said Whiskers. "I just know that they're not evil and that they bring all kinds of messages – some for direction, some are for warnings and others give hope. The messages vary."

This seemed to satisfy Boxer so Whiskers continued. "While near the area by Geseemo we looked back down and noticed that some of the seeds had fallen out of one of our seed pouches. Rabbit Grass seeds are tiny. We picked up as many as we could, but they were quickly scattered into the wind. Later during the growing season when we were checking on our Rabbit Grass, Stinky the turtle had come by to ask us why we planted Rabbit Grass so close to Geseemo. We told him the same thing we're telling you now."

Whiskers paused and then added, "Stinky doesn't come through here very often, so it's unlikely that you will meet him today, but he is a good neighbor. Even he knows how important it is to only plant the Rabbit Grass in certain places on the island."

"Why is it so important?" asked Boxer.

"Let me tell!" shouted Rocky as he scampered around Boxers feet, jumping up and down.

Sniffer laughed, "Go ahead little Rocky. Let's see how well you remember."

Rocky jumped on Boxer causing him to fall down into a sitting position within the tall Rabbit Grass. "Look Boxer," he said in his wise young voice, "I just pushed you down into the softest grass you ever felt. Right?"

Boxer bounced himself up and down saying, "Yes! Right!"

"Well," continued Rocky, "do you feel kind of warm and tingly on the inside? Do you feel good sitting there?"

"Why yes I do. I even feel like I could fall asleep. That's how comfortable I am!" exclaimed Boxer.

"The reason is this; being in Rabbit Grass causes almost all of the creatures or trees who land in it to feel peace and joy. Sometimes they might even have a vision or fall asleep and have a beautiful dream," continued Rocky as he walked around Boxer.

"Wow!" shouted Boxer. "I was having an awesome dream just before I met Sniffer and Whiskers!"

Sniffer came over to stand next to them, "That's right Boxer," he said. "What is amazing to us is that you landed on that small area of Rabbit Grass. That particular area of Rabbit Grass is only about ten feet by ten feet!" Boxer pondered that thought for a moment.

"Was it luck?"

Whiskers said quietly, "I don't think so Boxer."

Boxer looked up, not realizing that he had spoken his question out loud. With a puzzled look on his face he turned to look at

Rocky. "Why is it that only some and not all creatures and trees feel good in the Rabbit Grass?"

Rocky shuffled his feet, "Uh, let me think. Oh! I know! Some of the creatures and trees around here aren't very nice. *When* they stumble into the Rabbit Grass, they start to feel *uncomfortable*. And if they happen to fall asleep, they have nightmares." Rocky jumped up and down saying, "How'd I do Mom and Dad? Huh? Did I do good?"

Whiskers swooped Rocky into her arms. As he licked her face, she giggled. "You did wonderful son! You remembered it well!"

Rocky began to wiggle in joyful exuberance and jumped out of her arms, racing up the hill to beat them to one of their neighbors' homes, Betty Beaver. The LongEars and Boxer went back unto the road following Rocky up the hill toward the Beaver community. As they walked through the neighborhood, several beaver parents and their babies came out to say hello and to watch the new tree walk by. "I feel like everyone's staring at me," said Boxer shyly, as he looked down to the ground.

Sniffer chuckled. "They are Boxer. But they're looking at you with admiration. We don't see many trees around here these days."

Boxer looked at him and was about to ask why when Sniffer somberly said, "Why don't you save your questions until later, you've got a lot on your mind already. I think over the next few weeks we'll just show you a few places and introduce you to several of our neighbors as planned. We'll have plenty of time later to tell you why your landing here is so important to us. He reached out and patted Boxer on the shoulder.

"That's a good idea," Whiskers added as they went to introduce him to several Beaver families.

By the end of the day they had traveled many miles and Boxer had met several friends and neighbors of the LongEars. "Wow," he said as they headed back home. "You sure do have a lot of friends.

Your neighbors seem just as kind and good as you both are!"

Whiskers proudly smiled. "We do have good neighbors and we're a very close community. We stick together. Whenever a neighbor has any problems, we're all there to pitch in to help."

"You know," said Boxer as they turned down the road going back past the Rabbit Grass, "I'm liking this place more and more." Whiskers reached over and tugged at Sniffers' arm, looking at him with hope in her eyes. He squeezed her hand, acknowledging that he understood and felt the same way.

---

## *Webber & Dr. Tearrent*

Webber woke up the next morning feeling very empty and alone. The lighting in the sterile room was very dim. There was a small beam of light coming in through the bottom of the door. She felt disoriented for a moment, unable to remember where she was. Her thoughts were just coming out of a dream she had. In the dream she was tucked inside one of her mother's branches, when a powerful blow hit Webber's trunk, causing her to be swept away from her mother into the rushing, swirling water.

She made herself sit up so she could become more fully awake. At that point she realized that it wasn't just a dream. It had really happened to her. She had been swept away during the Naming Ceremony, just before her parents named her. *I wish I could reach into my mind and pull out some of the bad memories and pain,* she thought. Being inventive, Webber was sure that there must be a way to remove bad memories.

Instantly Webber had a memory flashback to a conversation she once had with her mother:

The rest of the seedlings had gone over to Wyo's house to

play. Webber had a slight fever and stayed home. It was a warm summer night. While sitting on one of Cedra's roots, Webber asked her mother if she ever had any bad memories.

"Yes, little one, I have lots of memories that are painful to think about."

"How do you get rid of the pain Mother?"

Her mother, being very wise and patient said, "There are many ways to get rid of the pain. Someday I will tell you what some of those ways are."

Webber thought about that for a moment.

"Mother, what about the memories? How do you get rid of those? Can't someone invent a way to get rid of our bad memories?"

Cedra looked down at her inquisitive and creative seedling and touched her small treetop.

"Well my daughter, here's something to think about. What if by removing one bad memory, they also accidentally erase all the good ones?"

Suddenly the lights in Webber's room were bright once again. A click in the lock sounded and Dr. Tearrent walked in with a smile on her face.

"Good Morning Webber, did you sleep well?"

Webber didn't sleep well at all, but in order to be polite she said, "Yes, yes I did. Thank you."

Dr. Tearrent stood admiring the painting on the wall by Webber's bed. "Isn't that a wonderful painting of the outdoors? Don't you feel like you're outdoors when you look at it?" she asked.

Again Webber disagreed thinking, *I hate it*. But out loud she answered, "Yes, it's very nice." Webber felt like she should just agree for right now and not cause any problems,

The Dr. smiled. "Today Webber, I am personally going to take you on a grand tour of our Research Facilities and the surrounding land in Krontia. I believe you will be very impressed!"

Feeling that the doctor expected it, Webber stood up and followed her out of the room where Klon was waiting. Webber imagined that he was Dr. Tearrent's top weasel. They walked down the two flights of stairs and down another corridor past the examination room that Webber had been in.

As they walked, Dr. Tearrent bragged about how clean everything was in the building.

"On the first floor are all of the examination rooms. It's where all new visitors are required to go when they arrive. The second and third floors are rooms for our guests."

Webber looked at her. "What's on the fourth floor?"

Even though the doctor smiled, the look on her face indicated to Webber that Dr. Tearrent did not like being asked questions. With the same smile on her face, she looked at Webber firmly. "Webber, why don't you just listen and learn today?"

"All right," said Webber quickly, noticing that Klon was closely watching their interaction.

They went outdoors and the sun was bright. Webber excitedly looked around, expecting to see many flowers, bushes and trees. But so far there were none, at least not around this building. They turned to their left and began walking. They walked past the building where she had landed in the trashcan. As Webber looked over, Dr. Tearrent said, "Yes, Webber, that's where we found you. Let me see if they cleaned up the spider web, you wait here." Webber waited as the doctor went over and spent at least fifteen minutes inspecting the area. Satisfied that it was completely cleaned out, she continued walking. Klon nudged Webber urging her to catch up with the doctor. They walked at least another half mile. Soon, from a distance Webber saw a little garden down a small hill to her right with a bench in it. She was sure she saw someone sitting on the bench. *Oh my,* she thought. *I think I see flowers and trees in that garden!* She wanted to say something but the doctor began walking faster saying,

"Yes Webber, that's our little garden, I'll show it to you sometime. Let's hurry now; my associate Dr. Crophyster is doing an operation this morning. I'd like to sit in on it."

Dr. Tearrent was a tall, staunch tree and moved very quickly. Webber practically had to run to keep up with her. As they walked further, Webber didn't see any trees, bushes or flowers in this area, except for that little garden they had passed. Soon they came to some winding stairs on their left. "We'll go up to the research building now!" said the doctor excitedly. Briskly she began walking up several of the outside stairs – two by two. "We're doing some fascinating research on various trees and their unique diseases. One of our goals in Krontia is to free the trees of all diseases and abnormalities!" When Webber heard this, her heart raced. *Maybe they can use some of my creativity and ideas in this place. Plus, if I keep real busy, missing my family won't be in my mind so much.*

## The Operation

Finally they all stood at the top of the long stairway, in front of the tall round glass building. It was extremely hot outside and there were no shade trees here. They all stopped to catch their breath, so Webber had a moment to briefly look around. To her left she saw rows and rows of trees that were stripped of their bark. They had no leaves on them. Every single tree looked exactly alike. It startled her immensely. The building in front of her was a huge glass dome. She looked to the right. It looked exactly the same as the left side. There were rows and rows of trees that had been stripped of their bark. None of them had any leaves. They all looked identical.

The front door suddenly opened. Rig, the weasel with white spots on his brown fur, greeted Dr. Tearrent and Klon. He didn't even glance at Webber. He swung the doors wide open on both sides. As Webber began to move, Klon held her back. The moment

Dr. Tearrent walked in, a loud roar went up as several trees and weasels clapped and shouted – welcoming her into the Dome. The doctor took it in stride as the crowd opened up a path for her to walk through.

*She's very well respected here,* thought Webber. Klon then released Webber to follow. Webber walked in slowly. Everyone inside the Dome gasped as they looked at her rich dark textured bark, and full branches. The doctor quickly silenced them with a look. She held out her left branch, pointing at Webber saying, "This is my guest. I have personally examined her. She is clean. I will tolerate no more outbursts." Everyone instantly quieted down as Dr. Tearrent walked in, closely followed by Webber, Rig and Klon. Webber noticed two circular stairways that led up to the balcony. One was on the right side of the Dome and one on the left. As she followed Dr. Tearrant up the stairs on the right, she felt humiliated. Everyone's eyes were watching her as if she were some kind of freak.

Once on the top floor, Webber saw many doors that were spread out in a circle. The doctor led them through the one that had a square doorknob. As they went, Klon stayed near the back row of seats by the door with Rig. Dr. Tearrent motioned for Webber to follow her into the seats next to a railing that overlooked an open room below. As Webber looked below, she saw a male tree lying down on an operating table with several other trees bent over him. Dr. Tearrent looked seriously at Webber. "You are very privileged to be watching an important part of history taking place. They are injecting a small device into that tree's head. It will erase all of his bad memories. We've done this with female trees, but this is the first time we've put one in a male tree."

Webber couldn't believe it! Just a few weeks ago she had asked her mother about this!

The doctor saw the excitement on her face and was pleased. "I'm glad to see your positive response. Not all trees like this idea."

She turned her attention back down to the operation. "You see," she continued. "The male tree is sleeping. He's been injected with a simple sleeping solution that we extracted from one of the small plants that grow in our greenhouse. It's quite safe." Webber had so many questions, but knew she had better wait until later to ask them.

Dr. Tearrent continued to explain. "So many of the trees that come here searching for their Destiny Land, have had horrible experiences. Most of them carry many diseases or scars on their bark. Some of their leaves have been chewed away by worms. We have developed a way to cleanse them of their bark and remove their leaves and their bad memories! As I told you earlier, we're now experimenting with removing the bad memories from the male trees. The female trees that we've already operated on, usually decide that they want to stay here. You've already seen many of those trees when you came into the Dome. They believe their Destiny is to guard and protect the Dome."

Webber was so excited about the bad memory operation that she didn't hear much of what the doctor was saying. She watched the operation below and nodded her head now and then, but Webber's mind was going wild. *I had that idea! I'm going to tell her that I thought of it long ago. I'm sure she'll be impressed and train me for something!*

Below them Dr. Crophyster, Dr. Tearrent's colleague, continued finishing his operation. Once finished, all of his assistants stood back and clapped.

"Bravo!" shouted Dr. Tearrent as she stood, motioning for Webber to do the same.

Dr. Crophyster looked up in surprise and waved at Dr. Tearrent, motioning for her to come down to his office.

Dr. Tearrent quickly got up, leaving the balcony to meet with him. Klon grabbed Webber's branch hand and ushered her out as well. As they walked back down the stairs, Webber noticed several more doors were all around on the bottom main floor; but they were all closed and no one was in the hall. "They're all working Webber," said the doctor. *She must be watching me all the time, she always knows where I'm looking*, Webber thought.

They came to a large door with the name Dr. Crophyster on it. Dr. Tearrent didn't bother to knock. As she rushed in, Dr. Crophyster stood up and they shook hands. "Well done Doctor," she said. "We're progressing! Now we've worked on both species of trees. We've perfected the operation for females and now we'll continue operating on the males. This is great progress!"

Dr. Crophyster smiled, looking over at Webber now and then. "Yes, yes Dr. Tearrent, we're well on our way!"

"I want you to meet Webber. I am going to personally train her and would one day like to have her stand next to you as you continue to perform this new operation." Dr. Tearrent said. She looked at Webber with a smile, "Would you like that Webber?"

"Oh yes!" Webber replied instantly. "I would really like that!" In her exuberance Webber blurted out her ideas. "Actually, I had that thought about removing bad memories - even before I came here!"

"Really?" said both doctors at the same time while Klon silently stood at the back of the room, guarding the door.

"Yes, I did!" Webber replied. "I just knew there had to be something that could remove painful memories. And now I find out that there is!"

"Well," said Dr. Tearrent. "We probably thought about it long before you did, but nevertheless, you did think about it and that shows initiative!"

Webber was overwhelmed by everything that was going on and didn't notice the sarcasm in Dr. Tearrent's voice. She naively continued talking excitedly. "I'm also very creative and have a vivid imagination. I'm sure that will be useful to you!"

Dr. Crophyster and Klon were silent as Dr. Tearrent just stared at Webber, who in her excitement didn't notice any of the negative looks that had just taken place around her.

"Well Webber," said Doctor Tearrent. "Let's get you back to your room. It's been a long day. Klon, take Webber back while I visit with Dr. Crophyster."

Webber smiled and turned away, walking out the door with a new lift to her step as she followed Klon back to her room.

Dr. Tearrent sat down. "Dr. Crophyster, I have a special reason for letting her keep her bark and leaves. Trust me."

He looked at her saying, "I do not doubt your intelligence Dr. Tearrent. You are my superior. I trust you totally."

She had a smug smile on her face. He knew she was working out a plan in her mind.

What Dr. Crophyster and Dr. Tearrent didn't know, was that beneath the soil under their branch feet - there were others - also making plans.

## Plasick Meets Adronack

The smell of heavy plastic was once again in the air as the guard walked over and kicked Plasick. Startled, she sat up, trying to shake off her sleepiness and gather her thoughts. She quickly stood and followed the guard up the hill to meet with The Mixer. He saw her coming slowly toward him. "There you are!" he said in his gruff voice, noticing that she was also leaning on a walking stick. "Hurry up!" he said while frantically waving the order form in front of her face. "I've got a huge 'special' order to fill! We have to build ten molded pink tables, one hundred molded pink and white chairs, and one thousand figurines of an alligator idol with real grass mixed in! That's not all!" he said while holding up a handful of backorders.

"Before the end of the week I'll need fifty gray cabinets trimmed with strips of tree bark!" Turning to the guard, he yelled out, "Take her to the work station! Now!"

The guard moved quickly, racing over to the large Idol Factory and pushed Plasick through the front doors. The noise inside was loud! Several machines were mixing and pressing things into shape. Hundreds of creatures and trees were working in different sections. Some were on assembly lines; others were in booths doing work by hand. There was a sign that said, *Tearing Section*. In that section were about fifty worker trees tearing the bark off of other trees and bushes that had been captured and smuggled in from other lands. Some of the trees were shorter than Plasick, others were taller, but none of them were over six feet.

Plasick was shocked to see that all of the worker trees had been totally stripped of their bark. It made her sad. She wondered why of all of her bark wasn't taken off. Some of the trees and seedlings stopped working to look at her as she approached. But they soon heard the crack of General Saguwas' extremely long tail, which he used as a whip.

"Until I tell you to stop, YOU DON'T STOP!" he yelled through the megaphone. All of their leafless heads quickly looked down as they continued the tearing process. Then he shoved Plasick over to the *Tearing Section*. All of the trees kept their eyes looking downward and didn't stop working. The lizard grinned, enjoying the power he had over them. He cracked his tail whip loudly and yelled out, "Stop working now!" They all stopped working at once. "Look up at me and listen!" They all lifted their heads and looked only at him. Even though he stood right in front of them he yelled through the megaphone again. "You also have my permission to look at our new worker!"

Plasick could hear all of the trees and seedlings as they turned their dry leafless heads to look at her. It was unbearable for Plasick to see the grief and sadness in their eyes. He screamed out to the tallest female tree of the group while pushing Plasick toward her. "Adronack! You will train Plasick! To the rest of you – BACK TO WORK!" Turning abruptly he walked off to take care of a problem in the fur section.

Adronack looked at Plasick with lifeless eyes. "What is your name seedling and why did they leave some of your bark on you?"

Plasick looked up at her. "My name is Plasick and I really don't know why they didn't tear all of my bark off. I'm still wondering about that."

Adronack shrugged her shoulders as if disinterested. "*The Tearing Section* is watched over very closely because of the scarcity of bark. You can't let your guard down for a moment. General Saguwas always pops in and has spies that watch everything we do. See those holes up there?" She pointed to six holes in the roof. "At any given time a spy-snake will slide in and come down to our section and listen to our conversations. You never know when they are watching or when they are listening. If they hear the word 'escape' or 'run away' they slither quickly over to General Saguwas and tell him. Several trees have been chopped up for trying to escape. They use those pieces in some of the furniture." A shiver went through Plasick's body as she listened.

Adronack continued. "Come over here next to me now and I'll show you how to strip bark off of the fresh cut tree parts and the dead tree parts. We also get a few live bushes that come in and we need to take off their bark as well. I'll warn you now; they sometimes struggle. Once the bark is entirely off, the bushes are put in that big vat and crushed up to be used as trim for some of the idols and furniture." Adronack mechanically began to show Plasick how to do the job. Several times Plasick felt tears well up in her eyes and tried to stop them from spilling out. She was able to contain them for a while. But, as the screams came out from some of the bushes in that section, her tears fell profusely. Adronack looked at her. "Don't worry, you'll soon stop crying. You'll get used to the screams and block them out. Hear that loud music? That's what they play when we work so other workers won't hear the screams. I've been here for three years. You'll get used to it, trust me. Tomorrow you'll have to start doing this yourself, just like I'm showing you."

Plasick quickly wiped her tears trying to block out the screams. It was hard because the bushes were on the massive table directly in front of her. Adronack continued, "Plasick, you've got to pull yourself together or you will be on this table someday."

Plasick sobered up quickly. "All right Adronack, I will," she said as she was given a fresh branch to practice on.

## Adronack Shares a Secret

Plasick worked in the factory every day from morning till night. Each day that went by was much like the one before it. Sometimes she and Adronack would be able to talk, but it was limited. One time, during a rare moment, Adronack shared a secret with Plasick. They were sitting on a huge rock taking a break outside the factory.

"Look," said Adronack as she held out the backside of her right branch hand.

"I don't see anything," said Plasick, leaning over - straining her eyes to see.

Adronack laughed quietly. "Look, there are three jewels Plasick. They are hidden, deeply imbedded into the underside of my little finger." Adronack lifted up her bark-stripped branch fingers as she continued speaking in a soft, proud voice. "See? There they are, my three tiny red stones. Two are just a bit smaller than the other one."

Plasick finally saw the stones as the sunlight briefly shone on them. "Oh yes, now I see them! They are very beautiful and unusual looking Adronack. Why do you have them?" she asked while reaching out to touch the barely visible jewels.

Adronack continued to smile. "These are rare and precious stones which symbolize my children. I dug small holes and embedded them into my little finger when my seedlings were born. I also had one matching red jewel embedded on the inside of each of their little finger branches. This way if we ever got lost, we could find each other." She sighed deeply. "The day I was captured and shipped over to Barren Land, I told my children to run and hide, so they did. I had to leave them behind. Someday I'll find them. I'll know them by the matching stones on their branch finger. Look at the unusual way they reflect gold in the sunlight!" She lovingly looked at the jewels turning her hand in the light. "They are my three tiny red jewels. Whenever I think I can no longer bear the suffering, I look at them and remember that they escaped. I miss them terribly."

Plasick looked up at Adronack's face. Seeing her sad countenance, Plasick reached over and touched her arm. But Adronack pulled away quickly and stood up.

"Oh, don't feel sorry for me Plasick. I'm tough. You'd better get tough too or you'll never make it here!"

Plasick nodded her head and stood up next to her. They both began to slowly walk back to work. As if she were all alone, Adronack spoke in a whisper while touching her little finger, "They'll never find my jewels. They'll never take them away from me."

Although they saw each now and then, Adronack and Plasick were never able to have another long meeting again. Plasick thought that Adronack probably kept to herself most of the time, so she wouldn't endanger Plasick. It was well known that very few workers in Barren Land became friends. The guards separated anyone who looked like they were forming friendships. The workers were always kept very busy.

As time went on, Plasick learned her job well and worked hard.

The Mixer and General Saguwas noticed. They saw potential in her, so they began training her to make idols. Designing and creating idols was a very tedious job. They began to call upon her more and more, making her workload much more difficult than the others.

All the trees stayed in a huge building up another hill past the Idol Factory. There were rows and rows of flat beds in it. The trees were constantly monitored, so they were careful about what they said to each other. At night, there was a little more freedom because the Armadillo guards usually never disturbed their sleep. Of course, there were always exceptions.

## The Dark Sky

One night in particular, after a long day working in the factory, Plasick was extra tired. She quickly fell asleep and began dreaming. In the dream she was fighting with her siblings again and her father was trying to teach her that kindness worked much better than anger. A loud voice broke into her dream and suddenly she was jolted back into reality. The Mixer came barging into the bunkhouse yelling. "We just got a rush job order for fifty Snake and fifty Alligator idols from a very important company. I need all of you at the factory now!" She jumped up out of bed, grabbed her cane and hobbled, trying to quickly follow several other trees, as they all raced over to the factory. The Mixer was close behind.

Once inside the worker trees immediately began pulling out the molds of various Reptile idols. Pots with hard plastic were already heating up. Bins of fur and tree bark were pulled out from under the big working tables. General Saguwas barked out orders, cracking his tail whip, letting it cut through some of the workers dry branches when necessary. Plasick took her place and was looking for Adronack, but didn't see her. She knew this was no time to ask questions; so she pulled out the molds she would need and went to work. The place was loud with activity. Some trees bumped into each other as they tried to hurry. Plasick's leg began to pound with pain. She knew it would be a long, long night. While dragging the heavy molds over to the ovens she thought, *Will I ever be able to leave this place?*

The trees worked long tedious hours – well into the morning. They were still working when Plasick came out into the yard and hobbled down the hill with her cane to do more work for The Mixer. She looked up to see a few birds fluttering around, trying to escape the heat from the melted plastic as it began to fill the air. It was a rare sight to see so many birds at one time.

Going down the hill was not easy for Plasick, especially after having stood all through the night. The Mixer was working her overtime and seemed especially anxious to get a new batch of mix worked up for some wealthy Reptile customer who was looking for unique furniture. He actually wanted a lot of earth mixed into the furniture. The Mixer didn't often sell earth, because it took away from the land where his factory was.

As she came close to the edge of the water, where she first landed, The Mixer showed her the large kettle that he was stirring over the fire. The mixture was yellowish green. The round table top molds were already laid out on the ground near the water. The Mixer began shouting out orders. "Fill the molds with this mix! The guard will pick up the molds and submerge them in the water – so they cool faster. He'll pull them out quickly. They'll start to harden, but should still be soft enough for you to work with." He handed her a bucket of pale brown earth . . . for the soil in Barren Land was not healthy. "Pour some this dirt into each mold and stir it. Use it sparingly, just enough so it's sprinkled here and there. Wait one more hour for it to completely set and then pull the table top out of the molds."

Plasick started to work, not understanding why she was the one he picked to do this job. *Anyone could have done this,* she thought to herself. *It's as if he always wants to overload me with work and keep me weak with tiredness.* The Mixer raced back up the hill. *I must have another purpose other than this,* she thought as she mindlessly continued working. She looked up at the sky. *That's strange, it's almost daylight and the sky is getting dark. Burning so many unusable bushes and all that plastic must be making the atmosphere darker than usual.* Plasick didn't want to think about it. She was growing weary of this place, but hopes of leaving seemed so slight. Where would she go after all? She didn't even know how to get home – or if there was a home to go back to.

❧ ❦

# Greedo & The Cave

Sand City's population continued to grow. Numby knew that there were many new opportunities for advancement coming his way. During the training sessions he paid special attention to Greedo's progress. He saw that Greedo was becoming extremely sharp witted and clever, so he quickly promoted him to second in command. Greedo was efficient and self-motivated. Unlike the others that Numby had trained, Greedo didn't need to be told what to do. Because of that, he was able to work directly under Numby and rarely needed to check in with him. Numby was so confident in Greedo that he sent two new recruits, Jet and Fret, for Greedo to train. Jet was a thin, lanky tree that always took radically stupid chances. Fret was the shorter, stockier tree that worried a lot.

Greedo eagerly began training them but was frustrated at their slow progress. Then, one summer night around 10 p.m. as the three of them were walking down a dark alley, Greedo saw another prime training opportunity. His keen eyesight noticed an old Ostrich wandering down the alley ahead of them. He looked disoriented and was swaying a little bit here and there. Greedo knew those ostrich feathers would bring a good price or trade. "Come on you guys, now you can put yourselves to work – don't foul up this time!"

Jet and Fret ran ahead of Greedo and began slowly walking next to the Ostrich, pretending to help him.

"Oh thank you so much," said the Ostrich in a feeble voice. "I seem to have lost my way and it's so dark in here . . . I can't see very well."

Fret patted the Ostrich. "Sir, don't worry, we'll help you out."

In the meantime, Jet grabbed the Ostrich from behind and knocked him out with a club. The Ostrich fell to the ground never to be heard of again. Jet opened up the large bag he was carrying as Fret pulled out several of the Ostrich's long feathers and stuffed them into the bag. There were several trashcans near them, so they dragged the Ostrich over and hid him behind one of the larger ones. Greedo had watched the whole thing from a distance and now approached them. "You only knocked him out. Right?"

Jet quickly stammered. "Uh-h-h . . . Oh Yeh! – he'll wake up in the morning with a bump on his head, that's all!"

Fret looked down at the ground, knowing that the Ostrich would never wake up.

"Good job you guys. I couldn't have done better myself."
Jet and Fret smirked at each other as they followed Greedo down the rest of the alleyway.

At the very end of the alley, there was a small hill with a fence in front of it. There was a narrow winding path that led to the top of the hill. Greedo was curious to check it out.

"Fret, leave that bag behind the red building over there for now."

Fret did as he was told.

Having no idea where the path led to, Greedo leapt over the

fence and began walking up the hill. He called out to Jet and Fret to follow him. Once they reached the top, all three of them looked over to their right and saw a second smaller hill down below them.

"Right in the middle of the city!" pondered Greedo out loud. Being the explorer that he was, Greedo directed his two sidekicks to follow him. He ran down toward the short hill with Jet and Fret following. As soon as they reached the bottom, they began to climb up the smaller hill. Their branch feet were having a hard time gripping the dirt because it was like slimy mud. They shifted positions, moving their branch feet sideways. Slowly they crept up the hill, finally reaching the edge of the top. This top of this hill was flat and wide. They stood there looking around and spotted a small ledge that looked like a step to their left. Then they noticing that a lot of brush was covering up what looked like - an opening to a cave.

Greedo raced over and began moving and pulling the bushes and brush out of the way. Jet and Fret jumped in to help. Once almost everything was removed Greedo noticed a thin vapor of light coming out from inside the cave.

Amazed, Greedo watched it move. "It looks like a cloud of moonlight shining and waving in the air." All three watched the vapors move up into the sky. It was an odd thing to see because by now it was 11 o'clock at night. There were no Bug Lights in this area to help them see and the stars weren't shining. It was almost black all around except for a sliver of moonlight poking through the clouds. As the vapor moved above them, they continued pulling and moving the bushes out of the way.

Greedo shouted out, "Hey! It looks like an opening to a cave!"

He leaned forward and a musty damp smell filled his nose as cool air came out of the cave. He stopped and stood up. The smell stirred something in his memory. He frowned in frustration. *What does that remind me of? It's back there . . . still too vague in my mind.* He leaned over continuing to work. As he pulled the last bush away, he saw an entryway into the cave.

"Let's head on in!" he shouted.

While going in, he couldn't fully stand up, because although the inside of the cave was wide, it had a low rock ceiling. He bent over and squatted on his branch legs. As he shuffled in he felt damp, slimy, moss covered rocks beneath his branch feet, which caused him to slip now and then.

Jet and Fret stood outside the cave looking at each other - wondering if their boss really knew what he was doing. Crawling around in a musty cave was not their idea of a fun night. Although they were getting a little tired of being bossed around so much, they continued to follow Greedo. Wherever Greedo went, they went.

## The Blue Light

They too bent over and shuffled into the cave. Although they began to slide around a bit because of the wet moss, they were still able to move forward. Greedo was just a few feet ahead of them. Still bent over, Greedo started to venture in a little further, holding on to the sides of the wall that were cool and damp to the touch. Then, he heard dripping sounds – the kind one would expect to hear in a cave. He squinted his eyes and looked in further. *I see it! The blue light! That has to be where that vapor of light came from!*

To Greedo, it looked like a blue-white light that was coming from some kind of hole deeper in the cave. *What is it?* He felt the pull of energy coming from the light and was drawn to it. *I've got to see what it is.* Slowly he began inching forward, not realizing that his recruits followed right behind him. Fret kept creeping closer and closer to Greedo's left side, suddenly bumping into him. Before he knew it, Greedo's feet were up in the air and his back was down on the ground. There was a loud cracking sound!

"Oh-h-h," groaned Greedo, "that hurt!"

In anger he quickly recovered from the pain and was furious! Behind him, Jet and Fret were slipping, sliding and colliding with each other. Soon all three were sprawled on the ground of the cave – and they were only about nine feet inside!

Greedo was fed up with those two seedlings! Every time he went walking somewhere, they were so close behind him, he could hardly breathe.

"What's your problem?" he yelled out. In frustration he began swinging at them in the dark. The only light in the cave was the faint blue-white light coming from the hole behind him and a dim light coming through the opening of the cave. He figured if he kept swinging his fists fast enough, they would eventually land on one of them.

They couldn't see Greedo either, but Jet and Fret could hear the sounds. *Swoosh! Swat! Swoosh!* They knew he was furious and was trying to hit them. He was swinging hard! Every time they heard a swishing sound, they ducked as low as they could to get out of his way.

"You jerks! When I need you close you aren't there and when I don't need you around . . . there you are! You're getting in my way!"

Jet and Fret began to stumble over each other, trying to crawl their way out of the cave.

Greedo blasted at them. "GET OUT OF HERE!!!"

Frantically, Jet came crashing out of the cave first. Fret followed close behind, but then his feet slipped and he fell forward and began to roll out of the cave, bumping into Jet. Once out, they both scrambled to their feet, moving off to the right side of the opening of the cave. Standing very still they waited, hoping Greedo wouldn't be able to reach them with his punches. Out came Greedo, still cursing under his breath at the two of them. He looked to his right and saw them hovering. "Get over here!" he screamed. "Help me cover up the cave till daylight comes! I'll come back another time without you two bumbling idiots!" They all went to work pulling and stacking the brush. Greedo put the last bush over the hole. Fret and Jet still stood far away from him, just in case he started to remember how much he wanted to hit them.

But Greedo was lost in his thoughts about this new discovery. "Let's get going!" he said. "This time you two stay in front of me so I can keep my eye on you both!" Jet and Fret quickly ran in front of Greedo and began to jog down the smaller hill and back up the larger hill, disappearing as they headed down toward the alley. Greedo stood for a moment, looking back at the cave. "I wonder what that light was? I wonder where that cave leads to? Yeh, I'm coming back on my own! I'm gonna come in the daytime and find out just what's in that cave!" Greedo was so engrossed with his thoughts that he didn't realize he had just spoken them out loud. He also didn't notice that there was someone close by – listening to every word he spoke.

Chapter IV

# Histories, Visions and Memories

## Aya & The Toucan Seer

Several months had passed by since Aya and Wyo's incredible experience of escaping from the ditch. Throughout the journey, their friendship continued to grow. But now, they had entered into a new different land. Wyo knew they were no longer in the land of Valorous, but he still wasn't exactly sure where they were. A strange scent in the air was interfering with his sense of smell. Most of the land around them was very dry and yellow. The land was parched, in dire need of rain. "Aya, I'm not quite sure where we are," he said as Aya stood up, ready to travel again. He didn't tell her that they had actually been going in circles for a few days.

Aya's face began to frown with worry, but then brightened as her eyes fell upon a large section of lush green grass across the road.

"Wyo, look over there. See? On the other side of the road there's a large open field, full of green grass. It's beautiful! Maybe that's the way home, I'll bet we're closer than you think!"

"Maybe we are," he said as he tried to convince himself.

Aya called out again, "Do you see the field?"

Wyo looked to where she was pointing, "Yes, I see it. I also see a tree stump in the middle of the field."

Aya looked for the stump, just as a bright colorful bird came flying down and stood on it.

"Wyo, a bird just flew down on the stump!"

Wyo looked over at the vibrantly colorful bird standing on the stump. He noticed that she stood about two feet high and had a long smooth bright orange beak. He smiled.

Aya excitedly yelled out, "Do you see the bird?"

"Yes Aya, he replied. "That's the Toucan Seer."

Aya quickly turned to look at Wyo. "But how do you know that?"

"You probably don't remember, but she was at your Naming Celebration."

Aya shook her head as she looked back at the beautiful bird. "No, I don't remember."

Wyo then began to tell Aya what he knew about the Toucan Seer.

"She flies throughout Etainia at different times, for various reasons. No one knows where she lives; not even me. She is very wise."

"Wiser than you?" Aya asked in surprise.

"Yes," he replied. "Much wiser than me. She also has over seventy-seven different colors of Succor Feathers on her body."

Aya quickly asked, "What's a Succor Feather?"

Wyo explained. "It's a special Feather that will help someone who is in need or distressed. Some of her Feathers have 'Wisdom' inside of them; others might have 'Truth' and so on. She alone decides what kind of Succor Feather to release, and when to release it. Much depends on the particular *need or distress* – that is deep within the one seeking."

"I think I understand," said Aya as she listened intently. "But how do they get the Feather; does she just let whoever is seeking pull them out of her?"

Wyo explained, "No, she *feels or senses* the seeker's need for help and then she flies to wherever they are; perches herself on a rock, tree trunk, trees, shack or wherever she finds room – and then she waits. After a few moments, she decides what to do."

Aya listened in wonder. "But how does she know when a Feather leaves her body? And what happens when all her feathers are gone?"

Wyo grinned as he answered Aya's questions.

"She knows when a Feather leaves, because she feels a slight surge of energy released from her body – but just for a moment. And it never takes away her strength."

Aya reminded him, "And what about when all the feathers are gone?"

Wyo chuckled. "She never releases all of her feathers at one time. When a Feather is released, and the seeker needs to keep it, another Feather grows quickly in its place. The only time she doesn't grow back a Feather, is when a seeker doesn't need to keep it. Then, the Feather eventually finds its original place on her body, and settles back in."

By now they had crossed the road and were walking in the green grass toward the field. Aya earnestly asked, "Why is she here Wyo?" He looked at her quietly. "Because you are here Aya and she knows that you are seeking Wisdom. But don't rush her. She usually doesn't let anyone come too close to her."

Aya began to get nervous, "What do I do Wyo? I need Wisdom to know where we are, and which direction to travel. I need to continue on my journey!"

Wyo walked over and whispered into her ear. "Approach her gently."

Aya walked slowly toward the Toucan Seer. After she took a few steps, the bird flapped her wings and flew away. Aya ran and ran toward the tree trunk, breathlessly shouting, "No, no, don't go, don't leave me! We're lost, we're lost!" She stopped near the tree trunk, watching the Toucan Seer fly farther and farther away.

Aya dropped her head and began to sob. "Why did she leave us? Why did she abandon us?" Just as the last words came out of her mouth, Aya felt a brief tickle on her forehead, and then on the tip of her nose. She instinctively held out her hand and a Feather – the color of copper – landed. Wisdom had found Aya.

Even though the wind began to blow, the Feather did not move. As the sunlight shone on the tip of the Feather, it began to evolve into thousands of sparkling, silver and copper particles, that looked clear, like crystal. Aya stared in amazement as they floated around in front of her face. Then, for a brief moment, the particles spread out into a horizontal layer, and began to form into a tree standing at the edge of a brook. Aya stood back, mesmerized by this amazing vision in the atmosphere. As she continued looking at it, she remembered passing a Noble Tree and a deep brook that was near it. At the time, she didn't think there was a way to cross it . . . *or was there?* "Wyo! The Wisdom Feather showed me a vision! We need to go back to where we saw that deep brook and the Noble Tree. Do you remember?" she said excitedly.

"Yes, yes I do! It was less than a mile back!"

Aya began running, "There's got to be a way to cross the brook to the other side. That was the direction we should have gone! I believe that's what the Feather is telling me now!"

Wyo flew ahead as Aya ran, clutching the Copper Feather. Once Aya saw the vision, and accepted Wisdom, the Copper Feather had re-formed itself in Aya's branch hand. Soon, they saw the brook and the Noble Tree from a distance and began to run faster. They stopped and looked at the water behind the tree. It was very deep – very wide. The Feather began to tickle Aya's hand, causing her to open it. As she did, the Feather flew out and over the deep waters. Again the silver and copper particles appeared; but then they dropped into the water, forming seven white, flat Stones. Each Stone was four feet, by four feet, and had shimmering colors of silver and copper embedded within. Aya fixed her eyes upon them. The Stones looked like they were breathing!

She stood on the edge of the brook, frozen, unable to step onto the first Stone.

"I'm scared Wyo! The Stones are moving! Or wobbling – or something!"

"Aya! Hurry Aya! It won't last long!" yelled Wyo from behind her.

Fearfully, Aya stepped out onto the first Stone and was surprised at how solid it was! Feeling more confident; knowing that she must do this; Aya quickly began to step across all of them. As she did, each Stone left some of the silver and copper residue on her branch feet – which would never wash off.

Finally, they reached the bank on the other side. They both turned to look back. Aya's eyes grew wide as she saw the seven flat, white Stones, rise up out of the water, turning into tiny silver and copper particles – to once again form the original copper-colored Feather. The Feather then blew far, far up into the atmosphere and disappeared into the sky.

"Don't worry Aya, the Wisdom Feather will find the Toucan Seer. Remember? That's why she never has to worry about losing all of her Feathers."

Aya was still in shock, at all she had witnessed and experienced. *What is this strange and mystical place we are in*" she thought as she looked at the brook that was now behind them.

"Wyo, what is the name of this place? Are we still in Valorous?"

"No Aya," he replied. "Even though I've never been here before, I know where we are now." Wyo looked around as he continued, "I've only heard stories about this place. We're in the land called Sumatoria – it's a land where magical and mystical things happen. But, don't worry, because of the Toucan Seers' guidance, we can be assured that we're headed in the right direction." Aya looked at Wyo, wondering if he had just read her thoughts.

As they walked away from the brook and up a small hill, toward another road, Aya began feeling an unusual electric energy around her feet and legs. She looked down at her and saw wispy, light colored vapors swirling around her branch legs and feet. Astounded, she also noticed that some the silvery, copper residue was still on parts of her branch feet! All of a sudden the residue disappeared, only to reappear once again. Aya shook her head from side-to-side, while looking down at the strange happenings. Then, she looked up and smiled. As Perception opened her understanding she knew that every new land she entered would have secret treasures for her to take to the next place. From deep within she heard the words, "*Do not waste your moments.*" She hoped she would remember.

Wyo and Aya continued going toward the road. As they walked under a tall fifty-foot Seyama Tree, they didn't notice the Toucan Seer sitting high, high above, on one of the branches. Nor did they hear the simple, yet tender song that she sang, as her watchful eyes followed them down the hill:

> *"Little ones, little ones, do not fear. Little ones, little ones dry your tears.*
> *Follow the road that you've come upon. Not to worry. It won't be long.*
> *Keep on looking — open your eyes. Soon you will discover unusual things.*
> *Follow the road to the mysteries ahead. Be amazed to see what they bring."*

The copper Feather, having being soothed by the song, had already settled in amongst the other Feathers on the Toucan Seers' back – satisfied to have completed the task.

— ◆ —

## Boxer & Coconut Flats

It had been several weeks since Boxer blew into Rensamor Island. He met almost all of the nearby neighbors on the right side of the island. Now that he was getting acquainted with most of the community, Sniffer and Whiskers thought it would be a good time to take him to the other side of the island and tell him the rest of story.

It was early morning. Whiskers and Sniffer had finished all of their work around the house the day before, in preparation for an all day trip with Boxer. Sniffer looked at the time, "We'd better get those two up so we can cover all the ground we want to before dark."

Whiskers looked at him. "You're right dear, but maybe we can give them another ten minutes to snooze."

Sniffer smiled at her and nodded his approval.

Rocky was becoming a close friend to Boxer and was often found resting near his bed at night. He had appointed himself to keep watch over Boxer. But today, instead of being on the floor, Rocky was lying across Boxer's legs, sleeping. During the middle of the night, Boxer woke up crying; missing his mother and father. Rocky quickly jumped up on his bed to lick Boxer's salty tears and comfort him. Soon after, both had fallen asleep again.

Boxer sat up and stretched, enjoying the sunlight coming through the window. His sad dream was forgotten. He looked down at Rocky who was still sleeping and spread across his branch legs. *It's nice to have someone watch over me,* he thought as he laid his head back against the headboard. *I remember another time when father watched out for me in a different way. I got into a fight with the neighbor seedling who pushed me down and then ran off before I could do anything . . .*

Boxer got up and ran home, not saying a word to anyone. But his father noticed something was wrong, so he took him aside. He didn't correct him or even ask what had happened. He only said, "Sometimes you won't be able to do anything about the bad things that happen in life."

Boxer looked up at him. "But father, in this case, I was really afraid. I don't think I would have done anything – even if I could have!"

His father looked at him with compassion. "Everyone has their own journey to take, in order to find their individual courage. It's different for everyone. And it will be different for you."

Even though he was hurting, especially in his pride, Boxer listened carefully.

"Remember this. If you go through your life with honesty, making sure that you have the right motives, you will be able to face most any problem – head on. You might not be able to solve the problem, but you won't be afraid to look at it."

He knelt down and held out his arms. Boxer ran into the long arms and was quickly encased in the security of his father's embrace.

"Boxer, always be loyal to yourself and those close to you. Then, when you are accused of doing something wrong – even when you haven't – you can stand strong. Those who are your true friends will stand with you – no matter what."

Hugging his son tightly, he lifted Boxer up off the ground and looked into his eyes. "Will you remember these things?"

A tear went down Boxers cheek as he nodded his head yes.

"Good." He gently wiped away the tear before placing Boxer on his shoulders. "Let's go see what your siblings are up to. O.K.?" Boxer smiled holding on tightly as he and his father went to find his sisters and brothers.

*I miss my family so much.* While remembering the conversation with his father, he pondered out loud, "I know I can be fearful at times, but I'm also fiercely loyal and try to be honest!"

"Boxer! Rocky! It's time to wake up!" called Whiskers from the kitchen.

The sound of her voice startled him and he quickly sat up. Then he reached over and gently shook Rocky, who slowly opened his sleepy eyes to look at Boxer. "Today is a special day Rocky, I'm going to see the rest of Rensamor Island!"

Rocky woke up instantly, sat on his hind legs and raised up his front paws in anticipation. Jumping off the bed, he began to run in circles on the floor.

Boxer laughed as he shook his branches and walked out of the bedroom into the kitchen.

"Good Morning Boxer!" the Long-Ears' said in unison. "Are you ready to go exploring and hear the rest of the story about our Island?"

"I sure am!" he said with a smile on his face while following them down the front stairs.

"We're going to move fast today, we've got a lot of ground to cover before dark," Sniffer said as he and Whiskers headed back toward the Swamp area.

As soon they were close to the small section of Rabbit Grass, where they first found Boxer, Sniffer began to talk about the Swampland. "There many enemies in and near this Swamp. The Slime creature is primeval and comes from an evil place. She gave birth to two slimes, which are more evil than she is. We've never seen her mate. We think he's still hiding in the Swamp, but we're not sure." Boxer's eyes grew large as he listened.

"See that broken bridge on the left side of the swamp area?" Boxer nodded as Sniffer continued.

"It was once a very long bridge that connected to the smaller island, Coconut Flats, which was claimed and built only a few years ago. Most of the trees and creatures we know have set up their homes here on Rensamor Island. Several of them live near the Beaver Community. But there are some restless seedlings that come exploring around this Swamp, trying to see what Coconut Flats looks like from a distance. Some even venture out, attempting to cross the bridge. A few of the young seedlings and animals actually make it— but not very often."

"Geseemo's slimy offspring, Snitch & Snatch, are brothers. They always stay close to the bridge trying to catch and torment anyone who comes near it. Their friends, the Beetle Bites and Dragon Stingers, like to bite and sting the seedlings and animals.

That usually sends the curiosity seekers running back home. But there are other times when they don't get away. The Beetle Bites keep attacking until the helpless victim nears the edge of the Swamp and falls in. Then Geseemo takes over and devours them."

Boxer's eyes grew large as he exclaimed, "That could have been me!"

"We're amazed at that too Boxer!" exclaimed Whiskers as she continued filling in other details. "In the middle of the murky swamp are several huge leafy 'lily' pads where the Toadies and the Lapper Zapper Frogs like to hop back and forth on. The Beetle Bites and Dragon Stingers don't get near the Lapper Zappers because when they do - the frogs zap them with their long ropey tongues and eat them. Toadies also love to eat the BeetleBites and Dragon Stingers."

Rocky was standing near Whiskers and looked up at her asking, "Mom, do Geseemo and her children try to capture the Toadies?"

"No Rocky," she said, "because the Toadies have little sticky needlelike thorns on their backs. When Snatch tried to eat one of the Toadies, sharp needles went into his mouth. He bellowed so loud that the whole island heard him. Of course the Toadie took it in stride and hopped away!"

Sniffer laughed, "The Slimes haven't bothered the Toadies since!"

Rocky jumped up and down in front of his parents. "I know something!"

"Go ahead Rocky, what is it?" said Sniffer.

"Well-l-l," Rocky began. "Even though that lil' patch of Rabbit Grass wasn't supposed to be there, it helped a bunch of seedlings and creatures hide when they were trying to reach the bridge! Maybe while they were in the grass, they got a vision dream too, just like Boxer did!"

"Could be," said Whiskers, "Our mistake in dropping the seeds, actually turned out to be a good thing!"

They took Boxer further down a winding road and up toward another hill that overlooked the waters.

Boxer looked out at the clearest water he had ever seen. "Is it deep?"

"It's very shallow for the first ten feet and doesn't even come up to your waist," replied Sniffer as he poked Boxer in his tummy trunk. "But then it becomes very deep. It's too far to swim. The only other way to get there is by crossing The Broken Bridge, or by some kind of floating object."

Whiskers pointed past the water toward land. "Boxer, do you see where that small island is --- near those tall palm trees with the brightly colored coconuts in them?"

"Yes, I do," he said while squinting his eyes.

"It's a resort and vacation spot for all kinds of creatures. There's a reason so many young seedlings are willing to risk their lives to get there."

"Why?"

"Some seedlings feel they don't have a Destiny here. They want more adventure. In Coconut Flats there are hundreds of boats. The owners of the Island promise to take any seedling -one way to wherever they want go in Etainia. But there are two conditions. They must work at the resort for three weeks without pay. And, if they want to go back home to Rensamor Island, there is no ride for them. The owners hate us because they know we discourage everyone from going to Coconut Flats."

The four of them watched gold reflections of light ripple across the water as the sun went down. "We'd better head home," said Sniffer somberly.

As they turned to go back, Boxer noticed that Sniffer and Whiskers were extra quiet. He wasn't sure why, but thought it had something to do with the young seedlings and Coconut Flats.

"Are we going to look at any other places?" he asked.

"Not tonight Boxer," Sniffer said. "In a couple of weeks we'll take you to a place far up on the right side of the island and finish telling you the history of Rensamor."

As they turned down the winding road Whiskers added, "Yes, and we'll also tell you some of the problems we are facing."
Boxer looked up at her sad face, but she quickly recovered as she saw him watching her.

"Don't worry about that now Boxer! Let's all race back to the house and see who wins!"

Rocky jumped up in the air and took off running with Boxer racing close behind.

Sniffer watched the two of them racing toward home.

"Do you think he's too young to understand everything?"
Whiskers looked over at her husband as they started to jog. "He may be young, but Boxer is a very wise and mature young seedling. He'll remember what he needs to and what he doesn't remember, he'll ask about."

Sniffer nodded. "You're right. We'll present the offer to him after he meets Enobleus. Agreed?"

Whiskers placed her hand in his. "Agreed."

---

## Webber & The Memory Talk

Webber had been in training under Dr. Tearrent for over seven months and was learning rapidly. Joff, the weasel without a tail, was assigned to be Webbers' personal assistant. Webber was allowed to walk the grounds as long as Joff was with her. One day she decided to go to the garden she had seen with the bench in it.

As she headed toward it she heard Dr. Tearrent yell out,

"Webber, I need you in the Greenhouse. We're extracting some of the sleeping serum today."

She ran to catch up with the doctor.

"Webber, at this time I do not want you to go to the garden. I have my reasons."

Webber fearfully looked up. "All right doctor, I won't."

Dr. Tearrent was very impressed; as was Dr. Crophyster, at how quickly Webber was learning things and how quickly she took orders.

"Webber, you're doing very well, we're proud of you.

"Thanks to you doctor for letting me in on your experiments." Dr. Tearrent smiled. "There's only one problem Webber, it's all those bad memories that you have. I believe they are getting in the way of your ability to learn. Think about allowing us to ease your pain though our operation."

Webber tried to keep up with the doctor's long strides.

"I know what you mean Dr. Tearrent. I've been thinking about it a lot. But I keep remembering what my mother once said when I was little."

Webber looked sideways up at the doctor, wondering if she should say anything.

"Yes?"

"Well," Webber began. My mother once said, *'What if by removing one bad memory you also accidentally erase all the good ones?'*"

The doctor stopped immediately and stared at the young seedling.

"I'm sure your mother was wise Webber, but has she done what I have done? Has she performed operations? Did she ever run an organization like I am doing?"

Webber looked down at the ground. For the first time in her life, Webber felt ashamed of her mother. "No, she hasn't done any of those things."

Dr. Tearrent began walking faster. "Don't worry Webber, not everyone has the kind of intelligence that I do. But remember, I am alive and your loyalties are now to me, not to your mother. Don't speak to me anymore about her. Do you understand?"

Webber answered quietly; "No I won't speak of her anymore." Webber felt even more ashamed, feeling that she had just betrayed not only the memory of her mother, but also her entire family. Still, she remained silent.

Soon they were both standing in front of the Greenhouse. Heitenny, a large chameleon opened the door. Webber was amazed at this long skinny chameleon with a split tail that changed into several different colors while they walked through the door.

"Good morning Dr. Tearrent," he said, not looking at Webber.

"Good Morning Heitenny, this is Webber. I believe she will soon be promoted to Dr. Webber once her training is completed!"

"Oh," he replied without any expression.

"I've brought her to you because of your expertise in extracting various solutions and serums from several of our flowers and plants. Webber will be under your tutelage for four weeks. I expect her to have intensive, focused training," said Dr. Tearrent as they all slowly walked through the entire one-story glass building.

"You can count on me doctor," he replied.

Dr. Tearrent turned and saw a new species of flower to her left. "What is this? I've never seen this one before."

He walked over to the large flower that had three vines instead of petals. Attached throughout each vine were sticky nettles.

Heitenny got excited as he explained. "This is a new plant that recently came into our lab. Dr. Crophyster brought it in last week for me to test it. I discovered that the nettles, when cut in half and squeezed, have a mind-altering effect on some of our trees. The trees begin to hallucinate. They become very vulnerable during that time. I actually think this could be put into a drinking solution."

"Does Dr. Crophyster know this?" Dr. Tearrent asked.

"No, I just tested it yesterday. I'm still observing the trees that I gave it to. I felt you should know first and I knew you were coming today," replied Heitenny.

"You did well," said Dr. Tearrent. The chameleon let out a quiet sigh of relief.

"I'll speak to Dr. Crophyster and we'll be back tomorrow to hear more." She turned, preparing to leave the tall glass building. As he rushed over to open the double doors she looked at him with her piercing eyes. "Teach Webber all you know."

Over the next few weeks, Webber had witnessed several trees being stripped of their bark. At first it was hard for her and she had many nightmares about it. But, everyday Dr. Tearrent spent an hour or more with Webber, speaking to her about the good they were doing and how the advanced work in Krontia was helping others. Dr. Tearrent was subtly influencing and controlling Webber's thoughts, little by little.

Webber gradually got used to implanting the memory-removing device. She became quite good at it. Once they finished implanting the device into all the minds of the male trees, they were going to experiment on the little seedlings. Although she was becoming more accomplished and popular in Krontia, there was an unsettled feeling within Webber. Something inside of her questioned some of the strange things that were going on in Krontia. But she tried to ignore those feelings by justifying the work she was doing as *progress for the future.*

As of yet, Webber hadn't met anyone she could call a friend. On different occasions she tried to go visit the little garden she had seen, but was always distracted by something else. Joff usually went with her anytime she went out on the grounds. But, there were days of reprieve when he was off doing other work for some of the other doctors. Klon was always nearby but kept mostly to himself. *He seems to be the leader over Joff and Rig*, she thought to herself one evening while preparing for bed. *I don't know who I can trust with some of the concerns I have on my mind. The thoughts just won't go away. No matter how much Dr. Tearrent tries to convince me, those lingering thoughts of uneasiness keep coming to my mind!*

At the same time Webber was climbing into bed, Dr. Tearrent was meeting with Dr. Crophyster in one of the guest rooms below. "I'm worried about her good and bad memories. They will interfere with our plans." Dr. Tearrent said to Dr. Crophyster as they sat across from each other. "I've been working on her mind over the past several months. She's starting to weaken but she keeps remembering what her mother said about 'losing the good memories when you try to erase the bad.'" I've got to get her into the operating room before too long."

Dr. Crophyster listened and nodded, knowing that Dr. Tearrent would find a way.

～⌣～

## *Plasic & The Discovery*

Several months had gone by since Plasick landed in Barren Land. The hot sun rose up once again, shining its strong rays across Plasick's closed eyes, waking her up. There were no stationary trees or bushes to cool the land and shaded areas were hard to come by. She yawned and for a brief moment, remembered pieces of the dream she just had.

*One of her brothers was teasing her, waving his bushy arm in her face saying,*

*"Come on Slick, let's go chase butterflies!" He always believed that she got away with things because of her innocent face and big brown eyes. So he nicknamed her Slick. She started running after him . . .*

The thick smell of heavy plastic in the air pulled her thoughts away from the lingering dream. It was time to help The Mixer mold and stock up on more plastic images for the homes in the land. *Smells like he's cooking up a big batch now, he'll be looking for me,* she thought while walking out of the tree bunkhouse. Shaking the sleepiness off, she put the dream behind her and went searching for him to get her orders. Walking toward the factory, she saw him coming toward her. "There you are!" he yelled out in his gruff voice. Each day he was giving her more and more responsibilities that were usually given to Adronack. She hadn't spoken to Adronack for several weeks. No one seemed to know where she was, or else they weren't saying.

They stood in front of the factory door as he told her what he needed. After motioning her to start at a worktable, he briskly walked away to another project. The stiffness of the plastic parts on her leg was causing her great difficulty in walking. She kept her cane near because when she stumbled and fell, she wasn't able to get up by herself. She rubbed her leg and looked at the clock. *I'd better get moving.* She ordered the Sawflies to cut some of the wood in thin strips as she continued building several more custom designed idols. Staring off into space, her mind drifted once again back to that first day. She remembered how loud she had screamed as her bark was being torn off. But The Mixer had screamed even louder, saying that he would destroy her if she didn't shut up. She immediately stopped screaming. Her will to live was stronger than the pain she was enduring.

*I'm so weary of this place, yet how can I escape?* she thought while gluing a thin piece of bark unto the idol she was creating. Stepping back for a moment, she unconsciously admired her work. *I have only a few trading resources and I don't even know where I would go anyway.* Time went by slowly as she continued building the idols. Soon it was 3 o'clock and she prepared to take the idols to the Packaging and Delivery Building. Picking up her cane, she started pushing the cart of idols and went outside. There was only one road that led in and out of the Delivery Building, which was about a mile away. Mixer trusted her to do this job, but he always sent one the Mugruccets to follow her there and back. The Mugruccets, one of the few animals that still had fur on them, had many sharp teeth. They lived outdoors and roamed around. They stood only six inches high and were around two feet long. The guards trained them to bite and tear at the heels of the seedlings and creatures if they tried to escape.

By the time Plasick returned from delivering the finished products, it was 4 o'clock. She passed by the Resource Building and decided to see if they were low on any resources. The Mixer usually stayed on top of this section, but she knew he wouldn't care. Now that she carried extra responsibilities, he trusted her more. Although the guards still had the upper hand, she had been given little more authority than the other workers.

As she approached the wide open door, one of the many Armadillo guards blocked her from coming in. "I'm one of the Worker Managers," she said, holding out her wrist. He looked at the tag attached to her wrist and saw the stamp that proved she was a Manager. "All right, all right! But hurry, we close the doors at 5 o'clock!" Plasick walked into the loud noises of the chopper machines as they cut up the extra bushes and trees in the back of the huge building on the left side. She tried shutting out the noise with the earplugs the guard had given her. After putting the plugs in, she went near the wall, where all the excess tree parts and bushes were. She went through bin after bin, making sure they were filled and spilling over the top. Each bin was made out of heavy plastic with wheels attached to the bottom. It took her over thirty minutes to inspect each one of them.

As she came to the last row, she noticed a bin that was tucked further back, almost hidden. It didn't look full from where she stood. She moved several of the bins out of the way so she could check it out. If The Mixer found any bin that wasn't filled to the top, he screamed about it and then harshly punished someone. *I wonder why I haven't heard about this one back here? He usually lets me know when something isn't done right,* she thought as she finally reached the bin. She set her cane down and saw that it definitely wasn't full. As she put her head over the bin to look deeper inside, she picked one of the leftover tree branches up. "Hm-m-m, some of these bare stripped branches will work just fine on the new idols I'm building," she said while digging around in the bin. Finally she found a really nice branch hand that suited her. As she turned the hand around to get a closer look at the finger branches, the sun came filtering through the window, revealing golden reflections on three . . . tiny red stones.

Plasick pulled her head back, threw the branch hand back into the bin and gasped, "Adronack!" She quickly put her hand to her mouth so the guard wouldn't hear her. Her head dropped down then and she wept, trying to muffle her cries. The loud noises of the chopper machines helped. Her back was toward the guard and another taller bin was behind her, so he couldn't see her directly. She began to panic. "I can't breathe, I can't breathe," she whispered under her breath. "I can't cry now. I've got to get a hold of myself!" Her mind was racing and she nervously looked at the clock. It was almost 5 o'clock. The guard would be coming to look for her.

"Make yourself do this," she said to herself as she leaned over the bin once again and picked up Adronack's branch hand. It took all of her strength to fight back her tears. Somehow she found inner strength as she stood stiffly, clinging to the heavy bin for support. Speaking quietly through her tightly clenched jaw she made a promise to herself. "I will remove these jewels and hide them. I will one day find her children." Plasick looked around as she quickly hid Adronack's branch hand within one of her own bushiest branches. She knew she had to act fast. She couldn't let anyone know what she had found in that bin. She swiftly went past several tables in the back, pretending to inspect them. Then she went toward some of the resource bins on the right. *That way, when I come out to face the guard, he'll think I came out from the right side of the building.* This would cover her tracks in case anything came up later.

As she walked toward him he glared at her. "You sure took your time!" he growled.

Trying to act normal she simply threw the earplugs in the trash, walked by him, and left the building. Walking fast she continued moving, straining to hear the door slam and the snap of the lock behind her. But there was no such sound. She walked faster and before long heard the guard running after her yelling.

"Worker Manager! Stop, right now!"

She froze, slowly turning to look at him.

"For a Manager, you're kind of forgetful aren't you? You left your cane!" He thrust the cane toward her. Nodding, she grabbed it and turned back toward the bunkhouse/warehouse, letting out a deep sigh of relief, hoping no one would stop her again.

It seemed like forever, but she finally made it to the tree bunkhouse. *The trees won't be there just yet. It will take them around fifteen minutes or so to come back from work!*" She ran to the back toward her bed and looked around - no one was there. Having picked up a sharp rock on her way into the building, she sat down and began to fervently dig out the three jewels.

"Come on, come on!" She said out loud as she dug.

One jewel popped out and she set it beside her on the bed. Frantically she looked at the clock. It was 5:10.

*Got to hurry. Don't panic. Calm down.*

She desperately dug out the other two jewels. One of them popped out, falling to the ground. Stopping it with her foot, she quickly grabbed it, placing both stones next to the other one. She hid the rock and Adronack's branch hand under her mattress and picked up the three jewels. *Where do I put them? Where do I put them?*

She heard the shuffling of the other trees as they opened the door. Plasick's bed was on the right corner at the very back of the tree bunkhouse so she had only seconds before some of them came back to their beds.

*Where? Where?*

Desperately searching, her eyes looked toward the wall near the head of her bed. She saw a small loose brick! Nervously yanking it out, she set the three tiny red jewels inside, quickly putting the brick back the way it was. She fell back down on her bed, pretending to rest.

Once all the tree workers were inside, the guard did a quick walk through and left. Plasick turned toward the back wall and began to weep quietly, then louder. The other trees seedlings, young and old, were used to outbursts of tears from other trees, so they paid no attention to her. It was well into the early morning hours before Plasick finally stopped crying. She turned on her back, looking up at the ceiling. She felt a slight pressure of Adronack's thin branch hand pressing through the stiff mattress. It reminded her of when Adronack would sometimes lay her branch hand on the back of Plasick's neck and shoulders telling her, "Don't worry so much, somehow everything will be all right."

She remembered the day when Adronack had shared her secret. It was always rare to see Adronack smile or look happy, but her face lit up when she talked about her three little seedlings. Plasick sighed a deep sigh as teardrops once again, began to fall down her face. Suddenly remorse began to hit her like a wave. *There I was, not only inspecting the bins, but also looking for prime branches for the idols I was making! Have I become so hard and callous that I blocked out where the leftover branches come from?*

Then her thoughts went wild. *Why was she killed? Did she try to escape? There are three other trees missing. Did they get away or are they also in those bins? Or worse, were they burned? Was that the dark smoke I saw the other day?"* Plasick shuddered at the thought. Suddenly, even within the agonizing circumstances she was going through, Plasick felt a new resolve growing inside of her mind. It traveled deep down into her heart as she barely whispered to herself, "I am going to get out of here. I am going to find Adronack's seedlings and give them the red jewels. And then . . . I will tell them the story of their mother."

*In a little while, I'll throw the rock back out on the ground. Then, as hard as it will be, I've got to bury Adronack's hand branch so no one will discover it. I will find a way!* Out of sheer emotional exhaustion, she finally began to fall asleep just as she faintly whispered into the dark, "You were right Adronack - they will never find your three tiny red jewels."

❦

## Greedo is Restless

As Greedo grew, he began to wear his treetop slicked back. He was still slim, but his upper branch arms and thighs had grown thick and strong. His bark was a mixture of dark colors and light. One late afternoon as he stretched high and low, breathing in the salty air of the beach, he began to cough. Even though he was in good physical shape, he thought that somewhere in his bark, on his ankle, something was wrong. The dark tree beetles liked to hide under the bark of cedar trees and slowly infect them. Greedo's lifestyle tended to attract those kind of bugs. " I must have picked up some kind of bug somewhere," he thought out loud as he headed toward town. He had been at a party the night before and couldn't remember the seedlings name that had been with him. *What was her name?* Greedo prided himself on keeping track of each one of the female seedlings that he knew. He didn't want to accidentally call one of them by the wrong name.

Still trying to remember who the seedling was, he continued walking down Main Street heading toward Jimmies Pawn Shop. He thought about the discovery of the cave. He wanted to go back; yet, something inside concerned him about it. He couldn't forget that image of the blue white light. Something about that night was causing him to feel unsettled and restless. *Why is this bothering me so much? I'm happy with my life!* Although he would never admit it, there were many days when he felt empty inside. There were even moments when he felt pangs of guilt, about some of the things he was doing. *Maybe I'm just tired and overworked.*

Lately at night, he was having a hard time falling asleep. He would lie awake for hours, usually thinking about the hidden cave, and what else might be in there. *Aw, forget about it!*

"Hey Greedo!" yelled Jet and Fret from across the street - bringing Greedo back into the reality of his world.

"Hey yourself! Do you have the bag?" he yelled back. Seeing their nods he waved to them, "Come on, let's go to Jimmies."

Fret nodded as he and Jet ran across the street carrying a bag of Ostrich Feathers and other stolen goods.

The buzzer on the door rang loudly as they walked in. Jimmie quickly turned his head and saw who it was. "Be right with you Greedo!" He turned back to his customer who was handing him a small cage with two purple mice, in exchange for three feet of rattlesnake skin. "Thanks," said Jimmie with his hoarse voice.

The elderly bent over tree shuffled toward the door. "You're most welcome," he said as he walked outside, ringing the buzzer loudly once again.

"What's up Greedo?" Whatcha got for me today?" Jimmie yelled out, anxious to see what they brought.

Greedo grinned and walked over to Jimmie. "I have something

really special for you Jimmie. In exchange, I'll need three speckled rhino eggs."

Jimmie stood about four feet tall. He was a short, heavyset monkey with bug eyes and bat-like ears. He opened up the bag and carefully took out all of the goods that they brought. He liked what he saw, especially the feathers.

"These are prime feathers Greedo, you can barter for more than the eggs if you like."

"Sure, let Jet and Fret pick something out."

Jet and Fret wasted no time and began walking around the shop to search.

Jimmie excitedly looked at the Ostrich Feathers, examining each one carefully. "Boys, I also have a catalog of exotic items if you want to look at those!"

Jet kept exploring the shop to find some treasure while Fret went to look at the catalog.

Jimmie handed Greedo the Giant Rhino Eggs. "You know Greedo, these aren't your average growing eggs. A year from now these Rhino eggs will be huge, and they won't even be full grown yet!"

Greedo looked at the eggs. "I know Jimmie. But I already have an idea of how I want to use them."

Jimmie looked admiringly at Greedo. He knew that any plan Greedo had would be a really big one. After about an hour all three finished their bartering and went out the door. As they stepped onto the sidewalk, a couple of female seedlings walked by, checking out Greedo. Greedo was lost in his own thoughts and didn't even notice. Jet and Fret walked behind him muttering under their breath about how Greedo always gets first choice on everything. The sun was setting as the three of them walked down the street. Greedo looked up at the clouds. A flash of light sped quickly across the sky, disappearing into another cloud. It was rare to see a flashing star in the center of the city – because of the millions of Neon Bug Lights that flashed out of the buildings every night.

Again, he thought about the light in the cave and made a mental note to go back sometime, even though he was a little afraid. *Where is this coming from?* he thought. *I was doing just fine until I went into that stupid cave.* Lately he had been realizing how dark some of the areas of his life were. He often felt desolate and alone. He couldn't figure out why. Stopping in front of a brightly lit building he yelled out, "You two aren't coming in! Go back out and find some goods that I can sell!" Jet and Fret ran off then, quick to obey, even though they were beginning to resent Greedo more and more everyday.

Chapter V

# *Challenges & Decisions*

## *Aya & The Healing Flowers of the Snap-Dragon Field"*

ya and Wyo stood on top of a hill looking over at a field. "There it is, just as Willow told me," said Wyo, *"The Healing Flowers of the Snap-Dragon Field."* Since their encounter with the Toucan Seer, Aya and Wyo had traveled a long way. Several miles back, they had entered The Valley of Life-Giving Flowers, which was still in the vast and mystical land of Sumatoria. Along the journey Aya met several friendly seedlings who were also seeking their Destiny Land. She was beginning to feel more hopeful about her future. She didn't know, that one of the greatest challenges on her journey – was about to happen.

"Aya, something's not right here," said Wyo, as they stood behind several trees far away from the field of flowers. "Willow encouraged me to find this place and take you through the field, in order to be refreshed and healed. But it looks like there's some kind of trouble over there that she might not have known about."
Aya looked at him, not understanding what was going on, "We've been traveling for several months Wyo, and I'm really tired. What is this field?"

Wyo pulled his glance away from the field and looked at her. "One night when you were resting, Willow told me about this flower field."

"Wyo, on your journey, while you are still in Sumatoria, you will enter the Mystical Valley of Life-Giving Flowers. There are four flower fields in that land. In order to reach the Land of Visions, you will need to go through The Healing Field of the Snap-Dragon Flowers. There are thousands of colorful Snapdragon flowers – that have special powers of healing. They consistently emulate a wonderful, clean, healing scent into the air. Their main purpose is to refresh and heal – by breathing out their nectar into the air or by giving their nectar to insects, bushes, animals and small trees. The nectar also empowers and nourishes whoever receives it. By then Aya will probably need the refreshing healing."

"Willow also said that sometimes, those who experience healing, are allowed to take a small amount of nectar back for their families to drink, or scatter onto their land. At times, even lost strangers are allowed access to their healing powers. The flowers are usually around three feet tall and have several leaves." He paused for a moment. "But now they are bent over and look weak."

"They don't look very healthy to me either," said Aya flippantly, anxious to rest and then continue on their journey.

Wyo paused for a moment, noticing Aya's arrogant attitude. "They must not be getting replenished," he said.

Aya stretched her tired branches and yawned. "And how does that happen?"

Wyo, slightly annoyed, looked at her out of the corner of his eye before speaking. "From what Willow told me, each flower is mysteriously replenished by morning. The soil here is rich, dark and very healthy. That's where the flowers reproduce their young." He looked down at the field. "Normally, evil is not allowed to grow here. But, I sense something dark has come into this place. Even from this distance, it looks like there are strange creatures on each corner of the field. We need to find the Overseer Tree of this land and find out what's going on before we try to cross over."

They both turned at the same time and saw several trees standing around them. The trees began to whisper to one another while watching Aya and Wyo. One of the larger trees reached over and tapped Aya's shoulder branch.

"Hello, my name is Treeania. I'm the Overseer Tree of the Snap-Dragon Field and the area surrounding it. We've been listening to your conversation. Please, come with me and I'll explain what happened."

Aya looked up at Treeania and started to resist, "Well we're just trying to cross over to the other side of the field."

"You mean – cross over to the Land of Visions?"

"I don't know what it's called," said Aya. "I just know I *really* want to go home and *that* is the direction we should go!" Tears filled her eyes, as she thought about how much she did not want to be in this situation.

"Aya," Wyo spoke softly, "I know you want to get home, but the only way we can get to *The Land of Visions* is through the Snap-Dragon Field. There is no other way." Aya looked at Wyo, knowing that he was probably right. There was nothing she could do but resign herself to the situation, and at least listen to what Treeania had to say.

"We've been waiting a long time, to see who would be sent to help the Snap-Dragon Flowers and our community," said Treeania as they all began to walk. "The flowers are dying because the Blue Renegade Butterflies haven't been able to replenish them. The Butterflies are supposed to breathe into the flowers which in turn breathe air back out into the atmosphere, which nourishes the other flowers, seedlings, animals and trees. Then, when Time speaks and the Wind blows, all of us trees help by quickly moving the healing breath through our branches into the air."

## The Takeover

"Renegade Butterflies! Who are they?" asked Aya.

Treeania led them up into a hidden place in the woods. He lifted both of them onto the top of a fifteen-foot rock, so that when he sat down on the ground, they could all face each other directly. "Let me start at the beginning."

"The span of this field is five miles long and three miles wide. The four Dragon Eye Brothers, Siree, Uozoni, Yeto and Ketonday have overtaken it. As you can see, each corner of the field is guarded by one of them. The flowers are being held prisoners and the brothers want to destroy it. They've already conquered and burned the other three Life-Giving Flower Fields in the Valley. This is the last one left."

Wyo abruptly asked him, "How did all of this come about. You're the Overseer, didn't you see it coming?"

Immediately Treeania felt ashamed. "No, I didn't."

"I'm sorry," said Wyo. "I shouldn't have spoken out. I didn't mean to judge you. Please go on."

Treeania smiled weakly as he continued:

"In the beginning formation of this large valley in Sumatoria, it was occupied by no one. Then, the Master Seed Planter came and planted four flower fields. She named it *The Valley of Life Giving Flowers*.

The first field she planted in the valley was *The Harmony Field with the Morning Glory Flowers*. They produced harmony and peace in their nectar.

The second field was *The Happy Field with Buttercup Flowers*. They illuminated happiness and laughter.

The third field was *The Field of Hope with the Lilies*. The Lilies released hope and expectations.

The fourth flower field is ours, *The Healing Field of the Snap-Dragon Flowers*. They give out healings of all kinds.

These four fields were spread out over the Valley of Life Giving Flowers, which as you have seen, is a lot of land. The Master Seed Planter continued to nurture and groom each of the fields. Then, she imparted unique powers to each group of flowers. Most of their powers, but not all, were encased in their nectar and pollen. The fields needed to grow for about a year, before they were allowed to release their special powers. The main purpose of the flower fields was to keep the lands, animals, trees and foliage – free of bitterness, self-pity, defeat and sickness."

By now several other trees and bushes in the area, had gathered to hear Treeania share the history of the valley. Aya couldn't help but notice the somber feeling in the atmosphere. For a moment she forgot about her own needs. She too wanted to know more.

"At the end of the growing year, The Master Seed Planter appointed one Overseer Tree to each field. I was appointed to oversee this field. Our jobs were to guide, protect and watch over the flowers as they grew. Once each flower matured it was able to release its powers. Over time, the flowers fields continued to replenish and multiply. The land in the valley flourished because of them. The four fields were doing so well, that The Master Seed Planter decided that each field should duplicate itself. She appointed me as the Overseer to begin the new project, right here."

"Who is The Master Seed Planter?" asked Wyo, for even he didn't know.

Treeania answered, "I don't know that much about her. She roams all over Etainia. She stayed in The Valley of Life Giving Flowers until the flowers were fully mature. Then she called upon Time to speak over them through the Wind. No one knows what Time said. Soon after that, the flowers began to release their powers. Evidently she travels throughout Etainia and is able take on the appearance of various trees, in order to keep her identity obscure. She only appears to the Overseer Trees. We often don't recognize her, until she speaks. Sometimes, she looks like a very ordinary tree."

Wyo looked around. "Should you be sharing this information among so many other trees and animals?"

The neighborhood trees glared at Wyo, being slightly offended.

Treeania replied, "She guards her identity well. Remember, she only appears to Overseer Trees, and because she appears in different forms; it's a great mystery, even to them."

Aya pondered on that for a moment and said, "Go on."

Treeania cleared his throat as he continued.

"I was instructed to pick four out of the seven most flourishing giant Snap Dragon flowers in the field. They were to be groomed as helpers for me. I chose four brothers – Siree, Uozoni, Yeto and Ketonday. Ketonday stayed here to be trained specifically by me. I sent the other three brothers to be trained at the Field of Harmony and Peace, where the Morning Glory Flowers were. I admit - I was a bit hesitant thinking that they might not be ready to leave my area. Sorry to say, I sent them anyway."

"Are all the flowers able to walk around like we do?" Wyo asked.

"No, only the giant ones – and they must get permission from the Overseer Tree. Seven special seeds that yielded giant flowers were planted in each field. The Master Seed Planter planned it that way."

Why didn't you train all of the brothers here?" asked Wyo.

"I wanted the three brothers to have a wider range of experience; by being trained in an unfamiliar area, with another Overseer tree." He took a moment to catch his breath.

"After a year those three brothers were to come back to my field and join Ketonday. Then I was going to promote them to the position of Snap-Dragon Walkers - assistants to me! The idea being, that by having more than one trained assistant, I could grow another, *bigger* Snap Dragon field more rapidly! My Healing Flower field was supposed to be a model for the others. It was a wonderful plan and the training was going quite well until just before the year was up. It was then that a strange thing happened in the Harmony and Peace Flower Field."

"But how do you know what happened over there if you were here?" asked Aya.

Treeania looked over at her.

"I can only tell you that we Overseers have several secret

Messengers in the land. They inform us of some of the more important happenings that take place around our area, and throughout Etainia. Although they were hindered along the way, they were still able to give us the horrendous details of what was happening in the Harmony and Peace Field." Treeania looked around and saw that more creatures and trees had joined them.

"You see, Aya, in the entire *Valley of Life Giving Flowers*, the poisons of bitterness, self-pity, defeat, and sickness are not allowed. My field, the Snap-Dragon Flower Field is a healing and refreshing field. At any time, the moment dark thoughts and feelings attempted to imbed themselves into the flower field or within our community – *the flowers would sense it, confront it and distribute the healing nectar accordingly.*" "But this time . . . evil came subtly from within our field and infiltrated the Snap-Dragon Flowers. I didn't perceive it in time. I didn't even notice that the elder snapdragon flower, Yeto, was becoming extremely jealous of his three brothers, especially Ketonday."

"By the time the three brothers were sent to the Harmony and Peace Field Yeto's jealousy had grown and taken root inside of him. But he cleverly hid it from everyone. I know I should have perceived it! But I was so excited about being the model Overseer -chosen to grow another field- that I overlooked many things. It was my pride that deceived me." Another tree came over and stood next to Treeania, patting his back for encouragement. "Well Aya, there you have it. I wanted you to know the history behind this field – so you can decide if you want to help us." He wearily dropped his head down. "I'm feeling kind of tired now from all the telling."

Aya felt his weariness. "Don't worry Treeania, we can all come together tomorrow if you'd like to share more."

"Thank you," he said, with a grateful smile on his face. "And just so you know, you're very safe here. The Dragon Eyes can't see or hear us from this distance."

Wyo looked around at all the seedlings, foliage, animals and trees, as they said their good nights to each other and returned to their homes.

Treeania called out to them. "We'll gather here early tomorrow morning. Leave your youngest offspring at home. Some of the things I'm going share will frighten them."

Soon the area was empty and quiet. Wyo looked at Aya, knowing that this would be one of those times when he couldn't give her any advice. As Willow once told him, *"There are some decisions that only she can make on this journey and you will have to follow."*

⸺ ⸺

## Boxer meets Enobleus and Volante'

The weeks flew into months as Boxer explored Rensamor Island with Rocky. It had been three months since the LongEars' had shown him Coconut Flats. Now, they were finally going to take him to the upper part of the Island to meet Enobleus, the old Overseer of the Island. Once they reached the top of Hightop Hill, Boxer looked down to see several little seedlings running around causing mischief.

"What are they doing to that old tree?" he asked.

Sniffer sighed, "Believe it or not, that is the Overseer of this land. He is very wise and knowledgeable, but some of the newer seedlings come from rebellious homes and do not respect him."

Boxer took off running down the hill with Rocky close behind, "Get away from him!" Boxer yelled out at the group of tree seedlings that were shouting names at the older tree. Rocky began nipping at their tree feet, running away when they swatted at him. They looked at Boxer, who was only a bit taller than they were, and just laughed, running off to find some other mischief to get into.

"Thank you young seedling, what is your name?" said the old tree as he reached out his gnarled branch hand.

Boxer shook his hand. "My name is Boxer."

The old tree looked closer at him saying, "Oh! You're the Boxer that Sniffer and Whiskers told me about! I'm happy to meet you. My name is Enobleus."

Boxer noticed a strange looking band on the old trees' upper branch arm. He was shocked that this tree was an Overseer; he seemed too old and feeble to do any good.

Soon the LongEars' caught up with Boxer and Rocky. "So you've already met," said Sniffer as he saw the two trees talking. "Yes, indeed!" exclaimed Enobleus. "I like my young Protégé!"

"What's that?" asked Boxer.

"Someone who will follow in my footsteps." replied Enobleus. Whiskers looked at the elder tree. "Well Enobleus, he hasn't heard the rest of Rensamor Island's story yet. We were counting on you to fill him in."

"What's going on?" asked Boxer, with a confused look on his face.

Whiskers explained, "Boxer, we would like to give you the opportunity to train with Enobleus to become a temporary Overseer Tree."

Boxer raised his eyebrows as he looked at all of them. Even though Boxer thought Enobleus wouldn't have a lot to teach him, he knew from what his parents had told him –becoming an Overseer Tree was a great honor for any seedling in Etainia.

"Yes! I would like that!" he yelled out.

Sniffer continued, "Then all we ask is that you stay with Enobleus now and live with him for the next twelve months to learn all that you can. At the end of the twelve months we will come to bring you home. If Enobleus endorses you, we will be asking you to consider being the temporary Overseer of Rensamor Island."

Boxer's eyes grew large at such a thought! "Me? Me?" he exclaimed. Suddenly it dawned on him that he would have to be away from Sniffer and Whiskers for a year! "A Year! A year away from you and Whiskers? Can't I see you at all during that year? What about Rocky?" Boxer said in anguish.

"Boxer it will be hard for us too!" said Whiskers as she wiped a tear from her eye. "It's important that you have focused training during that year. But, here's what we can do. Once every four months Sniffer and I will walk to the top of the hill, and let Rocky come down and stay with you for a couple of days and then we'll come back to the top of the hill and pick him up."

Boxer sadly complied. "O.K., and will you wave at me then?" Whiskers and Sniffer both came over to Boxer and gave him their biggest rabbit hugs.

"Yes, we'll wave at you."

"All right then. I'll stay here for one year to be trained. I'll do a great job and learn a lot. You'll be proud of me!" Boxer said as he slowly walked over to stand by Enobleus. The LongEars' shook Enobleus hand in agreement.

Whiskers gently leaned over and whispered into Boxer's ear. "Enobleus may be old Boxer, but don't think for a moment that he doesn't know what he is doing. His wisdom is beyond anyone else's on this Island. His words are few, but valuable – so take heed. You'll have to be alert to keep up with him."

With a surprised expression on his face, Boxer looked at Whiskers and wondered, *Could she read the thoughts I had earlier about Enobleus?*

"I will Whiskers, I promise."

She kissed him then and began to walk with Sniffer back to their home.

Rocky jumped up on Boxers knee, waiting for the familiar stroke on his head. Boxer knelt down and spoke in a broken voice as he rubbed Rocky's head and back "Well Rocky, stay close to Sniffer and Whiskers while I'm gone."

I will," said Rocky as Boxer stood up. "I will. And Boxer, I'm already missing you and can hardly wait to see you in four months!"

Rocky turned quickly before anyone could see him cry, as he sped past his parents and raced to the top of the hill to wait for them.

## The Rest of the Story

Boxer wrenched his eyes away from the sight of Rocky and his parents disappearing over the hill. Enobleus tapped him on the shoulder. "There's no time to waste Boxer. Let's go over there under that Oak Tree and I'll tell you the rest of the history of Rensamor Island."

As they walked closer to the humongous Oak Tree, she greeted them. "Hello Noble One."

Enobleus smiled, "Hello Volante', you're looking well."

"Thank you," she said as she looked at Boxer.

Standing next to this beautiful tall Oak tree, with incredibly bushy leaves, Boxer felt like a tiny two-inch tree.

"Hello young seedling, I noticed you admiring my leaves!" she said as she leaned down to gently tap Boxer.

"Oh! I'm so sorry! I was staring!" Boxer quickly said.

"No need to be sorry, it did not offend me," she said with a smile on her face. "And what is your name?"

Enobleus stood back a ways so he could watch how Boxer handled the conversation. Boxer nervously looked toward Enobleus.

"My name is Boxer."

"Oh is it now? I don't think that's your real name is it?" Volante' said as she looked down upon him.

Boxer looked worried then, because he didn't want her to think he was lying.

*Should I tell her the whole story about the Naming Ceremony?* he thought wildly.

The beautiful Oak tree laughed gently.

"Don't worry Boxer, I'm only teasing you. The LongEars' filled me in on your landing here. Welcome!"

Boxer relaxed then as she invited him to sit down near her trunk.

Enobleus smiled at Volante'. "I'm going to tell him the rest of the history, so if you have anything to add, please feel free to do so."

Nodding her full leafy head Volante' laughingly replied, "Don't worry, you know I will."

Enobleus sat down and began to speak. "Boxer you have landed on a unique Island. On the upper right side and in the middle there are mostly good loyal neighbors and trees. On the left side down by the Swamp, there are a few more enemies." Boxer leaned forward, listening carefully as Enobleus continued sharing.

"Many years ago when I came here and found my Destiny as Overseer of Rensamor Island, there were numerous young seedlings and their parents. At that time only trees lived here. They brought fresh air into the island. They provided shade and cool breezes with their branches. Soon various creatures came here to live. They were welcomed by the trees and seedlings. It was a happy place and the waters surrounding the island were clear and fresh.

Then one night a thunderous tide came rolling in and washed away part of the Island. Many seedlings and trees were washed away also. Coming in with the tide were various kinds of sea creatures, in particular two Giant Slime Fish. Some of the tidewater lingered. The Slime fish were close to death having been out of water so long. They slithered further into the island and slowly dug a huge deep hole. Exhausted they lay in it expecting to die. Overnight the heavy rains came and filled up the hole. The female slime, the one we call Geesemo, fought to live because she was giving birth. The male slime died that night. His body eventually dissolved into the waters, which still remain stagnant to this day. That area is now called The Swamp."

"Where Geseemo and her slime kids live?" asked Boxer.

"That's right – it's the same place where you landed." Enobleus replied. "Most of the baby seedlings were washed away, leaving only a few of the older trees to protect and cover this land." He looked over at Boxer. "Have you seen Coconut Flats?"

"Yes. Whiskers and Sniffer showed me."

"The water around our Island is shallow for up to about ten feet out, and then it becomes very deep," said Volante'. "The only reason why Geseemo and her children didn't move out is because the shallow water is too low for them to swim out into the deeper waters, and the tide has never come in that high again."

Enobleus continued. "The young seedlings are leaving this land little by little. Some are even being killed by the Slime's when they try to escape. Many of them are bored here."

Boxer spoke out, "Yes, Whiskers and Sniffer told me about that too."

"I'm glad you were in their care," replied Enobleus. "They are wise and compassionate and have always been very good to me. Boxer, my time here is ending soon and I'll need another Overseer to take over. Our island needs to be built up once again as it was – *alive and flourishing - with many young seedlings being nurtured and taught how to find their Destiny Land.*"

He looked at Boxer again, "Do you know about Destiny Land and the Soil of the Earth?"

"Yes," replied Boxer. "My father and mother made it a point to instruct us very carefully about what it means. Of course, some of my seedling friends didn't think it was that important, but I always did." Enobleus smiled at Volante' in silent agreement, appreciating the knowledge that Boxer already had.

"Boxer," he said. "Now and then there are still a few trees and seedlings who come here seeking their Destiny. Those that come by way of The Broken Bridge are usually destroyed by either Geseemo or her sons, or by other pestilence. There's always lots of pestilence that are on the lookout to destroy some of the weaker seedlings and trees. We have very few trees to shade the land and very few fruit trees are left for the squirrels and other animals to eat from."

"Do the Slimes ever eat the animals?"

Enobleus frowned, "Sometimes they do, but not always"

Boxer opened his mouth to ask 'why' but Volante' interrupted.

"Enobleus will tell you more about that later."

Boxer closed his mouth, knowing that he needed to listen carefully to what she was about to say.

"In order to help protect the seedlings that travel into this Island," said Volante'. "The Noble One sets up various troupes within the entire community to watch out for each other. Because of Enobleus, this island has not been overtaken by the evil that washed in. He has set in place and established a powerful network."

Enobleus grinned. Although he was uncomfortable hearing Volante' admire his work, he was proud to have served this land well during his season.

"See that field over there to your right?" Enobleus said pointing it out to Boxer.

"Yes, I do." Boxer looked out toward the land, which was far below them.

"Those sparse groups of seedlings that you see moving around, have traveled here from other places seeking their Destiny. It will take a while for some of them to find the right spot. There are a few of them waiting to see if they will be accepted by the Soil of the Earth. It's up to me to protect them."

"Oh," replied Boxer quietly, trying to remember everything.

"I know you're young Boxer," continued Enobleus. "But you are smart, alert and mature. You landed on this Island and were spared. I believe there is a good reason. I believe you are meant to help Rensamor Island – but . . . we will see."

Boxer looked at Enobleus somberly. "I'm here to learn from you and anyone else you appoint to train me."

Enobleus stood up, smiled at Boxer and thanked Volante' for her shade and for her wise additions.

"Noble One, you are always a welcome sight. Come back soon!" she said as she touched his arm branch with her full leafy hand. "As for you little seedling . . . "

Boxer stood up and held his breath, unsure of what she would tell him.

"That same invitation goes for you!" she said with a smile on her face.

Boxer ran over and attempted to hug her massive trunk. She held him for a moment.

"Run along now, Enobleus is already ahead of you."

Boxer looked up and sure enough, Enobleus was several feet ahead of him. Boxer had to run to catch up! *Whiskers was right. I'll have to pay close attention to him during this year of training.* He began to run, trying to keep up with Enobleus long strides.

Enobleus looked down at Boxer who was out of breath, but keeping up with him. Here we are, he thought. *Two generations walking side by side into our futures. This is good.*

❧

## Webber & The Garden

Webber woke up and couldn't get back to sleep. So on a whim she went to her door and tried to open it. It was unlocked! She wondered about that as she went through, closing it behind her. As she walked down the corridor to the bottom floor she noticed that no one was around. *I think I'll go to the garden that I've wanted to visit for the longest time. I've been here for almost eight months and still haven't seen it!"* Quickly she walked through the front door.

The entire grounds were quiet, except for the Weather Station Building on the very top of the hill above the Dome. She couldn't see the station from where she stood, but she could hear the cranking noises that often came from that direction. *It's unusual to hear those noises at this time of morning. I wonder what's going on? I wish they would give me a tour of that building!* She continued walking toward the small garden.

From a distance she saw a huge beautiful maple tree standing in front of a small bench in the garden. There was a rose bush on the right side of the tree with white roses on it and a red rose bush was on the left. As she came closer she saw a cardinal perched on top of the bench. *Wow, that's interesting, the bird isn't flying away.* Sitting on the bench were three little tree seedlings. *What are those young trees doing outside at this early morning hour?* When she approached the fence around the garden, the seedlings were looking up at the maple tree and didn't notice her. The gate was locked but the fence was low enough for her to climb over, so she did. Curious to speak with the little seedlings she tapped one of them on the shoulder.

She waited a moment, but the seedling didn't turn around. Actually, none of them moved. Not only that, the cardinal hadn't uttered a sound or moved! She went around to look at them from the front. As she reached out her hand to touch the seedlings, they still didn't move. She looked closer and then gasped out loud. "They're not real! The cardinal looks like a statue!" She turned to get a closer look at the Maple tree. "It's not real either!" She rushed to smell the red roses – they were scentless and the petals were hard. "This is a fake garden!" she said out loud, forgetting that someone might hear her. "Nothing here is alive! They are all dead!" She looked at the bark of the Maple tree, seeing a piece that was loose, she pulled at it and underneath she saw stripped tree bark - exactly like the ones on the outside of the Dome! "It was a real tree at one time!"

With tears in her eyes she looked over at the three seedlings, realizing that they too were once alive. "I'll bet they ran and played together like I did when I was growing up." Still in shock, Webber just stood there staring. *No wonder Dr. Tearrent didn't want me to come here. What did they do to make the trees and bushes look like this? And what about the bird?* She shuddered as she thought about what the answers might be. Suddenly loud blasting wind sounds came from the direction of the Weather Station. Then she heard loud voices yelling, "Hooray! We did it!"

*I'd better get back to my room before someone discovers I'm gone.* She climbed back over the fence and headed back toward the Research Building. Her heart was pounding with anxiety. Crazy thoughts ran in and out of her mind. It was as if her eyes were opened to see the truth for the first time since her arrival in **Krontia**. *Why are all the trees stripped? Why are there no birds or animals? Where are all the young seedling trees that I saw a few days ago?* She stopped in her tracks with a sudden revelation. "Then again, why does Dr. Tearrent want to remove my bad memories?" She continued walking and talking out loud. "Or . . . maybe that's not all she wants to remove!" She opened the front door, which was still unlocked and ran upstairs to the second floor toward her room.

She pulled on the door handle to her room. It wouldn't open! "Oh no! I closed it! It self locked!" She started to shake uncontrollably.

"Calm down! Try again!" said a whisper of a voice.

She looked around but didn't see anyone. *It must have been my imagination.* She tugged and tugged at the door, pulling harder. Finally it opened! She hurriedly raced in, as it slammed shut behind her. She tested it and found that it self-locked. *Since it's locked, they won't suspect me of leaving the room. But I've got to act like I don't know anything.* She began pacing back and forth. *Oh-h-h what will I do? Who can I talk to? Who can help me?*

With her heart racing she went over to the steel chair and sat down. *They weren't real! The trees, the bird, the bushes - weren't real!* She looked at the wall. No windows, only paintings on the wall! Why? Why? Then she remembered how angry Dr. Tearrent was about seeing a spider web on the building. Webber continued to piece things together. "And when she took me on a tour – she spent a long time making sure that the area was disinfected and clean."

A noise at her door startled her and she sat upright in the chair. She closed her eyes to get her composure. As the door opened, she saw Klon walk in first.

"Dr. Tearrent would like to see you in her office." He said in his stone cold voice.

Fearfully she followed Klon wondering, *Do they know? Did she see me?* Soon they were in front of Dr. Tearrents' office. Klon opened the door and directed her to go in. Webber went over and sat in the same chair she usually sat in during her weekly visits to see Dr. Tearrent. *I wonder what she wants at this early morning hour?* She waited nervously.

The door swung open and in walked Dr. Tearrent and Dr. Crophyster with big smiles on their faces. Webber had learned long ago not to trust their smiles. They exchanged greetings and sat in two chairs directly across from her.

Dr. Tearrent leaned forward in a friendly manner. "Webber, we have a surprise for you!"
Webber waited anxiously.

"Dr. Crophyster and I have watched how quickly you've learned about Krontia and the goals we have for the future - and how well you listen to orders! We're both impressed at your operating skills.

As you know, we will soon be operating on the little seedlings."
Webber nodded.

Dr. Crophyster spoke in his raspy voice, "I have been pleased to work with such an astute learner. Your creative ideas have been logged into my book of future inventions."

Webber's heart briefly lifted. "I'm so honored that you think my ideas are worthy of being put in that book!"

Dr. Crophyster had the book in his lap. Lifting it up he said, "One day, when we begin to test and work on some of your ideas, I will put those details in this book and your name will be placed there too! But for now I mainly wanted you to know that several of your creative ideas are already in here."

Webber looked at the unusually looking old red book with thick pages. Many symbols were etched on the outside. There were also words written on the binding that she couldn't make out. He noticed her intense observation of the book. He stood up and walked over to Dr. Tearrents' bookcases. He quickly put the book back onto the shelf and locked the glass encasement. Dr. Tearrent continued to speak as Dr. Crophyster sat back down.

"Webber," she said in a serious tone. "We are going to give you your certificate of completion in one week. You will then be called Dr. Webber!"

Webber jumped up out of her seat! "Oh my gosh! Oh my!" she said as she jumped up and down. "This is an awesome honor! Do you really think I'm ready?"

Dr. Tearrent smiled, "Of course you are! You passed all the tests with the highest points we've ever given! - with the exception of my scores and Dr. Crophyster's. You also did excellent in the area of extracting and mixing solutions and serums from the flowers."
Webber exclaimed, "Heitenny is an expert. I simply listened and fol-lowed directions."

Dr. Tearrent stood up and walked over to her desk chair to sit down. "That's commendable Webber. How well you *do listen and follow* directions." She leaned forward, putting her arm branches on the desk and clasped her hand branches together as she continued speaking. "Webber, there is one more qualification you need to fill before we can give you your certificate and allow you to continue operating here." Webber looked at her, listening carefully. "Webber," said Dr. Tearrent, "You must have the bad memory removal operation first."

Webber was stunned. Everything within her limbs felt paralyzed, stiff. The excitement that she had with the news of becoming a doctor, quickly turned into dread. She tried not to show the dismay on her face. They were watching her reaction very carefully. She hesitated before speaking.

"Well, uh, do I have time to think about this?" she asked timidly.

Dr. Tearrent stood up again and put her branch arms behind her back as she came to the front of her desk. She sat down on the corner of the desk placing her right branch leg on the floor and the left leg swinging in the air, as she folded her arms in front of her. Looking directly at Webber she said in a monotone voice. "You have no choice and there is no time to think about it." She switched then to a friendlier voice. "You see Webber, all upcoming doctors are required to have this operation. It's for the benefit of all as I have explained to you many times. You can willingly choose to have the operation and become a doctor. Or, you can refuse and eventually become like one of those loyal trees that stand, guarding the Dome."

She looked at Webber's worried face. Webber's mind was going crazy. *Either way I choose, I'll be given the operation. If I choose to become a doctor I'll have a better chance of escaping."* She looked up at the two doctors, while they waited for her answer. *I wonder if they can read my mind?* she nervously thought.

She found herself saying, "I accept your offer with honor." Both doctors stood up and came over to shake her hand.

"You'll not regret it," said Dr. Crophyster as he patted her shoulder.

"Yes, yes!" echoed Dr. Tearrent. "You've made the right choice. You will be much happier! We'll set up a time one week from today to do the operation! Shortly after that we'll have a Graduation Celebration just for you. On that day, everyone will be commanded to call you Dr. Webber!"

With mixed feelings, Webber smiled lamely as Dr. Tearrent continued, "This week as a special graduation gift I'll have Klon give you a tour of the rest of the grounds, except for the Weather Station Building. I'll even give you a week off from doing any operations!" "Thank you so much," said Webber as she stood to her feet - thankful that there was a sudden knock on the door.

Klon opened it to let Heitenny in. "Sorry to disturb you Doctor Tearrent, we just got that new flower in – the one you wanted to see," he said.

"Oh yes! Webber. Dr. Crophyster. Come with me to the Greenhouse!" Dr. Tearrent said as she walked past Heitenny and Klon - expecting everyone to follow her.

While walking up the hill Webber realized that she must escape this place before they could operate on her. *But how? How?*

Most of the day in the Greenhouse was spent observing the new plant. Dr. Tearrent extracted some of its pollen and mixed it with another type of pollen. Once she was finished mixing it she exclaimed, "There! This solution should have the potential to temporarily burn and blind any creature or tree if necessary. You never know when we might need something like this for protection."

She walked over to wash her branch hands and spoke over her shoulder to Heitenny and Webber. "You two stay here and continue working on this solution until it is perfected!" On the way out of the front door, Dr. Tearrent and Dr. Crophyster turned back to look straight at Webber. "Don't ever forget this," said Dr. Tearrent in a serious voice. "We have many enemies who hate us and are jealous of the technology being discovered here. So keep what you learn between all of us." Webber nodded as the two doctors turned away from her and left the building.

## The Experiment

After working fervently all day long, Webber and Heitenny had perfected a new solution. It was burning powder. They tested it on a nearby tree and it worked. The old trees eyes watered and burned, causing him to bend over and rub them. It took at least one hour before the tree could see anything clearly again.

"What do you see now?" asked Webber.

"Everything is still blurry," said the tree quietly. "But it's slowly starting to clear up." Satisfied that the solution was working they dismissed the old tree and logged all of the information into the <u>Serum & Solution</u> book.

It was late evening so Webber cleaned up, preparing to go back to her room. She hoped she wouldn't run into Dr. Tearrent. *I need some time to myself to think about all that's happened today.* She finally made it back to her room without having to interact with anyone. Once inside, she heard the lock automatically click into place. Sure enough, when she tried the door, it wouldn't open. Exhausted and frightened at the prospect of having her memories removed she climbed into bed and lay down with her thoughts once again running wild. *Who will help me? The only creatures I know are the weasels and they are loyal to Dr. Tearrent. The only trees I know are either doctors or researchers. I don't trust any of them!"* She rubbed her head, trying to wipe her mind free of any more thoughts. After several hours she finally drifted into a fitful, restless sleep.

# Plasick and the Medic

Plasick looked over at the new resource building on the grounds of the Idol Factory. It had been almost a year since she buried Adronack's hand behind the tree bunkhouse. Try as she might, Plasick couldn't figure out a secure escape plan, but she hadn't forgotten the promises she made to herself. Several other worker trees had tried to escape. When they were found, depending on what condition they were in - they might be burned up in order to keep the big pots heated or their limbs might show up on an idol or piece of furniture. But even when that happened no one really knew because once the trees were stripped of their bark, they all looked alike.

Plasick's manager tag now had a shiny badge on it. Indicating that she was promoted to Supervisor over all the trees, bushes and creatures work production. Mixer even appointed two Armadillo guards to watch over her since many trees and bushes wanted her destroyed. *I know so many of them hate me*, she thought. *Most of them just don't realize that I've been forced to do this.* The scars in her deformed left leg proved that. Whenever she wouldn't do what Mixer asked, he would cut a piece out of her branch leg and replace it with plastic.

Today they were bringing in new potential workers. She walked toward the training building with her Armadillo guards following closely behind. General Saguwas and several of his web-toed lizards had captured and brought in a few new trees. They had already been taken to the Peeling Building and stripped of their bark. Over time Plasick had finally realized that the only reason Mixer let her keep her bark on, was to give false hope to some of the trees. He also did it to make her feel grateful and obligated to him. She pretended to be, but she wasn't. She didn't trust him one bit.

Now and then Plasick would find little ways to make the workload less difficult for the workers. She knew how it was to hate some of the jobs they were commanded to do. Today she had to tackle many hated jobs. She would have to select workers from the new group that just came in. The trees that she didn't select would be taken away to the Resource Building where they would be chopped up and used in idols, furniture and other areas.

She walked into the training building to see the group. Her first guard went over to the new crop of trees and hit one of them. "Stand to attention!" he yelled at a Thorn tree. The Thorn tree stood up reluctantly as Plasick came over to the table. She noticed that it was the same table she was led to when she first met her trainer, Adronack. Plasick put on her toughest look and stern voice and told the group the same thing she told every new group that came in.

"You are here to work, and work you will. You are not indispensable. One day you might even be released for good behavior. If some of your children or relatives end up here - because of your hard work, they might be able to keep their bark on, as I have." When the trees heard this, they were relieved for many of them had seen their children being captured and taken away.

Plasick saw that it worked and continued. "I will now select ten of you to be trained in my group. As I call you out, stay at this table. You three dried out fruit trees – stay. You four oak trees standing together - stay. M-m-m, let's see. Oh yes, that Olive Tree. I want you to stay."

The trees stood tall and tried to look healthy and strong as Plasick kept looking them over.

"O.K., two more. Elm tree – stay and . . . " Plasick scanned the small group and noticed the Thorn tree watching her. *Is that a defiant look I see on his face?* she thought as they continued looking at each other. "Thorn tree, stay. The rest of you will be trained by someone else."

Of course she knew that the rest of them would be taken to the

Resource Factory. She called out to the second guard to escort the unusable group out. The guard came over and one by one they walked out of the factory. Some of them were trembling, wondering who their boss would be.

Plasick looked over her group of ten, motioning them to them to follow as she gave them a tour of the factory and grounds. This task took most of the day and her leg began to throb and was hurting more than usual. So she ordered her second guard to lead her group to the tree bunkhouse and then take the night off. Mixer had given her permission to dismiss the guards when she didn't need them.

The sun began to set as she walked up the dusty hill to get more medicine from the Medic. They had become good friends over the past year. He knew about her plan to escape and today he said he would help her. *It's strange, but I trust him, even though he's an alligator,* she thought as she started to open the door. But someone on the other side was opening it too.

"Why hello Plasick!" said Medic as he opened the door to let his receptionist leave for the day. Plasick nodded at the receptionist and walked into the building.

"Hello yourself Medic, can I come in?"

"Of course, of course! Come on in," he said while shutting the door and locking it. They walked into the kitchen and sat down, both weary from the day's work.

"You look more tired than usual Plasick. How's your leg?"

Plasick propped her leg on the chair opposite from her. "It hurts pretty bad. We got some new trees in and I gave them the speech and a long tour. I'll be extra busy for the next few weeks."

He looked at her as he examined her leg. "That could actually prove to be a good distraction from your escape."

She looked up quickly, "So you think I can leave that soon?"

He shook his head yes. "It's getting to the point where *you need* to leave. I know you have compassion for some of the trees and creatures. But Plasick, I've also noticed that you sometimes enjoy being able to control them."

At first she shook her head no, but then she stopped. "It's true Medic, I don't know what comes over me at times. Once I was beating one of the worker trees so hard that one of my Armadillo guards had to stop me." She lowered her head in shame.

"I know Plasick, that's why you must leave soon. You're starting to become like those that you hate." He wrapped her leg and rubbed some ointment on it to ease the pain. "There, that should help for about a week or two," he said as he gently patted her shoulder branch.

She looked up at him, "What did you want to tell me tonight?"

He picked up her cane and asked, "Remember when I gave you this? It was the first day you arrived here. I knew then that I was going to help you one day." He began to unscrew the top off and turned it over exposing a long thin dagger underneath. "This has always been here Plasick. I wanted you to carry the cane around for a long time, so Mixer and the others would get used to seeing you with it. This dagger can pierce through alligator and armadillo hide because it's razor sharp and won't break."

He turned the straight part of the cane upside down. Out came several packets of black powder. He went on to explain. "Each of these packets has powerful potions of sneezing powder. When thrown directly into someone's face, they will begin to sneeze violently. Their eyes will water constantly and they will also have a hard time breathing or speaking."

Plasick's eyes lit up in wonder. "Medic, can I actually begin to hope again? Can I pull this off?"

He looked at her with compassionate eyes. "Yes Plasick, you will pull this off. I'll help you. By the way, they've hired another Medic who is younger than I am. He will do exactly as they tell him. Mixer hates it when I argue with him. They are replacing me in the next three weeks. That's why I called you here on such short notice. Before I leave, I must know that I helped at least one tree to escape. If there is anyone else you want to take with you, let me know in two weeks. Make up an excuse to come here. Then I'll tell you my plans. Plasick, you must leave before I do! We're going to have to act fast. Mixer trusts you more and more these days. I have a feeling you won't ever get another chance to leave."

Medic screwed the top of the cane back on, handing it to Plasick as she stood up. She took it and reached out to him. They hugged tightly. "Go on now," he said stepping back. Plasick turned and went out the door, feeling a bit sad to be leaving Medic, but excited about the escape. Walking toward the bunkhouse she noticed that the pain in her leg was letting up. *Who else should I take?*

## The Thorn Tree

The next three days Plasick worked overtime training the new trees. On the fourth day of training as Plasick was shouting out orders, The Mixer went over to her and said, "Next week focus on training the Thorn Tree. He looks like he might make a good manager. I'll get another manager to work with your group. Finish up this morning and you and your trainees can have the rest of the day off. She worked extra hard that day and sure enough, he gave her and the trainees the afternoon off. They were actually allowed to walk around the grounds and visit with each other. Medic was right; The Mixer trusted her more and more each day. Of course there were plenty of guards still standing around them.

Plasick couldn't remember the last time she actually had a day off. As she started walking down the road from the tree bunkhouse she felt someone following her. She turned and saw the Thorn Tree.

"Hi," he said. "Do you mind if I walk with you?"

She nodded her approval. Plasick was unfamiliar with socializing. She had been in the role of Manager and Supervisor and rarely associated with the trainees. It was a bit awkward, but inside she was glad he was there. As they walked down the road to the clearing below, where many of the trees were visiting, he looked over at her. "Sure is a nice afternoon isn't it?"

"Yes it is. Having some time off is a rare occasion around here."

"Do you mind if we go over there and sit on that large rock and visit a bit?" he said while briefly touching her arm.

"All right." Plasick replied wondering why he was paying so much attention to her. She knew she was unattractive so she imagined he wanted to talk about work. They sat down facing each other. "Did you want to talk to me about work? I guess you've heard that The Mixer has his eye on you for being a manager. Is that it?"

He leaned forward toward her, "Well, that's great, but I really just wanted to get to know you. My name's Thorn by the way. Can I call you Plasick?"

She nervously covered her left leg with her branch hand. "Well, uh, of course if you like, but not in front of the other trainees." All of a sudden she felt very vulnerable.

"Listen Plasick, I'll get to the point. I like you. Since the first day I saw you, I liked you." Thorn said as he touched her hand. She looked at him with surprise showing through her big brown eyes. He continued, "You don't have to cover your leg in front of me either. I don't even care about that. I admire your strength and ability to handle your position. I like strong female trees." He smiled and held her hand with both of his.

She wasn't sure what to think about all of this! But she timidly smiled back; hoping no one else saw them.

"Don't worry, they're all busy visiting," he said. "Why don't you tell me about yourself and how you came to be here. I'm really interested."

No one except for Medic had ever asked her about herself. All of a sudden, Plasick opened up and began to share with Thorn. She told him how she landed in Barren Land, about the torture she went through and the humiliation she had experienced. Thorn moved closer to her and patted her shoulder. She began to cry, sharing about the loss of her mother and her friend Adronack. Plasick left out the part about the jewels and finding Adronack's hand. That seemed like a secret she was supposed to keep to herself. But she did begin to talk about escaping and then she stopped suddenly, realizing that she might have shared too much.

"Don't worry. I won't tell. You see Plasick, I want to escape too and I think if we work together we can do it."

"Maybe your right." She replied as she told him about the Medic, the secret in the cane and meeting with him next week to plan her escape. "Mixer will be replacing Medic soon, so we're going to have to act fast. He told me to let him know if there was anyone else I wanted to bring. I'll bring you!" she said smiling.

Having formed a bond, the two of them began talking more of their escape. Thorn had a few ideas that she liked.

"Thorn, The Mixer wants me to focus on training you all week, so we have a reason to be together and can plan more!" Plasick said excitedly.

"That's great Plasick, but I will be happy just to be able to spend time with you without having to explain why."

Plasick put her head down and smiled. *What's going on with me? I feel like I could really like him*, she thought as they continued talking.

Over the next week Plasick threw herself into the pretense of training Thorn. They were diligently planning out how they would get past the guards. Thorn assured her that she wouldn't have to kill anyone. If that came up, he would take care of it. Plasick was relieved. Although she had abused many workers, she told him that she couldn't imagine killing any of them, or even one of the guards. He looked at her seriously and asked, "Plasick, if you had to do it in order to save your life or mine, you would, wouldn't you?"

She looked at the seriousness on his face and replied, "I guess I would if I absolutely had to Thorn."

He looked relieved. "Another thing Plasick, I'm going to pretend I hurt myself on the day that your going to the Medic, that way you have a reason to take me. Does he know about me?"

"Yes, I told him about you and he said he trusted my judgment and to bring you along. Thorn, there is one thing he told me and you might not like it." Thorn listened to her while giving the outward appearance of being trained.

"He said that we should get married secretly and he would do the ceremony since he's also qualified to do that."

Thorn looked at her with a frown. "Why?"

Plasick got nervous, thinking she saw anger on his face. He recovered quickly. With a gentler look on his face he said again,

"Why Plasick?"

"Well, he said we would have an easier time once we're out of here. Something about the land he's sending us to has a law forbidding male and female trees traveling together unless they are married. He'll marry us and give us the paper to take with us."

"I'll be happy and proud to marry you Plasick."

She looked at Thorn, with tears starting to well up.

"Don't cry now, someone will see." He said sternly.

"Don't worry Thorn I won't let you down." Still she thought to herself, *I can feel happy in my heart, surely that can't hurt anything.*

## Escape Barren Land?

Another workday and the horn blasted loudly in the factory yard. Five o'clock. Thorn held his arm as he walked over to Plasick, pretending to be hurt. As they walked out together, Plasick dismissed her personal guards. This was the day they were getting married. This was the day they were getting the plans to escape.

"Come in," said the Medic as they knocked on his door. "Lock the door behind you!"

Thorn locked the door and they went into the kitchen where the Medic was waiting.

"Medic," said Plasick, "This is Thorn."

Thorn and Medic shook hands and they all sat down.

"First things first!" said the Medic. "Our time is limited. Here is your marriage license already filled out, I just need you both to sign it." He looked over at Thorn. "Did Plasick explain everything about this to you?"

Thorn nodded.

"Good! Both of you stand now and I'll proceed to marry you."

The ceremony was over quickly, but Plasick didn't mind. The important thing to her was that she would be escaping this place in a week, not alone, but with *her husband*, who loved her! After they said, "I do," Thorn and Plasick briefly hugged. Plasick had a smile on her face as she handed Medic her cane and sat next to Thorn.

Thorn was looking at the open window. "Medic, you'd better close that kitchen window, someone might hear us."

Medic looked up and quickly shut the window.

Plasick was still was pondering her love for Thorn when he nudged her, "Let's pay attention to Medic." Medic spread out the map. A long hour had gone by as they all sat back in their chairs mulling over everything they had spoken about.

"Now, There are two other things you need to know," said Medic. "First, after midnight they release the Sticky Bats to roam at night. If the bats hear any sounds that are out of the ordinary they begin to send signals back to a machine that is in General Saguwas office. Here is a bundle of Wild Rue Berries, the bats love them, but I've injected poison into each one. Drop them on your way out. It should take care of the problem."

Thorn said, "What if it doesn't?"

Medic looked at him seriously. "Then run! Run fast! Once you pass the gate and the two guards that are there, no one can follow you. Cellberth people own the land outside of the gate. Cellberth is a town with very strict rules. That's why I joined you two in marriage. Once you get to the town, show the officials your marriage certificate and tell them you're just passing through to go to CreatureVille. It's a long journey, but with perseverance you will make it."

"How do you know all this Medic? And what's the second thing you wanted to tell us?" Thorn asked as he handed the poison berries to Plasick.

"Thorn, I know all of this because I've been here for almost ten years. I've explored every inch of this area! I'm an alligator, so they didn't keep track of my coming and going." He looked at them both. "The second thing you need to know is that Barren land is having their ten-year celebration in two days. Only the Officers know about it so far. You *must* leave on that night!"

Thorn looked confident. "Sounds good, we're ready."

Plasick didn't look as confident, but trusted her friend and new husband.

Medic walked over and stood in front of her. They reached out to one another with a long embrace.

"Will you be all right Medic? I know they are replacing you shortly after we're gone."

Medic smiled as he looked at her through his aged, yet tender eyes.

"When I see your familiar branches go by my window on the night you leave, I'll be the happiest 'gator' you ever saw!" He threw his head back and laughed. But after seeing the concern in her eyes he became somber. "I know how to take care of myself Plasick, don't worry."

Thorn watched them and said impatiently, "Come on Plasick, we've got to go . . . now!" Plasick turned toward Thorn. With sadness gripping her heart she followed him out the door and down the steps toward the tree bunkhouse. She didn't dare look back or she knew she would break down. Medic had rushed to the window to watch her walk away.

The next two days flew by for Thorn and Plasick. Today was the day of the 10-year Anniversary of the Idol Factory. Mixer and his wife did not intend on inviting any of the creatures, worker trees, managers or supervisors. But he did give them the option of having the afternoon off, if they would serve their guests, run errands and clean up afterward. Most of them agreed to do it. A few chose to continue working.

Plasick told Mixer that it was important that she spend the afternoon and evening finishing the final training of Thorn. Being preoccupied with preparing for the special event, Mixer approved her request. Now all Thorn and Plasick had to do was wait until dark. While Thorn was in the factory, Plasick went to the tree bunkhouse. It was empty so she hurried to pull out the brick where the three red jewels were hidden. "O.K. little ones, you're coming with me now." She used the dagger in her cane to cut three small, deep holes on the inside of her right thigh and pushed the stones in with the tip of the knife until she was sure they couldn't be moved. It was painful, but she managed to do it without crying out. "No one will find them Adronack," she said as she left the bunkhouse.

By late afternoon most of the guests had arrived. Music was playing and congratulations were being made. Everyone was happy and excited to be a part of the celebration. They all followed The Mixer and Messer into the resource room to take a thirty-minute tour. After that they would go down the hill to the clearing where a platform and chairs were set up for The Mixer's speech. Of course, a few guards were milling around making sure things went well.

Thorn and Plasick casually watched as they went into the building. She had already released her personal guards to go and join the party. They left without any questions, eager to join the festivities. The Medic had gone out the night before and dropped several poison berries on the ground. He hoped that all of the Sticky Fur Bats would eat them and be dead before Thorn and Plasick came though the woods.

Everything was set. It was time to escape. Slowly walking up toward Medic's building behind Plasick, Thorn looked around. As Medic promised, the usual Armadillo guards were not patrolling in front of the house. Medic had given his guards the night off. He also gave them and the Border Gate Keeper Guards several special 'feel good' pills to take during the celebration. He had told them, "Consider it a gift for all your hard work." They thanked him profusely, especially for the pills. Thorn and Plasick walked toward the rear of Medic's house. Plasick looked to her left and saw Medic's smiling face looking out the window at her. They waved good-by to each other. Once he saw them enter the woods behind his house, he closed the curtains. As he lay down on his cot he thought out loud, "As long as those Border Gate Keeper Guards take those pills, Thorn and Plasick will be sure to escape."

"It's dark out here, but the moonlight is helping," said Thorn as they walked through the forest.

"Yes and it's so quiet, I don't see any of those Sticky Fur Bats in the air."

They both continued to run down the path toward the edge of the grounds. They had been running for about fifteen minutes when Thorn stumbled, almost falling. As he looked down to see what he tripped over, he saw two Sticky Fur Bats dead on the ground.

"What's this?"

Plasick came over and saw a several berries lying near the bats. "Medic! He must have come last night and thrown the poison berries around. Look at all the dead bats over there!"

Thorn looked around and saw several dead bats. "Wow, there must be around fifty them! We never could have handled that on our own."

Plasick silently thanked her dear friend as Thorn called out, "Let's keep going; we only have a few more miles to go."

They finally came within about ten feet of the hidden road that would take them out of Barren Land. As they stood behind a tree they could see beautiful country in the distance past the row of thin poplar trees, which were usually well guarded. Only two Border Gate Guards were there and they were sitting on the ground, slumped over near one of the poplar threes.

"I wonder if they're drunk?" whispered Thorn.

"I don't think so."

They waited for several moments. Thorn took out the black sneezing powder that Medic gave them. "We've got to try, it's the only way out of here."

The closer they got to the guards, the more they realized the guards were out cold.

*I'll bet Medic had something to do with this too*, thought Plasick.

"It's our lucky day Plasick, let's get out of here, we're free!"

They both climbed over the gate and rushed past the Poplar trees and down the hill toward the beautiful hill they had seen earlier. Thorn had memorized the map to save time. "Let's head on to Cellberth Town," he said as he pulled out their marriage certificate.

Plasick ran to catch up with him thinking, *I can't believe it was so easy to escape! I was so afraid! They are all so afraid back there. It's like another world yet it is so close to freedom! If only I had told Medic earlier that I wanted to leave. He could have helped Adronack too!*

Soon they were both over the hill, gasping for breath. They were finally, really safe from The Mixer! He would never enter this land because of the strict laws. Also, the creatures in this land didn't really like alligators. Plasick began to laugh and laugh, enjoying the freedom. Although Thorn had only been in the Barren Land for less than a month, he too was happy to be out and free. With added energy they forged ahead toward Cellberth Town.

Medic was right; it took them three days of walking to get to Cellberth Town. They had no trouble being allowed to come in after they showed them their marriage certificate and told them they were only passing through and wouldn't be staying in town for very long. In the beginning, Thorn was nice enough, but much less attentive than he was in Barren Land. Plasick imagined that he was just preoccupied with getting them to safety. After around three weeks they left Cellberth Town and continued walking on their journey to CreatureVille. Thorn was impatient to get there and complained to Plasick that she was too slow and needed to hurry and keep up with him. She noticed that he often avoided looking at her and didn't treat her as nice as he did when they first met. Since they escaped from the Idol Factory, he had changed a lot. He treated her roughly and hurt her wrist when he cut off her Supervisor I.D. Each day, he talked to her less and less. What have I done to upset him? She shrugged off her thoughts. *Still . . . we're married. I'm so-o-o happy about that! Once we find a home, I'm sure he'll be less anxious. We're out of Barren Land! We escaped! We escaped!*

## Greedo has an Unusual Day

Greedo had become a very powerful icon in Sand City. He did have his share of enemies, but there were many trees and creatures who were intensely loyal to him. His progress under the tutelage of

Numby was impressive. Sand City, now boasted of a population of over one hundred thousand seedlings and creatures.

Business Opportunities and other doors opened wide when they knew Greedo was involved. He now owned his own apartment building in one of the wealthiest neighborhoods. His apartment was on the top floor of a five-story building. Without trying, he had become more powerful than Numby.

It was the middle of the week and Greedo was on his way to an important investment meeting at the Brawnvin Hotel in CreatureVille. CreatureVille was only about two hours away from Sand City if he rode The Wheeler. He was enjoying the cool wind that was blowing as he went to see if The Wheeler was prepared for the trip. Greedo didn't like having to always walk so far to other villages and towns – it took up too much time. So he came up with a unique design for traveling and called it "The Wheeler." No one else had this special means of traveling. He had drawn the plans out himself. Now and then he would rent it out to some of his wealthier friends. Of course, his good pal Numby never had to pay.

The Wheeler was a ten by ten foot flat piece of wood that was cut out of a dead Redwood Tree. Greedo had it covered with rare soft cream-colored fur from a Giant Winter Tiger that had been captured in Sand City and killed by some evil outside hunters. The wheels were made from the same tree. He had traded several of his prize goods for the wood, fur and rhino eggs, but it was worth it. He incubated the Giant Rhino Eggs for several weeks and witnessed their hatching. He was the first face the three baby Rhinos saw, once they were able to open their eyes. He personally nurtured and trained them from birth. Because of that they were extremely loyal to him. They did excellent work as carriers whose main job was to pull The Wheeler. They also enjoyed the prestige and respect that the community extended to them.

"This is the life!" He said out loud as in no time at all he was at the Brawnvin Hotel in CreatureVille. Several other bank and shop owners were looking out the seventh story hotel window as The Wheeler pulled up. Greedo knew they would be watching for him and he was satisfied that he made a good first impression. As he jumped off The Wheeler he looked intensely at the Rhino Trio. They knew the look and nodded their massive heads in agreement. They would not leave until he came back.

Greedo took care of his business in less than an hour. He bought up several other businesses that he was going to resell, along with a few franchises. He socialized for a while, signed all the necessary papers and started back down the stairs of the hotel. Once outside he heard someone yelling with a loud voice. He looked to his left and saw a large gathering of creatures and trees listening to someone speak. Being curious, Greedo motioned to the Rhino Trio to wait for him. After he subtly hid his business papers in a secret compartment under the seat of The Wheeler, he began walking toward the crowd.

As he got closer he heard a voice cry out, "That's right Creature Preacher! Tell it like it is!"

Greedo pushed his way through the crowd trying to see who was yelling so loudly. There was something about that voice. As he moved closer to the front of the group that was gathered around the platform he saw the female seedling that was shouting. She was standing next to an unattractive thorny tree, holding his hand. The thorny tree was only about a foot higher than she was. She excitedly jumped up and yelled out again when he roughly pushed her down. She stumbled, falling over a nearby creature and then crashed to the ground. She was struggling to get up, but no one would help her. The other trees and creatures stood back and stared at her. Some even got angry and looking at her with disgust.

Greedo couldn't understand why no one would help her. But as he edged closer - he saw why. She was part plastic and part tree and had several gouges in her trunk. Many of her limbs were broken. Her left tree leg looked deformed.

"Poor sap, she should go to Sand City, they wouldn't care how she looked there." Feeling a moment of compassion, Greedo walked over to her. Reaching out his right tree branch arm, he bent over to help her up. She was facing the ground struggling to get back up when she saw the tree arm extended toward her. She quickly grabbed it and held on tightly. She wasn't very heavy and Greedo easily pulled her to a standing position.

She shyly looked up at Greedo and for a moment, they just stood there, staring at each other. Finally she spoke, "Thank you so much!"

"Not a problem." replied Greedo as he smiled down at her.

"Let's get out of here!" yelled her Thorny Tree husband, who was watching her every move. She quickly turned away from Greedo to rush over to her husband. Greedo watched as the Thorny Tree grabbed the deformed seedling and left the meeting.

Greedo shook his head and started walking back toward The Wheeler. On the way he looked over at the platform, stopping for a moment. It was a Creature Preacher and he was preparing to travel again. He had gathered quite a following. Several creatures and trees began to pick up their already packed bags to go with him to the next town. Greedo saw the glazed, unseeing look in the preacher's eyes as he continued to yell out. "You are worthless, you are sinners. Without RELIGION what do you have? Get your life straight and follow me to the RIGHT RELIGIOUS, RIGHTEOUS WAY."

The more Greedo heard the words, the more irritated he became. All I hear is condemnation from this creature!! Why would those trees and creatures join in with someone who is heaping condemnation on them and then pretending to love them? No thanks! He briskly walked away from the loud preaching and stepped up into The Wheeler. Taking up the reins, he barely tapped the Rhino

Trio and they began their journey back home. As he slowly rode out of town, Greedo looked ahead and on the right side of the road he noticed the female seedling that he had seen just moments before. *She's the one who fell down.* She was limping and in obvious pain while trying to catch up with her husband. While passing them by, Greedo turned to look at her and waved. She saw him and timidly smiled and waved back, hoping her husband didn't see her. *Looks like she's got it tough,* he thought. *But, at least she didn't follow that Creature Preacher. I don't know why, but I'm glad about that.*

## Greedo's True Friends

The next day, after Greedo had returned from CreatureVille, it was raining. Not a stormy rain, but a steady, soft, all day rain. Although yesterday was a successful business day for him, Greedo was feeling restless and decided to walk over to *The Bear's Neighborhood Shoppe*. Mr. and Mrs. Fuzzy, also known as Momma and Poppa, were the two bears that owned it. Both of them looked up as they heard the tinkling of the bell on the front door. In walked Greedo.

"Hey Momma and Poppa!" He stood at the door and closed his eyes for a moment and took in a deep breath. "Something smells s-o-o-o good in here!"

It brought back a memory, yet he wasn't sure if it was an actual memory or a dream of a memory he would like to have. Nevertheless, he liked it.

"Hello, hello, our little Greedo" they both called out in unison.

By now, Greedo was almost five feet tall, so he stood a little taller than Momma, but a little shorter than Poppa. Momma reached out giving Greedo a big bear hug.

"Oh my, you must have those young female seedlings going crazy for you with your slicked back tree top and your broad shoulder branches."

Greedo blushed, "Awe Momma, you know you're my favorite girl!"

Poppa slapped him on the back. "I love you little Greedo, but don't you go flirting with my Frejeea, she's mine!"

The couple laughed, pulling out the tall chairs at the table while Greedo went and got a cup of coffee for Momma and sat down. Poppa went behind the bakery shelves to pull out a plate of different pastries. The atmosphere of their unique Shoppe and just being in their company had a calming effect on him, at least for a few moments.

Momma and Poppa's children had moved to Cordaya Valley a long time ago and since the Great Storm, they hadn't heard from them. They were hopeful that somehow their children survived, yet they feared the worst. They unofficially adopted Greedo as their son. They loved him deeply and although they worried about his rough lifestyle, they accepted him for who he was.

"My little son," said Poppa as he brought over the pastries and sat down. "What's on your mind today, you seem very somber today." Momma walked over to the table then, sitting between Greedo and Poppa. Greedo slid the coffee over to Momma, enjoying the smell and watching them together as they ate their treats.

"Momma. Poppa. I was over in the town of CreatureVille yesterday and saw this weird Creature Preacher. What he was saying really annoyed me! He yelled out and heaped condemnation on the creatures and seedlings in that land. Then he had the nerve to collect money for some strange cause! When he walked off the stage I saw him turn and look straight at me. I got the eeriest feeling that this guy was a real con artist. I should know I am one too! It made me sick to look at him, yet as I walked away I thought, 'Am I looking into a mirror?' It was so obvious to me that he was giving everyone a big line. And then I thought, 'Well, so do I!' He robs creatures all in the name of his own made up cause. Then I thought, 'Well, I rob creatures and then justify it as an o.k. thing to do!' Then I realized that I sometimes steal just because I'm angry. My attitude is . . . if I've been hurt why shouldn't I hurt them?"

Momma and Poppa looked intently at Greedo as he stood up, walking around restlessly before sitting back down again. Greedo continued, for a moment, unaware of his surroundings.

"I'm a pretender. I'm prideful and so was the Preacher Creature. He's living a lie but pretending to be truthful. On the other hand, I know I am living a lie, but I'm not pretending to be something I'm not! Doesn't that kind of honesty make me better than him?"

Greedo rested his head in his hand branch as he looked out the window. "What is the truth anyway? He talks about others being bad and yet he won't admit that he is just as bad. I know what I'm doing is wrong and I keep on doing it. At least I'm honest about what I'm doing wrong. What makes us different?"

Poppa knew this was one of those soul-searching days that Greedo often had lately. Numby wasn't someone he could go to for help, so he often came into the shop to share some of his troubles. As Poppa watched Greedo staring out at the gentle rain falling against the window, he knew that this time it was different. This conversation was more serious. And Greedo looked sadder that usual today.

## Pop Shares His Wisdom

"Greedo, I don't have all the answers for you. But here is something that might help you. I have heard about a secret place where a very tall and enormously large tree grows. They say it is a tree like no other. I don't know its name and I don't even know where it is. But, I do know this.

It's not just the size of this tree that makes it so spectacular, although it certainly is huge and breathtaking. It is the Wisdom that this tree carries that makes it so special. The Wisdom inside of the tree produces leaves of many colors and each leaf has a message on it. I have also heard that these Wisdom messages have the power to heal. Some creatures and trees have received gladness and joy through the Wisdom from the tree. For others, their eyes of understanding are opened. I have also heard that many receive answers to some of their most difficult questions in life. Questions like the ones you are asking me."

Momma touched Greedo's arm as she spoke. "I've heard that everyone who encounters this tree has an amazing experience. I've never seen the Tree, but I believe it exists. Last winter the mysterious White Neoflight Birds came by and shared some stories about the Tree to several of us here at the Shoppe.

"Who are they?" asked Greedo.

"They are birds that are sent out by various Overseer Trees to give out hope and encouragement to others," said Momma. "Because of their messages, many creatures and trees now have hope that there is something more to be discovered outside of Sand City. Of course, there are still some who are afraid to venture out and see other lands. Poppa and I know we're meant to stay here. But not everyone feels that way." Momma looked at Greedo. "Perhaps you're not meant to stay here Greedo. Maybe that's why you keep feeling restless now and then. Huh?"

Greedo looked at Momma, knowing she was very wise.

"You might be on to something Momma. I just don't know."

"You are my little Greedo – that's for sure. You are also an adventurer. Maybe that Tree can give you some answers. Maybe you should think about taking a journey to find that tree? Huh? Poppa nodded his head in agreement.

For a few moments all was silent at the table except for the occasional 'slurp' as Momma drank her coffee and a 'smack' now and then as Poppa enjoyed the pastries. Greedo started to open his mouth to speak, when the door flew open and the bell above it began ringing wildly. Fret popped in his head.

"Hey Greedo, where have you been. I was lookin' all over for you. Big Yellow wants you to sit in on his elite high stakes card game!" Greedo stood, trying to cover up his disappointment at being interrupted.

"Sounds like a winner, let's go!"

As he left the shop he turned to look back and winked at his favorite 'adopted' parents. *They mean so much to me.* "See ya Poppa, later Momma!" Before they could wave back the door slammed shut and off he went with Fret down the street toward Big Yellow's place. The bell finished its last dying tingle. Momma Bear and Poppa Bear looked at each other with sadness in their eyes as their favorite seedling left the shop. The quietness was almost deafening. Poppa got up slowly to start another batch of hot cross buns. Momma somberly began to clean off the table. Each one was lost in their own thoughts, not realizing how similar those thoughts really were.

Chapter VI

# Clarity, Truth & Moving On

## Aya & The Evil Wasps

Treeania began to stir. It was already early morning. Soon Aya and Wyo also woke up.

"Good Morning," he said. "Did you sleep well?"

Aya stretched her limbs, "As well as can be expected I guess." Realizing that she sounded ungrateful, she quickly added, "But I'm looking forward to hearing more about the history and background of the valley."

Time moved within the atmosphere, whispering though the wind.

"Wake up all. Come. Wake up."

Little by little, nearby neighbors began to gather. When Time spoke in this land, even when it was a whisper, everyone listened. Knowing the seriousness of the situation, they shortened their greetings and conversations. They didn't want to miss a thing. Several of them came up to shake hands with Aya, hoping that she that would help them save the field. Time nudged them to move along, so they quickly found their favorite spots and sat down.

Aya was amazed at the large group. She asked Treeania, "How did they all know to come here now? You didn't call out."

Treeania looked at her, "Did you hear the Whispering Sounds in the Wind?

Aya thought for a moment, "Well, I heard a faint sound, like a voice. What was it?"

"It was Time. He comes and speaks through the Wind now and then. We're all accustomed to hearing his voice."

Aya's eyes grew large. "My, what incredible mysteries are in this land! A place where Time speaks!?"

"Actually, Time's voice is not limited to this land. Time travels everywhere. It's just that - not everyone can hear his voice. The fact that you even heard a Whisper of a voice is hopeful for you Aya. One day I imagine you will hear him clearly."

Puzzled, Aya was about to ask him another question. But he had already turned his attention toward his community.

Suddenly, it became very still as everyone waited for Treeania to speak. "Good Morning! I know you're all anxious to hear the rest of the history. In my respect for Time . . . I won't waste any."
He looked around at those in his community, proud of the unity they represented.

"As I shared yesterday, the three brothers were being trained in Harmony Field. About a month before their return home – they began grumbling among themselves about how mean their Overseer Trainer was. Then they began talking badly about their brother Ketonday. They felt he was given special privileges – by not having to leave The Harmony Field.

Also, they didn't like the foreign land of the Morning Glory field that they were in. Day by day their anger grew stronger. Yeto had been thinking and thinking and fuming about his situation for a long time! His nectar was gradually turning bitter and he knew it. Actually, he had known about it for a while, but said nothing. Now he simply didn't care. His jealousy was totally taking over, turning into deep-rooted Bitterness.

One night, long after Siree and Uozoni gone to sleep, Yeto walked off into an isolated area outside of the borders of Harmony Field. He leaned against a tall dead tree, not realizing that just a few feet above his large flower petals, was a nest of Wicked Wasps. Although he knew he had Bitterness, Yeto didn't realize that for many weeks, the bitter aroma had been seeping through his nectar. The aroma attracted the Wicked Wasps and

brought them into the land. They had been on the lookout for a
long, long time to find some way, through their sense of smell, to
find an opening that would allow them to attack and destroy the
Flower Fields. But they could never smell evil coming out of any
of the flowers – until Yeto developed a jealous heart."

"Wicked Wasps!" gasped six of the middle-ager rabbits. "What
do they look like?"

"They're black with a triple layer of large silver colored, metal
wings. The lower set of wings stays flat against their sides, ready for
emergencies. The middle set is used for flying, and the top layer is
for weaving into other Wasp wings, in order to carry objects. Their
eyes have no eyelids and are dull yellow, with black in the center.
They have extremely long; poisonous stingers that are on the tips of
their noses. They have two thin, long stick-like legs, with hairy ten-
tacles on them. Four sharp dagger-like toes are on each foot, to help
them grasp things with a strong grip."

The rabbits pink little eyes grew huge with fright, as they listened to Treeania's description. Treeania noticed that even though
the middle-ager rabbits were older than the baby rabbits, which were
not allowed at this meeting, they were becoming afraid.

"Don't worry," he said. "They don't attack animals."
In unison, all six rabbits let out a gasp of relief as Treeania continued
the story:

"Three of the Giant Wasps flew down; one went inside Yeto's
petals, to the pollen area of his flower and stung him with Hatred.
One flew to the core of his stem and stuck him with Poisonous
Revenge. The other one attacked and ravaged several of his petals.
Yeto tried to run, but the poison went into his veins instantly and
he fell down. The Wasps then pulled back to watch the evil transformation take place.

First, Yeto's white petals fell to the ground and withered. His
stem turned into a black, snake-like tail and traveled up his entire
body, causing him to have a slippery, scaly body like a Dragon.

One of his eyes turned white, the original color that his petals once were. The other eye turned black.

The Wasps then heard some noise and saw Yeto's brothers walking out of the Harmony Field looking for him. Once they got close to the dead tree, the Wicked Wasps seized the moment, attacking both of them in the same way that they had attacked Yeto. Only this time there were six Wasps.

When the attack was over, they fiendishly watched as Siree lost all of his red petals and his stem began to turn into a dark, reddish black color. Scales soon followed, forming him into a Dragon. At the same time, Uozoni's beautiful yellow petals were torn off. As the poison totally took over, his stem began to turn into a grimy, yellow and green color. His eyes took on the yellow color of his petals, which were crushed under his feet. The three brothers had been transformed into evil. Now the Wasps could use them to devour the Harmony Field and have access to the other three."

## The Bitter Roots

"But how could that happen?" said Aya.

Treeania looked at her sadly and explained. "It wasn't just Yeto who had Bitterness. His brothers also did. It began when they allowed their anger and murmuring to take root. Then Bitterness took over their nectar and it turned into Jealousy. When they hid it and didn't seek healing, the bitter nectar aroma attracted the poisonous Wasps. This is what gave the Wasps an opening to attack them.

"So then," said Wyo. "They began as three Snap-Dragon Flowers that provided healing to others and now after being distorted by the poison stingers – turned into evil Dragons. The Wasps even twisted the Snap-Dragon Flowers' name, by calling each one – Dragon Eye!"

One of the neighborhood bushes looked up at Treeania and blurted out, "What happened to the Harmony Field?"

Treeania sighed and closed his eyes for a moment, repeating what he had heard from the Messengers:

"Within hours, thousands of Wasps flew in and attacked the Overseer Tree. Once he died, the field was open for them to feast upon. The Dragon Eyes and the Wasps attacked the flowers mercilessly, and then Yeto burned the field with his fire. The Wasps moved quickly. They sent signals into the atmosphere, for other Giant Wasps to meet them at the Field of Hope and then the Field of Happiness. Everything happened at lightening speed, so each field was caught unaware and unprepared."

"How did the Dragon Eyes get to each field?" asked Cindy Quail.

"Thousands of the Giant Wasps formed three large mesh rugs, by intertwining their top layer of silver colored, metal wings. Once formed, the Wasps waited on the ground, as each Dragon Eye stepped onto the incredibly strong, mesh rugs. Once they did, the Wasps middle wings began to move and flap loudly. From what I understand, the noise of the thousands of Wicked Wasps flapping their wings was deafening! They wasted no time and immediately flew into the Field of Hope, destroying the Overseer Tree and all of the Lilies. Then they speedily went on to the Field of Happiness, viciously destroying the Buttercup Flowers and the Overseer Tree."

Aya's eyes grew round in awe. "Why wasn't your field burned too?"

"By the time the Dragon Eyes got here, we had been warned by the Messengers of what had happened in the other fields; so we were a little more prepared. It also took the Dragon Eyes and Wicked Wasps a long time to get here. But, by the time they did, it was the Seven-Day Birthing Time in the Healing Field. Every year, for seven days the Snapdragon flowers give birth. This is a very vulnerable time for them."

"Why couldn't you destroy the Dragon Eyes?" asked one of the lightly spotted fawns.

"My Destiny is Overseer and Trainer – I have no powers over

this type of evil."

Robby the Robin was perched near Aya, and began to jump up and down to get Treeania's attention.

"Yes Robby, what is it?"

The little Robin quietly spoke, "What happened to the Wicked Wasps?"

"Before they came Robby, I told all the Snap-Dragon Flowers in my field, to breathe their Healing Vapors into the air. The Wasps hate any scent in the air that smells like healing, because it causes their evil powers to weaken and eventually disappear.

When the Healing Vapors blew on some of the Wasps, they lost their flying power and soon dropped all three Dragons unto the ground. Some of the Wasps shrunk from the breath of the Vapors and flew away; like little flies. Others died from the overwhelming Powers of Healing that blew through the atmosphere – because their evil bodies rejected it."

The entire community was intense as they listened to Treeania:

"The three Dragon Eyes were close enough to the ground when they fell, so they weren't killed. They shook themselves off and crawled to the outside of each corner of the field. Ketonday was already in my field; when his brothers first came in on the mesh rugs of the Wasps' wings. He didn't recognize his brothers at all.

Little did I know, that he too, had developed jealousy inside of his heart. One of the last Wicked Wasps had picked up the bitter scent. He flew down and stung Ketonday very hard. But, because of the weakened strength of the Wasp, Ketonday was only partially changed into a Dragon Eye. Both of his eyes turned orange and all of his petals fell to the ground except one –he still has one orange petal left, under his slimy neck. He tried to shake off the last petal, but it couldn't be removed. The Giant Wasp that stung him, died immediately."

Everyone turned then, to look down at the Snap Dragon Field of Flowers. Treeania sadly observed his community and said,

"Now, they are waiting for the flowers to weaken even more – which they will – during the next three days that are left in the Seven-Day Birthing Time. As long as the Healing Vapors are blowing, the Dragon-Eyes are limited to what evil they can do."

"Will the Healing Vapors blow for a long, long time?" asked the Peanut Tree.

"No Nutty, once the Birthings take place, the Winds must subside, so they don't blow the little Snap-Dragon Flower seedlings away. It's important that we now begin to prepare a plan of action and put it to work within 24-48 hours. Everyone . . . we must prepare for battle."

All of the forest animals, trees, bushes and others, became very quiet, as they thought about how impossible it was going be – to win this battle against such evil. Wyo watched as Aya turned away from the group, and quietly walked down the nearby hill. He knew she wanted to be alone.

---

## Boxer's Tough Decision

A year had passed by since Sniffer and Whiskers left Boxer to be trained by Enobleus. Every four months they had come by to wave at him from a distance, as they dropped Rocky off for his two day visit. The training period for Boxer had finally come to an end and they were very excited.

"Today is the day we go to pick up Boxer!" Whiskers said to Rocky. Immediately Rocky began to run in a happy circle around the room. Sniffer came in through the porch and laughed.

"Looks like you told Rocky the good news!"

"I hope Boxer stays with us Sniffer." Whiskers said quietly as

Rocky ran up and down the porch steps in anticipation of Boxer coming home.

"I know," he said, "I do too."

They practically ran all the way to gather around the Oak Tree Volante'. As Sniffer, Whiskers and Rocky came toward Volante', she began waving to them with her bright colorful leaves.

"Hello there!" she shouted out. "And how are the LongEars today?"

"A little nervous, that's for sure," said Whiskers.

"Come on over and have a seat, the ground is nice and soft. Enobleus and Boxer should be along shortly," said Volante'.

After a few moments Rocky took off running. As Sniffer and Whiskers looked to see where he was headed, they saw Boxer!

"Oh my," yelled out Whiskers as she and Sniffer began running toward him. "He's grown at least two feet!"

Rocky rushed over to Boxer, jumped up into his arms and knocked him over. Boxer fell to his knees and rolled over on the ground with Rocky, laughing so hard he couldn't get back up. Rocky began licking him all over his face and nuzzling his neck.

As they reached Boxer and Rocky, Whiskers and Sniffer fell on top of Boxer and began hugging him, crying unashamedly. They all started talking at once.

"How are you?"

"You've gotten so tall!"

"Wow, you both look great!"

"I missed you so much."

Enobleus couldn't tell who was saying what as they hugged, laughed and cried. In his wisdom he stood back, letting them enjoy their moments to the fullest. He watched tenderly as they kept grabbing and touching each other's hands and arms, simply wanting to hold on to the moment. Then all was quiet as they looked at each other with watery eyes.

"Let's go sit over by Volante' now," said Enobleus quietly.

They all stood up walking arm in arm, careful not to step on Rocky who was right under their feet.

"Welcome Noble One," said Volante'. Over the past year she had often visited with him. She also had regular interactions and training sessions with Boxer. She watched Boxer approaching, knowing that two paths of Destiny were going to open up for him today. Enobleus stood near Volante'and began to speak.

"Sniffer and Whisker's, you are to be commended for sending me such a teachable and wise protégé. It was a great sacrifice for you not to be with him for an entire year. Your love for Boxer and the trees and creatures in this land is evident." Rocky looked up at his parents who were weeping.

"Boxer, come here."

Boxer walked over and stood in front of Enobleus and Volante.' Sniffer and Whiskers stood behind him.

"Boxer you have been personally trained by me. You and I have formed a solid relationship of trust and loyalty. You have passed all of the physical and mental tasks that you were assigned. I believe you are ready to be a temporary Overseer Tree. Today, you can leave the island in search of your Destiny Land somewhere else, or you can stay here to oversee Rensamor Island for one year and then wait to see if The Soil of the Earth and The Sun of Splendor will allow you to root. Do you accept this challenge and honor?"

Volante' looked at Sniffer and Whisker's drawn faces as they anticipated his decision. Volante', being a Perceptive Tree, already knew his answer.

Boxer had been nervous all week long. He had tossed and turned many nights knowing this question would one day be presented to him. Thoughts of his family had come in and out of his mind for several weeks. He had asked himself, *Should I try to find them? Or is this where I should stay and seek my Destiny Land?*

But now, today he knew what his answer would be. He looked straight at Enobleus with confidence and said, "Yes, Enobleus, I accept this challenge and honor you have presented to me. I will be the Overseer Tree of this land for one year."

A gasp came out of Whiskers mouth as Enobleus continued, "This week at the celebration, I will publicly endorse you. In the meantime Boxer, congratulations, you are a valuable asset to this land." Volante' waved her branches over Boxer accepting his proclamation and endorsing his decision. They all stood beneath her, laughing and crying all over again with great joy and new hope in their hearts. After the proper amount of time, Enobleus said his goodbyes and went to prepare for the Overseer Celebration that would seal everything that had transpired tonight. He knew all the creatures and trees would be happy about this transition.

## The Celebration

A loud clanging sound woke Boxer up out of his deep, restful slumber. Boxer sat upright and looked around, rubbing the sleep from his eyes. As he scanned the room he saw Rocky. He was staring at him to see what Boxer's next move would be.

"Rocky, did you knock over those pans so I would wake up?" Boxer said as he looked out his bedroom door and saw a pan still wobbling on the floor.

Rocky jumped up on the bed as if he wanted to make sure Boxer was still at his home. It had been a week since Boxer's return. Time was on a mission and had moved through the days quickly. Today was the day the island was celebrating his position as temporary Overseer.

Everyone in the community was preparing for the special night. Several of them came by the LongEar's home to congratulate him and visit. They were all looking forward to new fresh beginnings - hoping to build up the community. They were sad to see Enobleus step down, but they knew he would be around to instruct Boxer whenever needed. Boxer jumped up to prepare for the day. Sniffer and Whisker's were already outside on the porch in their rockers waiting for him.

"Good Morning," he said to them as he walked out to the porch.

"Hello! Are you ready to be commissioned?"

He reached over, grabbed their hands and gently pulled them out of their rockers.

"Yep! I AM READY!"

Whiskers grabbed her best hat and gave Sniffer his as they hastily followed Boxer and Rocky up and down the winding road to meet Enobleus and the community under the Oak Tree, Volante.' The celebration was taking place under the shadow of her massive leaves. She was excited to see Boxer, Rocky, Sniffer and Whiskers approaching her. They were the first to arrive. The island was alive with excitement – she could feel it generating through the air. *How wonderful. The little seedling who almost lost his life - brought life to this dying community.*

They were coming from all over Rensamor Island to see Boxer. There was Billy Beaver with his parents. He began showing off by posing on his tail and then bouncing down the hill on it. Following Billy were the Sunflower Kids, four rambunctious rowdy middle-ager seedlings. They weren't baby seedlings and yet they weren't quite adults. Most everyone loved them, even with their fun-loving pranks. Right behind them came Millie Muskrat and her family. Harry Hamster and his wife brought their six young hamsters who loved to smell everything in sight. But when they got a little too close to the Sun-Flower Kids, who liked to pick them up by their tails and hold them upside down, the baby hamsters quickly ran back to their parents, jumping up onto their mother's back. The Ladybug Clan hitched a ride with Fanny Pigeon by clinging onto her feet while in the air.

*It's going to be a fun day, a wonderful day!* thought Boxer as he watched everyone come streaming down the hills and roads to congratulate him and find their seats. Spotting a slow moving turtle who was making his way through the crowd, Boxer thought, *that must be Stinky Turtle. I'll finally get to meet him today!*

Whiskers and Sniffer watched proudly as they waited for Enobleus to arrive.

"There he is Whiskers," said Sniffer as he looked to the right.

"Attention Everyone! The Noble One is entering the grounds," announced Volante' with her strong voice.

Everyone stood, giving Enobleus their respect, as his tall gnarled, body walked toward Volante' with pride.

*I didn't realize how respected and loved he really is,* thought Boxer as he listened to the audience clapping and whistle, shouting, "Honorable Enobleus! Our Great Overseer!"

### Boxer's Endorsement

Enobleus stood before them, putting his branch hands out so everyone would sit down. A loud "P-O-P!" went through the air as Mr. Warthog plopped down on a puffy bag that had been filled with air. "I'm so sorry!" he said as he stood up looking at his seat as if it would tell him what happened. He then put on his spectacles and sure enough, he saw the Sunflower Kids giggling in the back row. Mr. Warthog glared at them but knew he must quickly sit down so he wouldn't disturb the ceremony any more than it already had been.

The giggles and laughter soon quieted down. Enobleus didn't mind the ruckus.

*They needed a good laugh,* he thought as he looked out at the crowd. *It's good to see so many of them happy.* He cleared his throat.

"It's a joyful day today and wonderful to see so many of you come to this special occasion. Our community is now in a great transition and we will all go through many changes. That will require more flexibility from all of us. While we go through these transitions, I hope you will show Boxer the same teamwork and unity that you have shown me."

A loud roar from the crowd was sounded as they agreed. Enobleus continued, "I have personally trained the young seedling Boxer, who will oversee this land for one year. I believe he is capable of building up this land once again. Let's now show Boxer our support as I call him forward and commission him!" Everyone stood up clapping loudly and screaming out "Boxer! Boxer!"

Boxer came forward, nervously standing in front of Volante' and Enobleus.

Enobleus voice rang out into the air.

"Boxer, as we stand in front of your family, friends, neighbors and Volante', the Tree of Perception, I now appoint you as temporary Overseer of Rensamor Island for the period of one year. During that time Volante' and I will here if you need us."

Boxer stood proudly, listening to every word that was being spoken.

"Boxer, I now endorse and release you to fulfill your position and commitment!"

Another deafening roar of approval went out from the crowd! Volante' shook her whole tree, allowing some of her colorful leaves to fall upon Boxer and Enobleus. Then she shouted loudly into the atmosphere. "It has been proclaimed this day!"

Music started playing. Everyone stood and hugged each other. Conversations of joy and hope were being spoken and shared throughout the crowd. Many went over to personally congratulate Boxer. In the meantime, the offspring of all the creatures and trees grabbed some goodies as they raced out into the big field to play. Several trees began dancing a victory dance, as others went over to thank Sniffer and Whiskers for finding Boxer and bringing him to the community. It was a grand celebration that lasted into the night.

When it was over, every creature, every tree and every seedling pitched in to clean up.

After several hours the entire place was left spotless and very quiet.

Enobleus stood next to Volante'.

The night was still.

"Did you capture the proclamations?" he whispered.

"Yes I did. I absorbed them into some of my leaves."

Enobleus paused, letting out a long sigh. "What if he doesn't seek you out when he gets discouraged and wants to quit?"

Volante' spoke quietly. "I will instruct a letter leaf to search him out and give him the words he will need."

Enobleus was very tall, but he still had to reach up to hold one of Volante's lower branches. As their hands connected he spoke somberly.

"There are so many other mysteries and secrets that I wanted to impart to him. But my life-span is soon ending."

"I know," she replied. "But Time spoke to me last night and said to tell you not to worry. You will be given the moments you need to share the most crucial mysteries and secrets with Boxer."

Enobleus released her branch hand as he excitedly stood back to look up at her.

"I'll make every second count!"

Immediately several of Volante's leaves softly fell upon him, expressing her approval agreement.

"And I will be here when you need me."

⸺ ⸻

## Webber & The Underground Renegades

She was dreaming again. Her mother was smiling at her saying;

*You have a wonderful creative mind. Don't be afraid to use it, no matter what anyone tells you.* Webber woke up suddenly. Looking around the dimly lit room, with her heart beating wildly, she sat up and leaned against the tall silver backboard railing. She looked to her left at the large painting on the wall. "Fake!" she said. "All fake!" The locked door was to the far right of her bed. Even in the dim light she noticed how sterile the white walls looked. She stretched out her legs, touching the bed rail beneath her branch toes. Still staring at the rail she thought, *I feel like I'm in a prison.* Feeling disoriented and unsettled, she closed her eyes. Fear was jumping all over her as she thought about the possibility of them operating on her mind. "It's only a week away! What if they remove my good memories too? Is there no way out?" she said out loud.

*Tap. Tap. Tap. Tap.* Webber opened her eyes, but saw nothing. *Tap. Tap. Tap.* The sound came again. She jumped out of bed, kneeling down to look under it. It was dim in the room but the slit of light coming through the bottom of the door caused her to see a small object rolling toward her from under the bed. She fell back and went to the other side of the room where the chair was and stood behind it. The brown object continued to roll toward her so she ran back to the bed and jumped on top, pulling her feet back up onto the bed. As she looked back at the chair she saw the little brown object bump into the chair leg and stop rolling. As she stared at it, to her amazement - out popped two legs! Right after that, out popped two arms! Then, something that looked like a helmet popped up on the top and two little round eyes blinked up at her.

Her bed began to rattle as she shook uncontrollably. She felt like she was in a nightmare! The little object stood only about three inches tall and began to speak to her!

**"Come Out Now!"** - came a small yet commanding voice!

Thinking he meant her, she mindlessly began to obey and started to get out of bed. But just then several other brown objects came rolling out from under the bed! Little arms and legs began popping out of all of them! Right after that, one by one little helmet hats began to pop out exposing their eyes barely peeking through.

"Why they look like acorns!" Webber said out loud.

"Yes we are!" shouted the one with a commanding voice. "But we're not like any acorns you've ever seen!!" he said defiantly.

"March Comrades!" he shouted loudly. After scuffling around, one by one they got into formation. There they were, a long row of over one hundred acorns, dressed for battle. They stood facing the picture on the wall. In a uniformed manner they marched to the right and then to the left and began to climb up to the top of the rail where Webber's feet were earlier.

She pulled her feet far away from the rail. Wrapping her arms around her knees she pulled them close. Trembling, with her chin on her knees, her eyes grew large as she watched all of them, now lined up on the railing - staring at her. The commander stood in the middle of the row. She especially noticed him. Not only because of his commanding presence, but also because he was about an inch taller than the rest and because his helmet was green. All of the other acorns had beige helmet heads.

"We're here to help you," he said calmly. "We're your friends."

Webber kept blinking and rubbing her eyes to make sure she wasn't still dreaming or in one of her creative trances.

"No, you're not imagining us, we are real!"

He then jumped off the top rail unto one of her feet and started hopping up her legs until he reached the top of her knees. Now they were face to face, with direct eye contact. For some reason she wasn't afraid anymore. He's so confident and unafraid!

## Commander Detoro

He took off his helmet and bowed down before her.

"I am Commander Acrono Detoro – at your service. You may

simply call me Commander if you like."

Still in shock, Webber just stared at him.

"I know you're in shock. That's to be expected. After all, I realize that I'm not your average looking acorn. Now just listen for a moment and I will fill you in on what's going on here in Krontia. You see, I am in charge of the underground world below you. We have been listening and watching your interactions ever since you arrived here. There is a hidden world of renegade nuts, trees, flowers and other honorable creatures beneath every building in this land. Several of us went underground when Dr. Tearrent and her forces killed the Overseer Tree and took over this land. Actually, Krontia used to be called Fruleea Land."

Shaking her leafy head, Webber came out of shock and finally spoke up.

"Do you know who I am?"

He smiled. "Yes Webber, we've been listening to your conversations and to your dreams for a long time."

"My dreams?" she said.

"Yes," he answered. "You revealed much to us when you spoke your dreams out into the air."

Exasperated and confused she said, "I don't understand any of this!"

He put his helmet back on and became very serious. "We only have a little time before they unlock your door. Until then, I'm going to give you as much information as I can. Are you ready to listen?"

Webber looked at him with her round green eyes wide open.

"Yes I am." She said with a new strength in her voice.

Commander Detoro walked back and forth on her knees as he continued. "We're able to hear you because of our underground antennae devices. We have carved out tunnels and rooms below each building and throughout the grounds. We've drilled little holes all over Krontia that lead to our troops and the others. When newcomers stumble into this land, or when some of the trees are searching for their Destiny Land, we try to reach them before Dr. Tearrent does."

He paused then as he reflected on the losses, "We've missed several of them," he said sadly. "But then again, we've saved many of them from the stripping of bark and experimental operations. You probably have already noticed that Dr. Tearrent wants land that's sterile and according to her standards, free of germs and diseases. She wants total control of every living creature or tree – including you Webber!"

A shiver went up Webber's back and into her neck.

"And the Garden?" she asked.

"We saw you go there - no one else did so you are safe in that area. It's too gruesome to tell you how she designed that garden with creatures and trees who were once alive. You have enough to think about right now with your pending operation. We have a plan to help you, but you must listen and do everything I tell you to do. She is planning on removing all of your memories, good and bad. That's how she will get more control over you. You will eventually become more dependent on her and the only memories you will have are the ones she puts in there."

"What do you mean . . . puts in there?" Webber asked.

He looked at her sadly as he continued, "You didn't know this, but every time you did an operation on a tree, she went back in later that day and implanted words and ideas into that tree's mind. She never let you know because she has been planning to remove your memories since you arrived. She knew you couldn't forget what your mother had said to you. She knew you had a level of integrity that would be hard to break down. So she had to keep many things secret from you." He looked at Webber's serious expression and knew that she believed him. "She has other plans for you Webber. We must intervene in your case. It's your only hope. It's our only hope. Will you trust us? Actually, will you first trust me?"

Webber looked at him. Tears welled up in her eyes as she realized there was a time when she thought this 'memory removal' was a good thing.

"Commander, I'm remembering what my mother Cedra once said," '*There are other ways to heal your pain.*' I imagine she wanted me to learn about that one day, but not like this - not Dr. Tearrent's way!" She reached out her large branch hand turning it face up toward the Commander saying, "I do trust you and I will listen to all you tell me. I'm so afraid and I don't know how I'll get out of that operation, but I believe in my heart that you will help me find a way."

Commander Detoro reached out his small but powerful hand and slapped hers in agreement.

"I already have a plan. We have insiders working for us. They are hidden in various buildings." He abruptly turned around on her knee and called out to his troops.

"March forward troops, back to our quarters!"

He waited as they filed down the rail, one by one, onto the floor and under the bed. Then he too started climbing down Webber's legs and onto the floor calling back to her. "I'll be keeping in close contact with you. When Klon gives you a tour of the place, pay attention to the signs. Don't let your guard down at all!"

Just as he was about to slip under the bed toward the small secret tunnel hole underneath - he looked up. Webber was leaning over the side of the bed, looking at him. Once again they had eye-to-eye contact.

"And Webber . . . if this all goes planned, you will soon be heading back to Cordaya Valley – but not in the way that you might have expected."

—❧—

# Plasick . . . A Moment in Time

It was burning hot outside. Plasick was exhausted. The plastic on her body was causing her to feel the heat even more. Passers by gawked at her now and then, turning away quickly, pretending they didn't see her. For the most part she was used to it and usually didn't even notice. She and Thorn had only been in CreatureVille for one day. When they first entered the village they stumbled upon an outdoor meeting and had stayed to watch what was going on. While there, Thorn spoke to a couple of drifters who told him that Sand City had more opportunities for his line of work and was only about 3 days away on foot. They even gave him a contact person to look up - a Monkey Puzzle Tree named Numby.

Once Thorn heard about Sand City, he made the decision not to reside in CreatureVille as the Medic had suggested. Thorn had become more and more impatient over the last week. He continuously yelled at Plasick to hurry up - telling her that they would travel to the outskirts of town, spend one night there and then move onto Sand City.

*What am I going to do about her?* He thought as he looked back at Plasick limping along. It made him angry to look at her so he kept going at a faster pace.

"Come on! Come on!" he shouted. Turning away he began to walk even faster shouting out to her. "We're almost at the edge of town and then we'll stop to rest."

Plasick struggled to keep up with him, not understanding why he had become so mean to her. *Why is he so angry? He should be happy with me! After all, I'm the one who introduced him to the Medic and helped him to escape.* Still pondering while she walked, she had another thought. *Maybe he'll change when we get to Sand City. He* seemed very excited about that. Plasick was trying not to think that - he just used her to escape Barren Land. It was easier for her to block that thought and believe that he really loved her and that eventually - everything would work itself out.

It was nightfall by the time they reached the edge of Creature Ville. They found an empty lot and set up to stay there for the night. Thorn looked at Plasick with that charming look he gave her when he wanted something.

"Plasick, once we're in Sand City, we'll probably need to trade in that cane of yours for a place to live."

Plasick looked sadly at the ornate cane, remembering the Medic and wondering if he was safe. She looked at Thorn with sadness, yet realized that he was right.

"O.K." she said quietly, rubbing her sore leg. Too tired to argue, she lay down and began thinking about the events of the day. *I actually started feeling like I was one of the crowd at that meeting earlier and for a while no one seemed to notice my leg. They were all staring at the Creature Preacher. It was fun being able to shout out with the rest of them and get caught up in the moment.* She drifted back into the memory:

> *They entered CreatureVille in the early afternoon. When they walked into the outskirts of town there was a large crowd of trees and creatures. She asked Thorn if they could go over and see what was going on. For some reason he had agreed. Plasick read the sign on the platform that said, CREATURE PREACHER. When she looked at the crowd they seemed so happy. Some of them were shouting out, "Creature Preacher! Tell us more!" She had gotten excited and yelled out, "Yeh, that's right." Then without thinking she started to join their shouts. "That's right Creature Preacher! Tell it like it is!"*
>
> *She kept yelling and then suddenly felt someone shove her to the ground. When she looked up she saw Thorn's angry face. She tried to get up, but the stiff plastic on her leg wouldn't bend. "Help me Thorn," she whispered, feeling embarrassed that he just stood there, staring at her. Soon the other creatures and trees around her actually began to make a small circle,*

*trying to move away from her! When she looked at their faces, she saw them*
*frown. As usual, some were even pretending she wasn't there.*

A noise brought her back from her thoughts. She looked over
and saw Thorn rustling around. She smiled at him, but he just turned
away, pretending he didn't see her. She didn't know it but he too was
lost in his own thoughts, thinking about all the pockets he had
picked at the meeting earlier. Plasick felt a stabbing pain in her heart
at his reaction toward her. But she quickly shrugged it off, looking up
at the stars in the moonlit sky – as her mind went back to the memory of the day. *I remember, I kept struggling to get up.*

*While laying on the ground struggling, she saw a thick branch hand*
*extended out to her. She couldn't see who it was but gratefully grabbed at*
*it. In no time at all she was lifted up to her feet. As she stood face to face*
*with the stranger who helped her, he flashed her a big grin. She was thank-*
*ful to be on her feet. His long body shielded her from the some of the other*
*creatures who were still glaring at her. Plasick thanked him as he smiled at*
*her. She barely heard him say "No Problem," when Thorn yelled out at her.*
*Embarrassed she turned away from the stranger and quickly ran over to*
*Thorn. "You fumbling idiot, you embarrassed me again! Let's go!" he said,*
*while tightly grabbing her arm.*

*They walked for several blocks. As usual Thorn was way ahead of*
*her. While she walked on the edge of the street, she heard a loud noise to her*
*left. When she turned, she saw three strange creatures pulling an odd con-*
*traption past her on the street. She looked up to see who the driver was and*
*saw that he was turning to look at her! It was the tree seedling. The stranger*
*who helped her up earlier that day. He smiled and waved.*

Not able to sleep, she sat up looking at the sky. *He was so kind*
*to me, she thought as tears welled up in her eyes. I'm not used to that.*
*I'm so glad I waved back at him, even if I took a chance with Thorn*
*being upset. He always is, so what's the difference?* As she lay back down
under the clear skies she wondered who the stranger was. *Maybe he*
*was heading toward Sand City like we are. Who knows, maybe I'll run*
*into him again.*

She closed her eyes, finally falling asleep, but all to soon she was awakened roughly by Thorn's loud yell.

"Come on Plasick, wake up! Let's get a move on!"

She woke up and was immediately grateful that they weren't in Barren Land anymore, working in the hot sun. Even though he treated her badly at times, she loved Thorn and couldn't imagine her life without him. It took her a while, but she stiffly got up and began following Thorn out of CreatureVille - as they headed toward Sand City.

---

## Greedo . . . Going Back to the Cave

Greedo woke up in a sweat just before the sun came out. It hadn't been that long since his visit with Momma and Poppa. His days and nights were becoming even more restless than usual. He had been dreaming a lot about the cave and kept wondering about the color blue that he had seen there. *Today I have to go back to that cave to see where that light is coming from,* he said to himself as he rose abruptly and prepared for the day. He went out, locking the door behind as he continued talking to himself. "No one will know where I'm at and they won't start looking for me till late afternoon. I'll be back by then."

The city was quiet as Greedo walked toward the alley that led to the cave. He quickly got to the hill and was jumping the fence when a flock of birds flew up out of a nearby bush and startled him. He ran up the first hill and down to the next one. He reached the flat top of the smaller hill just as the morning sun began to shine on the bushes in front of the cave, as if leading the way. He quickly pulled the bushes away. *I don't know why, but I'm kinda scared about this . . .*

He stooped down and entered the cave, using the light he brought with him to see more clearly. "What's this?" he said, noticing several shiny silver objects stuck in the walls. After about twelve feet in he was able to stand upright. The ceiling of the cave was at least twenty-five feet above him. He noticed a stream of filtered sunlight coming through another opening on the opposite side of the cave - around thirty feet away, directly across from where he was standing. In between where he was standing and the window type opening on the other side, was a huge hole. "There's the light!" he shouted as a blue hazy light glowed from within the hole. He walked carefully over the slimy ground to get a closer look. Then a cloud of various colors of blue began to emerge from the hole, moving in a circular motion. "What's that? This is crazy! It looks like a cloud that's growing!"

The cloud of colors broke up into thin blue and white smoky vapors that extended high up into the air. Trying to focus his eyes and get a better look, he inched forward. As he did, the circle of blue lights began to slowly move in a downward spiral. Then, he heard a soft humming noise coming from within the cloud! "It's heading straight at me!" Startled, he ran back toward the opening of the cave. He lost his footing, slipped and almost fell, as his Bug Light shook loose from his branch hand and flew away.

The sunlight from the opening of the cave helped him to see the low slope as he neared the entrance. Trying to remain calm, he stooped down and shuffled forward to get back out. Finally he reached the opening breathing heavily. He slipped and instinctively put out his arm branch toward the wall to catch himself.

Immediately he felt a sharp pinch on his hand. The silver objects in the wall had cut him. *Ah, nothing serious Greedo, get a grip,* he told himself as he finally reached the outside of the cave. Leaning over and out of breath, he started to turn around in order to cover the opening once again with the bushes.

"SMACK!" A terrible pain went through his head as a heavy crushing blow hit him on the back of his neck. Falling to his knees on the ground, he immediately felt another powerful blow on his back. Someone began to fiercely kick him over and over again. The pain was so excruciating that he was unable to defend himself or see who was beating him. He fell flat on his face in agony. Then a large rock slammed down on his right ankle. He heard a loud CRACK! Then another crashing blow struck his head. From deep inside Greedo, wrenching cries came out into the air. The hollow echoes sounded into the atmosphere, frightening the animals of the forest. He barely rolled over onto his back, briefly catching a glimpse of the fast moving clouds as he tried desperately to grasp what was happening to him. Then suddenly . . . he was quiet.

Jet walked over peering closely to see if Greedo was breathing, but he couldn't hear anything.

"Is he dead?" said Fret fearfully, while standing away from Greedo's limp body just in case Greedo was faking.

"Come on idiot!" Jet yelled out. "Come check it out for yourself. Ha! He won't boss us around anymore."

Fret came closer and let out a relieved sigh as he leaned over and looked at Greedo's still body.

"All right!!" shouted Jet, "Bring over the dark beetles and put them under his bark, right there were we broke his ankle. It's the same place where I inserted two of them several months ago when he was sleeping. By the time anyone finds him, it'll look like he fell and broke his neck and ankle. They'll think the bug disease eventually destroyed him."

Fret brought the disease carrying beetles and let them out of the box so they could access Greedo's ankle. There were six of them and they quickly hid under the bark, letting out a bitter smell as they began their work.

"Did you hide the rock? And where's the club we hit him with?"

asked Jet.

"Yeh, I already hid the rock and the club's in this bag. There's a bonfire going on at the beach tonight and I'll chop it up before then and throw it on the fire."

Jet looked around nervously. "Let's get out of here!"

They both quickly ran down the smaller hill and up the larger one toward the alley.

Jet was gasping and out of breath as he shouted out, "Wow, is Numby going to be happy about this!"

Immediately after Jet and Fret had gone, a silent but relentless movement around Greedo's lifeless body began. It was as if a moratorium was taking place. A blue butterfly pressed through the bushes in front of the small cave opening, landing on Greedo's heart, as he lay crumpled on the ground.

"Get those beetles out of his ankle!" shouted Rezanno, a large Aroma Tree. As he came running out of the thick forest from the right, outside of the cave, he bellowed again into the air. "Get those beetles out of his ankle!"

His twin brother Petanno was close behind him. Rezanno and his brother were the Scout Guard Trees who took care of and kept watch over the forest. The secret cave and the Ancient Forest were to be kept clean of diseases, pain and death at all times. Greedo didn't have a chance to see the outside of the cave on the right. If he had he would have discovered the beautiful flourishing forest. The brothers had been miles away overseeing the other side of the forest, when they heard loud screams of agony. As they came upon Greedo's limp body, they stopped and were quiet for a brief moment. Then they began their work. The Vulture Bug Bird heard Rezanno yell out and quickly came to the area. As he flew down to the scene, he saw the blue butterfly waiting for him, as Rezanno pointed to Greedo's leg.

The large bird drifted slowly near Greedo's ankle. At once, his eyes began to search for the beetles. It was important that he find and eat the bugs before they entrenched themselves into the wood of the seedling. The butterfly watched patiently as the Vulture Bug Bird finished the job.

"The first six were easy to find because of their bitter smell. Two of the beetles have been there for a while. But, I got them all," the Vulture Bird said to the butterfly. He looked at her as she moved her wings in approval. Then he began to slowly flap his huge wings and flew off. Having completed his job, he would now leave the butterfly to do hers.

Petanno and his brother picked up Greedo's body and scrunched down to carry him to the center of the cave. They took him near the same place Greedo had spotted earlier - the hole with the circle of various blue lights. The blue butterfly remained on Greedo's heart watching everything that was taking place. "All right," said Rezanno to his brother as they laid him down near the hole. "Let's go back out and seal up this cave with that boulder I saw." The brothers went out and together rolled the huge boulder over and sealed the cave. Rezanno stood back and looked at it. "No one can find this place or move that rock now." His brother nodded his head in agreement. They scanned the area, making sure everything was as it should be. After covering the boulder with a few bushes, Petanno started to run back into the forest. Running a few feet behind his brother, Rezanno briefly looked back. He saw three blue butterflies sitting on top of the boulder and smiled.

Chapters VII - XI

Aya's Journey

# Chapter VII

# Aya's Battle in the Field

## The Dragons

Treeania walked down a hill that was closer to the field, but not too close. He was looking over at the field and the Dragons as Aya approached him. She had spent some time alone all afternoon, thinking about the history of this field and how the Wicked Wasps were able to invade it. She spoke to Wyo, asking him what she should do. But in her heart, she knew he couldn't answer for her. Aya realized that this was an extremely important mission. Lives, future lands and generations were at stake. The trip here was not just about her getting across to the other land to find her family – it was much more than that. It had something to do with what her father once said when she was younger, *"You are more than just a daughter or sister –much more. But you won't really know this until you learn it through some of your experiences."* This was one of those times.

As she stood next to Treeania, looking out at the field, she noticed that there was some stirring among the desolate Snap-Dragon Flowers. It was as if they sensed something unusual was about to happen. Aya also knew that the evil Dragon Eyes were confidently biding their time, before destroying this last flower field. Treeania turned to look at Aya. "There's more I haven't told you Aya." She continued looking sadly at the field of downtrodden flowers and the four Dragons.

"Tell me the rest," she replied in a quiet voice. He looked back over at the field and began to speak.

"The Dragon Eye Siree is standing in the front left corner of the field. He's the one with dark red eyes. Right now he's moving in a semi-circle, retracting his six-inch knife-like claws."

From a distance, Aya could see Sirees' reddish colored body moving back and forth.

"He's restless, isn't he?" she said.

Treeania nodded, "Yes. Keep in mind that his eyes are able to roll around and see movements from all directions. Also, he enjoys tormenting the plants by tearing off their petals and leaves, one by one."

"Now, look over to the front right corner of the field. There's Uozoni. Right now he's looking around with his yellow, infected eyes and stomping his short legs. He's very jittery. See his grimy yellow/green body? See him flapping his short wings up and down?"

"Yes I do," answered Aya.

Treeania looked at her seriously. "He's only able to flap his wings up and down. He can't fly and he runs very slowly so he uses his massive tail that sweeps across the ground, or his long sticky tongue, to capture whatever gets in his path."

"Yeto is the oldest brother. He's the one guarding the back left corner of the field. His one black eye and one white eye are hypnotic. Looking into his eyes for too long causes victims to freeze up. Then he devours them with his huge mouth. There's one thing his eyes can't penetrate through – it's the unusual, vibrant blue color, which is on the Blue Renegade Butterfly wings. When they are near; if Yeto doesn't close his eyes right away, their penetrating blue color will burn his eyes, temporarily blinding him for several minutes."

A gentle breeze blew by just then, reminding Aya of the good that was still in this land, and how important it was to preserve it. Treeania didn't seem to notice. He was focused on giving Aya all the information he knew, so she could make a wise decision on whether to stay and help them.

"Do you notice Yeto's black shiny scales? They're slippery, like a snake and at night he blends in with the darkness. He seems to be the most evil brother of all four. Maybe it's because he was the first one to have jealousy in his heart and the first one to be poisoned by the Wasps. Yeto is the one who burned the other three Flower Fields."

"Look toward the back right corner of the field, over by that hill that leads to the Land of Visions. That's Ketonday, the youngest dragon. He's the one that I trained. Even from here you can see the one orange petal that is stuck under his chin. His eyes are orange and he is crippled on both of his front legs. He can barely move, but he's very tall and wide, with small, sticky claws. Whatever or whoever lands in those claws, will quickly get stuck.

"He doesn't seem as foreboding as his brothers," said Aya. "I mean; I know he's evil, but he doesn't seem as evil as his brothers. I'm not sure why, but from where I stand, that's the way it seems to me."

"You might be right Aya. I'm just not sure," answered Treeania.

## The Blue Renegade Butterflies

"You never did tell me who the Blue Renegade Butterflies are," said Aya.

"They came with The Master Seed Planter. They replenish flowers, bushes, trees and foliage in all lands, as needed."

Aya pondered upon this information. "Do they go everywhere?"

"No," answered Treeania. "They have to be sent. No one knows who sends them. At one time they were plentiful here. The Dragon Siree, was given instructions to kill all of them – that's why you don't see any around here right now. Sensing that the flowers were in danger of becoming extinct, a few of the Renegades hid in this area. I've heard there are three of them that the Dragon Eyes are trying to catch. Because the Renegades are in hiding –they are unable to replenish the flowers. That's one reason why the flowers look so sad and are bent over. The Blue Female Renegade Butterflies are the ones that replenish, *as needed,* the Snap-Dragon Flowers. When one lands on a flower, she breathes deeply into it. As the flower is replenished, it stands upright and begins to produce the healing pollen and nectar, at a fast pace."

"The Blue Male Renegade Butterflies are the Watchers, Depositors and Protectors. Throughout the year, they deposit the unique Birthing Pollen that they've collected, into each one of the Snap-Dragon Flowers. Then, *only once a year,* a Special Blue Female Renegade Butterfly comes through and releases a unique Birthing Breath deep into the flowers; within seven days they give birth."

"Oh," said Aya. "Is that what you call the Seven-Day Birthing Period?"

"Yes! I just know that one of the three Renegades that are hiding must be a female! It's amazing! Somehow, she was able to reach all of the flowers without the Dragon Eyes capturing her. That's why they're preparing to give birth!" He paused for a moment and said wistfully, "I hope to meet her someday."

After hearing this new information, Aya let out a deep breath. When she first entered Sumatoria, she had no idea of the hopelessness and devastation that was within the land. She had been totally caught up in her own life and didn't even notice. She looked up at Treeania as he was watching her.

"I have thought long and hard about this decision Treeania. I want you to know, that I am here to help you restore this land and this field, in any way that I can."

Wyo let out a sigh of relief. Aya turned then, surprised to see that he was behind her. Treeania reached over, grabbing her small hand branch in both of his.

"I'm so glad, I can't thank you enough!" He said while continuing to shake her hand.

"And I'm standing with Aya to help," said Wyo.

By this time Treeania was ecstatic with hope and joy. He knew that there was a wealth of Wisdom with these two. "There's so much to prepare for," he said.

"Well," said Aya, "let's go then!"

## Preparing for Battle

Treeania called the entire community to a special meeting telling them that Aya and Wyo were going to help. The whole group of animals, seedlings and trees got excited thinking that maybe, just maybe - they could actually win this battle! As they were conversing with each other, Aya called out to them, "I have an idea! What if we all call out to the Wind, perhaps he will help us."

"Yes," said Treeania, "That's an excellent idea!"

They all began to cry out to the Wind to come and speak to them. Soon there was quiet and then a huge gust of Wind blew in and said, "Why did you disturb me, I was just teaching the young Wind-Tots, how to blow a cool breeze into the desert."

They all began talking at once until Treeania held up his hand. He explained the whole situation to the Wind. Aya added the idea of the Wind stirring up the dirt in the fields and directing it toward the Dragons' eyes, so they would be distracted and unable to see clearly.

The Wind said he would be happy to help, especially after he heard that the field was at risk, and other generations would be affected. He looked at Treeania and said, "I'll have to call in my 'Target Wind Blowers' – their specialty is blowing in one particular direction. We don't want to chance blowing away any of the Snap-Dragon Flower babies, just in case some of them are born early!"

"Yes, of course you're right," replied Treeania.

The Wind continued, " On the way here I saw three Renegade butterflies, hidden inside a tree trunk. I'll go back and tell them what's going on."

Soon the Wind came back with the three Renegades, two males and one female, all flying low to the ground in between the trees, so the dragons wouldn't spot them.

Treeania was excited to meet and talk to the female Renegade.

"Are you the one responsible for recently blowing the Birthing Breath on the flowers?"

"No," she said, "That was Beshonna, she was called away on another mission. She's one of our lead Renegades." Treeania was disappointed, but silently hoped he would one day meet her.

The battle plan began to formulate as the Wind, Renegades, Treeania, Wyo and Aya, began to strategize. All of the animals, bushes, trees and animals chattered among themselves quietly, walking to the outskirts of the forest in order to give their Overseer more privacy. Aya looked down from the top of the rock that she and Wyo were sitting on, listening to everyone's ideas. "Well, we've got to do something soon – the flowers are wilting rapidly, and time's running out." They all nodded in agreement as she continued speaking, "This next idea might seem too simple, but it could work. I'll just walk into the field, and simply pretend that I'm traveling home and lost my way. I'll ask them if I can run quickly through the middle of the field, to the other side. Remember, the Dragon-Eyes aren't interested me." Treeania and Wyo looked at each other.

"You're right!" said Wyo. "They don't care about passers by, as long as they don't interfere with the Dragon's plans. You'll have to put on quite an act to fool them though."

"Yes, I know," she said. "Let's face it Wyo, I can be pretty dramatic when I want to be – right?"

He smiled and nodded in agreement.

"Wyo, once we reach the middle of the field, we'll release the three butterflies to begin breathing on the flowers – to replenish them. Just before we do that, the Wind-Tots can stir the dirt and direct it toward the Dragons' eyes."

"I like that idea!" said the Wind.

Several of the thorn bushes came running out shouting, "We want to help! We may be small, but we have long sharp thorns we can shoot at the Dragons!"

Treeania looked down at them. "Yes, that's a good idea! When I give my signal, you'll all scamper through the field and shoot at the dragons feet which are very tender."

The thorn bushes excitedly ran to a corner of the forest and began to prepare for the task ahead, happy to be included in such an honorable mission.

Aya asked, "What if Uozoni, the one that flaps up and down, sees us?"

Treeania pulled out of his trunk a small but strong leaf that held three tiny poisonous darts.

"Some of the neighborhood Berry Bushes, made these for me a while back. They put some of their deadly poisonous juice on the tips. The leaf is covering the tips so the poison won't affect you. They will slip out very easily when you're ready to throw them at the Dragon Eyes. We've kept them hidden until the right 'one' came along to do this job."

"What do you mean, the right one?" asked Aya.

"The Toucan Seer came through a few days ago and told us that a young seedling was coming this way and that she would be the one used to set the flowers free. She said to tell you that she left a Feather of Courage in one of your branches the last time you saw her. She said that you must trust it and hold it in your left hand," said Treeania. "When the Feather tickles your hand, you must let it go."

"The Toucan Seer . . . she remembered me?" said Aya as she

glanced over at Wyo and back toward Treeania. "Can I keep the Feather all through the battle? I'll need that Courage!"

"No," he answered. "She said the Feather will give you enough Courage to begin the trip, then you must let it go when it tickles you and then continue moving on through, using your own strength. She said the Feather will complete its' task and you must complete yours."

Aya turned and saw all of the trees, animals and plants approaching Treeania. He began to instruct and appoint each one of them to a task. She was amazed at their willingness to came forward and offer their help in the forthcoming battle. *I've been so selfish*, she thought to herself. *Always thinking about myself. Always thinking about what I want.* "All right!" she said. "Tomorrow the Renegades will hide in Wyo's wings and I will hide the darts in between the bark of my tree."

Everyone shouted, "Hooray! We can do it!" They stopped suddenly and looked seriously at each other, knowing that there was grave danger involved, especially if the plan didn't work out. The fire from Yeto could burn them. The claws of Siree could easily tear Wyo and Aya to shreds. If the plan failed, the flowers would remain prisoners. If for some reason Yeto didn't burn the field, the flowers, without the replenishing breath of the Blue Renegade Butterflies, would rot and die. They were all risking a lot. On the other hand, they were risking more, if they didn't fight.

Treeania sent out several Messengers to fly around the forest and let the other trees and animals know what was going on. Although they were making a lot of commotion, they were far from the field and couldn't be heard by the Dragon Eyes – who were hard of hearing to begin with.

Treeania called out. "All right everyone, let's calm down. Prepare in whatever way you need to and then get a good nights' sleep. We'll attack early in the morning, as the Misty Waters are rising from the ground. They will help keep things wet in case Yeto blasts his fire."

## The Time is Now

Soon it was morning. The Dragon Eyes were just waking up from their slumber. Siree and Uozoni, who were guarding the right and left front corners of the field, thought they saw two shadowy figures coming down the hill. It was Aya and Wyo, walking down the hill to the entrance of the Snap-Dragon Field. As they approached, the two Dragons signaled and alerted Yeto and Ketonday, who were way in the back of the field. Aya and Wyo felt the Dragon Eyes glaring at them, as they came forward.

"Why are you two here?" growled Siree.

"I only want to cross the field to the other side," said Aya.

"Who are you?" asked Uozoni, as the infection dripped out of his eyes and his mouth started watering.

Aya put on her most innocent look as she said, "This may sound strange, but I'm not sure who I am, my mother died when I was just a baby seedling and my father was swept away in a storm."

Siree and his brother began to mock her.

"So, you're an orphan, a nobody . . . ha . . . ha . . . and who is your 'little feathered friend' with the crooked beak?" asked Uozoni, swishing his long tail. Wyo was embarrassed. He didn't think anyone ever noticed that his beak was a little crooked. But he acted wisely. He kept quiet and just looked up at them, while pretending to laugh along.

"You're a nitwit – a fool!" yelled Siree. The Dragon Eyes continued to mock and make fun of them.

"Where are you headed - *mis-fits?* Did you miss the road and have a *fit?*" Uozoni began to laugh at his own joke and yelled back to Yeto and Ketonday. "Hey, we have a couple of orphans up here . . . *mis-fits!*" Aya could hear more laughter coming from the back of the Flower Field.

Aya and Wyo stood small before them and the Dragon Eyes in front started to boast.

"Too bad you don't have a strong team like we have!" said Siree, as he held up his knife-like claws, waving them in the air. "We're tough and we come from a strong line of 'tough' Dragons. No one can say we're orphans!!!! Everyone is afraid of us and that gives us great POWER!!!"

"Yes," said Aya, as she felt herself beginning to tremble. These Dragons *were* overpowering. She continued speaking, trying to keep her voice calm.

"I can see that you're very strong and powerful. But all we want to do is just cross your field to the other side and we won't be a bother anymore."

"Ha! What a baby you are!!!" yelled Uozoni as he looked at her with his yellow eyes. Aya and Wyo let them play their name game and just continued to pretend to be very shy and ignorant. Soon, the Dragon Eyes grew tired of making fun of them. They saw that the little seedling and her feathered friend were no threat to them.

"All right," said Siree. "Hurry up! Pass through the middle and be gone with you. And don't stop to talk to any of the flowers!"

The Dragon Eyes didn't notice a small dust storm stirring to the left. But some of the Snap-Dragon Flowers did and they began to stretch up as tall as they could - so the Dragon Eyes in the back would have a harder time seeing Aya and Wyo as they passed through.

Standing in the back, Yeto and Ketonday didn't pay much attention to them and could only see the very top of Aya's head from where they were. They assumed that Uozoni and Siree wouldn't have let them through if they thought there was any danger involved.

After they walked in a few feet, Wyo and Aya took off running. Aya held the Courage Feather tightly in her left branch hand. When they were just a few feet inside the Flower Field, the Wind-Tots began to quickly stir up the dust. Once that happened, Wyo released the three Renegade Butterflies, one at a time. Aya and Wyo were half way through the field, when the third Renegade was released. Then the dust storm grew thicker, specifically targeting the Dragons' eyes. Wyo shouted to Aya. "Keep on running –get the poison darts! Be careful!"

By then, the Dragons began to roar, feeling the agony of having dust in their eyes. The Wind Tots were making shrilling noises with their rushing winds. Even through the Dragons couldn't hear very well, the pressure of the Wind was piercing their ears with pain.

The winged dragon Uozoni began to flap his wings, moving up and down, sensing that something was up with these two. They were out of reach by now, and his tail couldn't swoop them up. Still partially hidden by the flowers and the dust, Wyo and Aya continued racing toward the back of the field. In the meantime the butterflies were swiftly breathing into the flowers – at an amazing speed! They had already covered half of the field on the front right side, only missing a few flowers that were close to the other Dragons.

"Hurry, throw the darts Aya!!!" yelled Wyo.
Aya's heart began to pump wildly as yellow-eyed Uozoni moved in slow motion as he tried to chase her. His sticky tongue was hanging out and almost caught her. She felt the Courage Feather tickle her hand. At first, because she was grasping it so tightly, she wouldn't let it go. It tickled her hand again and again until finally she released it.

Grabbing a dart she threw it at Uozoni. It barely touched the scales on his ankle and bounced off. Uozoni kept trying to come after her, but his little legs were causing him problems. Plus, the intense Wind had begun to press down heavy on his little wings, making it even more difficult for him to run . . . especially when he was feeling sharp needle-like jabs on his toes! The dust was thick dust so he couldn't see who was jabbing him. One of the little thorn bushes called out to his friends. "Hey, everybody, we got a few thorns into his feet, let's get out of here – f-a-s-t!"

By now, almost three fourths of the flowers in the field were nourished from the Renegades breath and were getting stronger. Seeing what was happening, Yeto blew short bursts of fire into the field. Several hundred flowers cried out and were instantly scorched, along with their unborn baby flowers. But his flame power was limited, because of the Healing Power that still existed in the field.

The Renegade Butterflies continued focusing on their mission - moving and replenishing flowers as they dodged the flames. Aya stopped abruptly in front of Uozoni. Just as he was swooshing his tail to capture her and lift her up in the air, she took careful aim and threw the second poisonous dart. It hit him in the center of his right eye! The poison quickly spread and partially blinded him. Still he fumbled around, trying to follow the sounds that she was making as she ran. "I'll destroy you for this!" he screamed out at her.

Siree was also in pursuit of her but was going in the wrong direction because of the heavy dust in his red eyes. He didn't realize that he was literally going in circles as he tried to chase her and Wyo. Wyo yelled out, "Five more yards Aya, five more! You can make it! You've got to get Yeto – fast!"

She looked over to her left and saw Yeto. He blew a blast of fire at her, just as she threw the last poisonous dart at him. The fire missed her, but the poisonous dart landed directly into his heart. He screamed out and instantly fell hard unto the ground and then was still.

Aya ran and Wyo flew toward the right side of the field where Ketonday was standing guard. At this point, she wasn't sure how to defend herself. She looked back and saw several fires burning the flowers. Still running, she turned back around and ran right into the tall, massive body of Ketonday! She knew who it was because of the orange petal she saw under his neck. He heard Siree and Uozoni yell out. "Keep her there, we want her alive!"

When Aya ran into Ketonday, a strange thing happened. As her branch hand touched his last flower petal, he closed his claw hands, so that his sticky fingers wouldn't accidentally capture her. She looked up at his eyes and he was looking down at her. Suddenly, his orange eyes turned to a softer color of Amber. A huge Amber tear fell down on Aya's hand. The same hand that held the Feather of Courage earlier. Sadly he looked out at the Field of Flowers, remembering that once, in another span of Time long ago, he was proud to be one of them.

He looked at the raging battle going on and saw some of the Snap-Dragon Flowers burning alive. A tightness gripped his chest as he remembered what his true purpose was – to help and to heal others. He looked down at Aya and yelled. "Go now! Escape! Save this land from the evil that tried to take it over!"

Aya touched his clenched fists before running off with Wyo, to the end of the field. All of a sudden, they heard loud thumping. Siree saw that they were escaping and was running after them! Aya turned around and saw Ketonday move to block him. But Siree was full of hatred and easily knocked him down. Uozoni finally caught up with Siree. They both were furious as they stood over him.

Siree shrieked at him. "You let them go!" He raised his knife-like claws and tore open Ketonday's chest.

Uozoni then stuck out his sticky tongue, trying to pull off the last petal on Ketonday – but it wouldn't budge.

Aya screamed. "Wyo!! Look what they're doing to Ketonday!"

The brothers heard her voice and started toward her.

Suddenly, several long thin feathers appeared! They traveled high, high into the sky and then rapidly shot back down, turning into rain. But this wasn't just regular rain. It was Burning Rain and the raindrops were extended and shaped like arrows. Strangely enough, as if the rain was designated . . . it only struck Siree and Uozoni. The brothers began bellowing loudly as the sheets of burning rain pelted them. The arrow-like rains that dropped on them had turned into sharp poisonous darts, which penetrated into their scales. Siree and Uozoni fell down to the ground unto each other and died. Immediately the rain turned back into long thin feathers and blew back up into the air.

Strangely enough, the Burning Rain didn't come near Ketonday. But he was lying on the ground, bleeding to death from his brother's attack. Aya ran back over to him and thankfully saw that the brothers' weren't able to remove his last orange petal from under his neck.

He looked up at Aya. "I'm sorry, I'm so sorry. I betrayed everyone."

Aya knelt down and looked straight into his face. "But you redeemed yourself Ketonday! You helped us take back the field! Because of you we won the battle!"

Ketonday lifted up his head and looked at her, hoping beyond hope that she was telling him the Truth.

Aya perceived his thoughts and said to him very seriously, "I'm telling you the Truth Ketonday."

He heard the Truth spoken through her voice. He believed her. He smiled then, a gentle smile and closed his Amber eyes and died.

Aya watched in amazement as his entire body began to transform itself back into the beautiful flower he once was. His coloring was even more vibrant. All of the effects on his body from the Wasps stinging him, and his brother's vicious attack, were gone. Watching this transformation unfold left a deep impact on Aya. One she would never forget.

Tears ran down her face as she wearily stood up, looking around at the Field of Snap-Dragon Flowers. Several cooling rain clouds, blown in by the Wind Tots, began to drench the fires in the field. Soon all the fires were out. Although it was smoldering in several areas, she saw that most of the field was safe; which meant many of the unborn Snap-Dragon Flowers were also safe, and would soon be born. Their generation would not be wiped out. She watched as another amazing thing happened. The Sun of Splendor came out and all of the surviving Snap-Dragon Flowers opened up their petals at the same time - to absorb his Amber Rays.

The Blue Renegade Butterflies had already replenished the flowers during the battle, so as the flowers opened up their petals, large clouds of Healing Air came out of them, vaporizing into the atmosphere. The Wind Tots began to blow on the Healing Clouds to help distribute the air among the trees. Treeania and some of the other trees began waving their branches, welcoming the Breath that was coming through. Other bushes and foliage began to do the same. It looked like a magical symphony of motion and healing. The Breath of Life came into the land that day.

The three Blue Renegade Butterflies came over to Aya and sat on her shoulder. The poison darts of the rain were gone. A gentle rain began to fall, just for a moment, as if cleansing the day. Then it slowed down, gathering together all of its raindrops to form a beautiful Feather, that looked like it was waving goodbye. The Feather then drifted off to find its place in the Toucan Seer, who had been nearby in the wilderness – watching the battle.

Because of the Breath going in and out everywhere, the Snap Dragon Flower Field was now full of activity. Things began to flourish at a rapid pace, right before Aya's eyes. The flowers became fuller, and the trees leaves turned a deep rich color green. Aya's heart was full as she stood next to Wyo at the back of the field.

"I knew this was an important battle to win, but I didn't realize how much the victory would affect everyone."

A huge Collywana Tree behind Aya touched her gently with one of his massive branches. The three Renegades left her shoulder and fluttered to a nearby bush. As she turned around he spoke.

"Aya, you didn't know this, but several of the trees in this area are Healing Trees. Without the Blue Renegade Butterflies and the Snap-Dragon Flowers breathing into and replenishing the air, some of our Healing Leaves wouldn't flourish. When you saved the field, you also helped us. Without our Healing Leaves, many throughout the land of Etainia and beyond, would die unnecessarily. Our leaves have traveled throughout Time through the direction of the Wind."

Aya listened in awe. "I didn't know," she said quietly.

Treeania walked over and stood next to the Collywana Healing Tree in agreement and said to Aya, "That's right. You not only saved a generation of Snap-Dragon Flowers, but you also saved the entire *Valley of Life Giving Flowers*, because now we can rebuild with what is left. You saved the life of millions, in more ways that you'll ever know; by having the courage to stay and help us."

Aya lowered her head with humble gratitude as she heard the Trees clapping their branches, the Butterflies flapping their wings and the Wind-Tots blowing through the clouds. Tears ran profusely down her face as Wyo flew to her shoulder. Both of them were exhausted, but very happy. Soon, the whole community had come to the back of the field to thank them saying, "We're going to celebrate; will you stay?"

Aya shook her head. "As much as I would like to stay with you all, Time is beckoning me to move on. Wyo and I couldn't have done what we did without all of your help. It took all of us to win it – even Ketonday . . . "

They all stood quiet for a moment, having already heard how he helped save the field.

"We will make sure he is buried with honor Aya," said Treeania.

Aya nodded. "Thank you all so much! My life will be forever changed because of this battle and having met you."

The large tree stepped up and handed her five leaves. "Aya, this is a gift of five 'leaves of healing'. Depending on what problems you and Wyo face, the leaves may be crushed into a broth or directly

applied to a wound. But use them wisely, for they cannot be reused."
Aya thanked him; putting the leaves carefully into the pouch that
Willow had given her when she and Wyo left Denotoria Forest. *That
seems so long ago.*

She waved to the Snap-Dragon Flowers and the others that
fought with her through the battle. They all waved back to her in
unison. As she looked out at the whole community and saw their
happy faces, she realized what she would have missed; had she continued on in her selfishness.

She and Wyo turned away then and began to walk up and over
the hill into The Land of Visions. What started out as a simple journey across the Snap-Dragon Field, *just to get to where she was going,*
became a life-changing event. One that would forever be etched into
her heart.

# Chapter VIII

# Aya . . . The Battle Within

## The Hidden Place

For a long time, after the battle in the Snap Dragon Flower Field, Aya felt elated. She realized that not only had she had helped to save the flowers in the field, but also, the next generation of flowers, along with several of the Healing Trees. For several weeks, as she remembered of all the amazing things that had happened there, it was easy for her to rise up each day and face the challenges of trying to find her way home.

But today, while still traveling within the Land of Visions, she began to feel discouraged. Aya had experienced numerous difficult circumstances on this journey. Although, she tried to learn from them, she was still a young tree. And today she felt more like a discouraged child.

"Wyo, it feels like we're still so far away from Cordaya Valley," she said in frustration. Today was a dreary day. The weather had been rainy and wet for several days. The dirt roads they were on became muddy. She constantly had to stop and shake the mud off of her branch feet.

Wyo watched her as she walked in front of him. He sensed that depression was beginning to settle upon her. It concerned him. He knew that even after winning a battle, leaders often felt discouraged. She stopped walking to turn and look at him. As she stood there, with her weather-beaten branches, torn leaves and deeply scarred trunk, he felt compassion. She had been through tremendous physical storms on this journey and had been victorious. But he knew that the storm she wrestled with now – was not on the outside, but within herself.

She turned back around and looked at the dirt road with all of the holes in it. A stormy battle was wrestling with her mind. Talking to herself she said, "You stupid fool – all of this traveling for nothing – all those seeds of optimism and goodness were for nothing – you're no better off than you were a year ago!" She tried to fight back the tears, but it didn't work. *Here we are, in the beautiful Land of Visions, walking down a torn up street!* As they reached the end of the road they saw a sign that read, "Small Town - Population 58". They turned the corner and there were three houses all sitting in a row on the right side. Except for a little flower garden in front of one houses, they all looked worn and rundown – similar to how Aya was feeling. *I'm so tired. I'm so very tired.*

As they approached the house in the middle, a buzzard flew out, quickly flying into the sky and disappearing. Wyo opened the creaking gate. By now, Aya was almost as tall as the entrance to the door, which was a little less than five feet. Once they stepped into the house, little creatures scurried away, aiming for the dark corners. The house looked the way that Aya felt.

They were only there for a few moments when there was a knock at the door. Aya opened the door and there was a tall, bent over Anteater lady standing there looking back at her. In a slow, wheezy voice she said, "H-ell-o . . . my name is Aloweeza. The house you're in is for rent if you would like to stay here. Mrs. Moleebeea lives in the house to your right. She's the one with the pretty garden." Wyo and Aya stared at her without speaking as she continued. "If you decide to stay, you're responsible to keep it clean and it will cost you three buckets of ants to be given to me. I'm on a diet." She yawned, "You can stay as long as you like. I need to know your answer right now, because after today – I don't want to be disturbed for the next three months."

*What a strange creature!* Yet, Aya thought about it for a moment and looked at Wyo, who obviously did not like the idea. But Aya was exhausted and didn't want to travel anywhere right now.

"O.K. But where should we put the ants, and how often, since you don't want to be disturbed?"

"I'm next door, to your left, near the empty field. Once a week, place a bucket of ants on the side of my house. There'll always be an empty bucket for you to pick up. When you decide not to live here anymore, just slide a note under my front door." She slowly turned around and scuffled back to the other run down house.

Aya looked at Wyo's face. "I know you're not happy about this, but I just don't feel I can go on right now. My heart feels very sad and I don't know what to do about it – my sadness is taking all of my energy. I'm sorry." Even while saying this, she looked at the filth all around her, wondering why she would even consider staying at such a dirty place.

"Aya, I don't think it's a good idea and I don't want to be here," said Wyo with a frown on his face. "But it's your decision. I respect our friendship enough to give you my support. Let's clean it up and take one day at a time."

Aya looked relieved and almost started crying again. Instead, she turned away and began to move things around, coughing, as the dust began to scatter in the air. Wyo knew to be silent. *She's in a dark place. Pushing her to leave wouldn't be the right thing to do – at least not now.*

## The Darkness of the Night

One day at a time, turned into over three months. It was a cool day as Aya looked out the only window in the old house. She held kept wiping an imaginary smudge on the window. Her thoughts drifted in and out of her mind. She remembered one night in the beginning of her journey, when she and Wyo were lying out under the stars. That night, while looking up at the sky she thought she heard music so she impulsively jumped up and started to dance.

Now, standing in the old house, it seemed as if she had sludge feet. Her roots didn't want to move; yet deep within her, she knew Time was pressing on her to leave this place. She had prepared to leave as much as her energy would allow. *I should have done more. So many things are still broken in this house – so many things are still broken in my heart.*

Aya continued rubbing the 'unsmudged' window. *I remember when I first moved here. Mrs. Moleebeea had a beautiful garden in her front yard and she used to take flowers to her neighbors. I haven't seen her since we moved in. She's like a bed lady now, never leaving her bed.* Aya also realized that Aloweeza was a recluse; they had only seen her one time, when she came out to get a bucket of ants.

*Small Town* was about three miles down the road. It was a lonely, desolate town. Most of the animals and seedlings sought the security of their homes and hardly ever came out. She realized how easily it would be to become like one of them; she was almost there. Having spent over three months in this place, it was very familiar to her, and she became comfortable, even in the lack of things. Aya quickly pulled back from the window, realizing just how close she was to becoming like those around her.

"I've got a journey to take and a Destiny to find – and there must be music playing somewhere. I haven't heard it in awhile," she said out loud. As she turned away from the window, a tear rolled down her cheek. She knew from her upbringing that without change, she wouldn't grow and if she stopped growing, she would die. "Time doesn't stand still, even if you do," Wyo would often say just before he dozed off to sleep. Other times he would look at her from across the room and remind her, "You're a trailblazer Aya. Don't forget, Destiny is often found by following the unmarked trails."

Aya let out a heavy sigh as she pushed open the front door and stood on the porch. The smell of pine was in the air. The setting sun was reflecting a soft orange glow everywhere. Wyo's words lingered on her mind, as the whistling of the evening wind mingled with the cool breath of winter in the air. She stood on the porch for a few moments longer, noticing that the smell of pine had grown stronger. She breathed in the aroma thinking, I'm walking through a memory and I don't know where it's from. While trying to remember what the memory was, she noticed the sun had disappeared below the horizon. *That's me all right, just like that sun. I feel like I'm going down, down and down again, because I'm feeling afraid. I'm afraid to get back out into the journey again.*

Aya opened the front gate and began to walk. She kept sighing deeply as she walked and walked - still feeling sad and lonely. Her head was bowed down facing the ground, and her step became slower and slower. She stopped for a moment and looked up. Suddenly she realized that she had walked into a strange and mysterious forest and it frightened her!

As the naked trees around her began walking, nervously her body did quake.
To her left was an Elm, to her right a strong Oak.
Up ahead was a tall Cedar saying, "Come now, don't poke."

Her step quickened and she hastened to see what was ahead.
Excitement rushed though her to find out what she would get.
Behind her were many bushes, of all kinds - what kind she didn't know.
She felt some twig branches on her legs; spurring her on to go, go, go.

Then all of a sudden before her, she saw an open field and stream.
She pinched her left arm, making sure it wasn't a dream.
For there stood in front of her, a lush Maple Tree.
With leaves of many colors, not just one, but over twenty-three.

There was orange and yellow and a really bright green.
Those were just a few of the colors, she was immediately seeing.
Was that a blue and a red and a purple there too?
How could a Tree have so many colors? She wasn't sure what to do.

All of the trees in that forest, in the woods she had just walked –
were all standing around her –and then yes, they all gawked.
For the Tree with many colors, kept changing them through and through.
It was the most beautiful sight Aya had ever seen,
and the Tree was looking at her too.

"Do you see all the different colors?" said the Tree loudly.
"Do you see them change?"
She blurted it right out, "Yes I do and they're all being rearranged."
"Do you know why I am here for you to experience this moment and see?"
"No," replied Aya. "No I really don't - are you doing it just for me?"

"No!" bellowed the Tree. "Look around you right now."
As she looked all around - she saw the other trees and bushes begin to bow.
"You see, I am the Great Tree and I will never grow old.
I have many different colors and several of them are bold.

Even now in this moment, you see, I am still growing very high. My
limbs and my branches are reaching up into the sky. I am teaching the
other trees to grow beyond their own space.
And you I am teaching- to reach out to others and give them grace.

For as you entered the forest and the path you did take –
You were thinking only of yourself and of all your bad breaks.
As you walked and you walked, there were others stumbling all around.
But you didn't notice them and your face wore a deep frown.

Now remove your burdens and lay them down before me.
And pick off a colorful leaf, off my branch, yes, off this Tree.
As you take that bright leaf with you, it never will die.
It will teach you to let go of some things, and learn how to say goodbye.

Say goodbye to your selfishness, say goodbye to your old ways.
Walk into your future now and find those brighter days.
A future that's new, a future that's right.
A future that will bring you out, of the darkness of your night.

While nighttime can often be soothing to some, indeed for you it is not.
You often feel dead, even sick- like the inside of a tree when it begins to rot."
Aya looked at the Great Tree, listening to every word.
She then began to bow down, so he would know that she had heard.

While down on the ground, a whisper of a breeze went by –
Was that a branch waving over me? She wasn't sure, because she began to cry.
She cried about things she hadn't done in her life. She wept deeply,
missing her mother.
She cried about things she couldn't change, and then she began to feel
smothered.

She cried for the missed opportunities on her journey, the ones that she
had passed up.
She cried for broken dreams, she sobbed and sobbed . . . and couldn't
get back up.
When she could cry no more, she felt her head being lifted up,
It was one of the Great Tree's Branches - and in the other he held out a cup.

Suddenly there was music in the air- joining the Great Tree as he
sang to her . . .

> *"Come now, you have cried enough, take a drink of my Tree,*
> *and when you walk back out of this forest, you will begin to feel free."*

Aya fell to her knees, looking up at the Great Tree standing before her eyes.
She knew this was something she needed; her heart had wanted a good cry.
But it wasn't just the tears that made her feel better . . .
It was the way that he spoke . . . and on the leaf – he had written a letter.

*"You feel deeply -what just happened and you'll see things more clearly now.*
*When a new situation comes up, you'll handle it, because you'll know how.*
*Long ago Xeraino singed your branch during your other- Vision of the Night.*
*You were told to collect Wisdom on your journey, so you'll know what is right.*

*For weeks and weeks, you've lived in sadness, thinking only of yourself.*
*You put the experience and victory of saving the flowers - up on a dusty shelf.*
*Focus now on what you've accomplished- not on the mistakes that were made.*
*Move forward into your Destiny; let unnecessary thoughts in your mind-now fade.*

*You've been allowed to step into this Vision, to experience what you just have.*
*Don't ignore these words or take them for granted — instead, use them like salve.*
*Only one other tree in the land of Etainia has living leaves, such as mine.*
*Another will seek her out during his dark season, in his season of Time.*

*So now Aya, take heed, keep this Letter on the Leaf, always with you.*
*As a reminder of the sadness you were once in and what I told you to do.*
*When you go back and lay down to sleep, you'll no longer feel fright.*
*Because during these moments, you've been reminded of your future-*

*You've been brought out of the darkness of your night."*

## The Letter on the Leaf

As she finished reading the words that were written on the *Letter on the Leaf,* her heart began to feel uplifted. She sensed things would be different now. Having been newly refreshed, she knew she would rise once again with Courage and Fortitude. Her eyes were full of happy tears as she stood and looked up. But the Great Tree was gone and there was nothing unusual around her anymore. It simply looked like a regular forest in the early season of winter.

A soft snow began to fall. She dropped her head back and allowed the snowflakes to fall upon her face, feeling their cleansing touch. She turned to start walking back toward the old house. But this time her head was no longer bowed down. Now she stood tall and straight - ready to face new challenges. The *Letter on the Leaf* was still clutched in her hand, proving that she had just walked out of a Vision in the Unseen World. - a world that, because of her desperate, lonely state, she was allowed to see and experience. In that realization, she felt comforted.

Deep within her mind she heard the words, *don't give up hope – you're almost there.* She stopped for a moment, noticing that the snow stopped falling and there was a smell of honeysuckle all around her. *Where did that scent come from? It's the middle of winter!* Then, she heard the sound of water trickling over pebbles to her right. She turned, catching a glimpse of a small creek that had a row of orange and yellow Honeysuckle flowers near it.

As she walked toward the creek, a yellow butterfly with red and orange markings, landed on her right foot. She didn't want to move for fear of disturbing it. Aya quietly watched the tiny fragile wings slowly moving back and forth. *What a beautiful sight. What a quietly confident butterfly.* As she watched the beautiful creature in it's small but significant stature, another thought went through her mind. *Well, here's a fellow who waited a long time in that ugly cocoon before it accomplished birth.*

"Oh" said the butterfly. "I wasn't THAT ugly!! In some circles I might have been considered quite handsome - *just in the state of transition!!*"

Aya stumbled back in amazement as this butterfly spoke -or rather- reprimanded her.

"Goodness!!!" Did I speak that out loud?"

"No," he said. "Since I'm so close to you, my antennas read your thought signals."

"My," said Aya, quite stunned. "That's an amazing gift you have."

The butterfly flew up near her face, looked her in the eyes and said, "Well, I do have some great gifts and I'd like to say this is one of them, but I cannot lie. Actually, the Great Tree allowed me hear your thoughts, so I could speak to you now."

Aya's mouth dropped open and her blue eyes widened. "You know the Great Tree?"

The butterfly landed on her nose for a moment, and then, seeing that it caused her to look cross-eyed at him, flew off to settle on a nearby bush. "Yes of course I do. You need to know that the creek and those flowers are another part of the Unseen World. It has been revealed to you for a purpose, but only for a few moments so LIS-TEN UP!"

Aya knew by this time to be quiet and listen while in this strange but magical place -especially after the experience she just had. The butterfly continued speaking. "If I had come out of my cocoon too soon, I might not have survived or turned out as strong and beautiful as I am now. On the other hand, if I chose to stay in the cocoon too long, and if I didn't push myself out, I would have died. Do you understand the meaning of this for you?"

"Yes, yes," she said. "I guess that's me too. If I allow myself to press in and learn during the dark seasons of my journey, no matter how dark it gets, I will eventually find the strength to break out and move into the next place of my Destiny. But if I stay in the darkness too long - I will die."

At that point she looked over at the butterfly to see if she was right. But he had already taken flight and was in the air above her. She watched as he began to fly away. Then, very faintly she heard his voice in the wind. "That's right, you got it - now go."

Suddenly, he flew back and began fluttering in front of her face. "Don't forget the scent of the Honeysuckle flowers, it's a good thing. Somewhere in your future you'll need them -their scent will guide you." And then he was gone.

She looked back toward the creek and flowers, but they had also disappeared. Or perhaps they were hidden in the unseen land of Space and Time. Aya turned and began to walk back toward the house. Another light, gentle snow began to fall softly upon her. Each snowflake that landed upon her absorbed some of her sadness; and then vaporized back into the atmosphere. As this happened, her mind began to clear and she realized how many wonderful and insightful things she had learned on this journey.

*I've met some amazing characters and seedlings. I've made many loyal friends along the way,* she thought. *And Wyo, my closest friend, has stayed with me all of these months - waiting and waiting until I woke up from focusing on myself!* She was almost at the gate to the old house. She stopped in front of the creaking gate and looked at all three houses - as if seeing them for the first time. *How dingy and dark they look! Wyo has stayed with me in this dark and ugly place! He's listened to me cry and complain and whine. He's watched me escape through sleeping, all the while looking after me.*

Sadness came over her then, as she realized how much she had neglected her friend Wyo. She walked through the gate, looking at the house on the left and the house on the right. *I've been totally absorbed within myself and haven't even reached out to help my neighbors.* Even though she felt free and cleansed of her own despair, she also felt terrible for the lack of kindness she had shown to her friend and neighbors. "I'll make up for it," she said as she ran to the front door and flew it open. "Wyo!" she yelled out. He ran to the front door. "Aya, what is it? What's wrong?"

"Wyo, I've had a most incredible experience in the forest!!" Relieved that nothing was wrong, Wyo closed the front door. He listened as she shared about her walk into the forest and the Unseen World. She told him about her life-changing experience with the Great Tree. Wyo listened closely as she spoke about her walk out of the forest and her conversation with the butterfly. "I have neglected you Wyo. I have rejected and ignored you while focusing on myself." She began to weep deeply. "I am so sorry. Can you forgive me?"

Wyo stood up and perched on the tall chair next to her. She looked at him with tears streaming down her bark. He placed one of his wings under her chin. "Yes, Aya, I can forgive you - with all my heart." Aya hugged him tightly. At that point Aya let it all come out as she cried, not out of sadness, but out of gratefulness, for having such a loyal, steadfast friend. Wyo spoke then, "Aya, let's put this behind us now, you never have to bring it up again, and neither will I."

Aya wiped the tears from her eyes, and hugged him once again.

Amber colors of the evening sun shown through the window, casting a warm glow over them, as once again they prepared to rest up for the journey tomorrow. Aya laid her head down – soon falling into a rare and peaceful sleep, while remembering the words . . .

*"When you go back and lay down to sleep, you'll no longer feel fright.*
*Because during these moments, you've been reminded of your future-*

**You've been brought out of the darkness of your night."**

Chapter IX

# *Aya Climbs Another Hill*

## *Reflections*

Before dawn even broke the next day, Aya woke up with renewed energy, and Wyo felt it!

"Wyo, one day I'm coming back here to help build up this community!" she said.

Wyo smiled in agreement, relieved that the depression had finally lifted off of her.

She ran over and hugged him. "I'm ready to move on today! Let's clean up here and leave a bucket of ants for Aloweeza and a note that we'll return one day to help Small Town."

Wyo hugged her back. "I agree, let's get to work!"

They both began to straighten up the house. Once finished, they went out the door, taking the last bucket of ants to Aloweeza, leaving a note under her door. Skipping and whistling, Aya began to jog toward the direction Wyo had suggested. Wyo bounced up and down on her shoulder as she ran, and finally flew into the air ahead of her. Both were excited to be continuing their journey to find her family and Cordaya Valley.

They had gone several miles before resting near a small stream, which had several large boulders on the bank. As they sat down Aya began talking.

"Wyo, the experience I had with the Great Tree was amazing. I'll never be the same. I've been so selfish and pitiful. Even after the victory of the Snap Dragon Flower Field, for some reason, I had lost hope of ever finding Cordaya Valley and my family."

Wyo looked over at her. "Sometimes that happens after a great victory Aya. Don't be too hard on yourself. Many leaders have gone through that experience."

"I've never considered myself a leader. But I have to admit, when they wanted my help at the field - although I argued with myself, it seemed natural to take charge."

Aya thought about what she just said. Wyo perceived that she was entering into another expansion of her mind and that her perspective was broadening. *She will be called upon many more times to lead*, he thought.

"I'll keep in mind what you've said Wyo. I've learned to listen." He smiled at her, "Yes Aya, you have learned that."

Aya began to walk toward another forest area that had several trees in it. Once inside the forest Aya shouted out, "Look Wyo, there's a small path, let's follow it!" As they went up the path Aya saw a small bridge that looked very familiar, but wasn't sure why. She continued walking toward it. "Let's cross this bridge Wyo, I have a good feeling about this." Anticipation was causing her heart to pound although she wasn't sure why. As they approached the bridge Aya sensed that somewhere in her past, she had been there before. *Did I dream about this?* She thought to herself. What Aya didn't realize was that they had entered the South side of Cordaya Valley and that she was actually walking on the land where she was born.

As they started to cross the bridge, Aya stopped midway. Leaning over the rail, she looked down at the running water beneath her and began to reflect her thoughts out loud.

"After the Great Storm, I was so afraid! That fear never left me until I fell into the ditch. It was in the ditch that my fears began to disappear. I had no choice but to face them. Once I did, I saw that I could get through to the other side of the fear."

Wyo quietly listened; amazed at the wisdom that was growing

inside her and pleased at the understanding she was experiencing. She turned around and continued walking across the bridge. Very soon after that, she saw a hill up ahead.

"Wyo, let's go up that big hill, I think there might be something on top that will give us a clue as to where we are." she said while running toward it. Wyo flew after her and came to her side. The hill had a long slope so it took them a while but they finally reached the top. Once they were on top, Aya looked around. She saw a huge tree trunk several feet away from her. The roots of the tree were partially buried in the ground and then extended about fifteen feet above ground.

"Look Wyo!" Aya said as she raced over to stand under the tree roots as they towered over her. The section of land that she stood on under the roots, measured about five feet by five feet. "I'm a tree standing under a tree!" She laughed at her own words, feeling happier than she had in a long time. She stood under the tree looking all around. "Wyo! I feel like I'm in a house that has roots as walls and open windows in between each root!" she said while whirling around.

Wyo sat on a nearby rock, watching her – enjoying the happiness that she was experiencing. It was a cool day. There was a fresh scent of cedar in the air. Aya closed her eyes and started to have another memory, but it flashed by quickly - too short to remember. She looked around inside the massive tree roots, noticing that in one of the corners there was some kind of box partially sticking out of the ground. She ran over, knelt down and began to dig it out. Soon she pulled out what looked like someone's treasure box.

"Wyo!" she shouted. "I think I've found a treasure box!"

Wyo flew in between the large tree roots and sat on a boulder that was near Aya.

"Yes Aya, I see it. Can you open it?"

Aya looked carefully at the lock and said, "I don't know, it has a strange lock on it. And look Wyo, there is an Amber Stone on it!" The stone was near the lock. The Amber light began to flicker when Aya's branch brushed by it.

### The Letter

As she leaned way over and peered at the box, her deformed branch – the one she always kept hidden, fell out, dropping close to the lock. At first she tried to hide it, vaguely noticing the similarity between the shape of the lock and the end of her branch. She tried to read the writing on the outside of the box, but it had been scratched and was weather worn. She reached out and touched the Amber Stone. It began to glow brightly, shining a stream of light on the end of her deformed branch and on the lock. She saw the similarity immediately! "They match!" she gasped. Slowly she moved her branch into the lock. Nothing happened. She tried it once again and suddenly – lock and branch connected! As they did, the Amber Stone flashed brighter than before. So much so, that it momentarily blinded her.

Gradually the stone's light subsided. Aya heard a loud clicking sound and the lock released its hold on her branch. The top of the box began to slowly open. Wyo jumped off the boulder he was sitting on and came near Aya. She hurriedly lifted up the Treasure Box and set it on the boulder where he had been sitting. The top of the Treasure Box then opened up all the way. She looked inside and she saw several rolled up scrolls. Each one had a special embossed seal on it.

"What's inside?" asked Wyo.

Aya looked closer and yelled out, "They look like scrolls of some sort. Oh, there's a letter on the bottom of the box." She hurriedly moved the scrolls and grabbed the letter. "Wyo! It has my name on it!" she exclaimed.

"Go ahead and open it!"

Standing over the treasure box, Aya took out the letter and began to read it to herself.

*Dearest Aya,*

*As I write this, it is now early evening on the day of the Naming Ceremony. You just ran over and gave me a big hug saying, "I love you Mommy." And now you're running off to join your siblings to go out and play with Wyo and Squeegie. Your father is talking things over with some of the Elder Trees, preparing for the important events of the night. Cordaya Valley is alive with energy — everyone is anticipating the moments of hearing the names of our seedlings. I am very happy tonight and feel so proud - although there is one thing that's troubling me. A few moments ago I noticed some dark clouds forming to the North of Cordaya Valley.*

*Although they are far away, I'm concerned that something dark is about to happen. I wish I didn't feel this way, but I know better than to ignore these intuitions. I believe a storm is brewing. I also believe evil messengers are involved — I'm not sure how, but I just have a deep foreboding sense that a storm might hit our valley tonight. For that reason, I am writing this letter to you — just in case. Once I finish the letter, I will place it inside the Treasure Box. Because of so much activity going on, I won't even have time to let your father know about it.*

*If you are reading this letter then you have found the Treasure Box. If you have found the Treasure Box then you have also found me and are standing within my roots. Your Father and I had an agreement early on in our union, that if anything happened to either one of us, we would hide the Treasure Box tightly within imbedded rocks under the tall roots of the one who died first. Those roots would then be positioned on a high, high land overseeing Cordaya Valley. Your father will explain many other things to you that even I don't know.*

*It's important that I tell you this Aya. I always knew you would be "A Leader to Many' — I also knew that if anything happened to my five seedlings, you would be the one to rise up with courage and take charge. I saw that courage in your eyes from the day you were born. I saw it every time you questioned your father and I about so many things. Actually, I knew that you would be a great leader, even before you were born. This kind of perception will one day be revealed to you. It's very important that you know - you are from the lineage of Great Overseer Trees — The Ancient*

*Ones. Your father and I were destined to be your parents. You are destined to lead. Ask him to tell you the history of your ancestry.*

*The reason you could open the lock on the Treasure Box is because I had a special imprint molded into the lock. The imprint is from the shape of one of my deformed branches that I've kept hidden since I was a young seedling. I've only allowed R.T to see it. Aya, your deformed branch and mine have the exact same shape. It is my responsibility to open Treasure Box tonight at the Naming Ceremony. But secretly, I know that if anything happens to me, I have the assurance that you will be able to open it.*

*You see Aya; the branch that you hid- because it was deformed- is actually the special branch that has not only opened the Treasure Box, but has also opened pathways for you and your brothers and sisters — so you can find your Destiny Lands. The Treasure Box holds each one of your naming scrolls. The Misty Visions will appear when your names are spoken out into the atmosphere by each one of you. Your father and the Toucan Seer will instruct you about this.*

*My strong little seedling - as you finish reading this letter, you will probably cry. It's important to let that happen, but don't let sadness rule you. Allow my healing oil to seep through your roots. Let it continue to rise up and reach every part of your body. Let it heal and strengthen you through and through.*

*And Aya . . . no matter what happens, don't ever stop following your path.*

*Love, Mother*

The moment Aya finished reading the letter; Cedra's roots began dripping Amber colored oil. It slowly seeped into the soil all around Aya's branch feet. As it absorbed into her trunk, her bark became a rich, deep brown color. Many of her scars were becoming almost unnoticeable. The oil continued to penetrate the soil she was standing on and gradually flowed down its predestined path into a section of land below. The Soil of the Earth opened up a wide area to encase it and soon a small pool of oil was formed. Realizing what her mother had given her through the writing of this letter, Aya wept deep and hard. Cedra was still giving life, even in death.

Though she didn't quite understand it all, Aya closed her eyes and allowed herself to cry. As she did the oil continued saturating her bark and healing her. She stood there for several moments taking it all in and then slowly bent over to place the letter back into the Treasure Box. She wiped her eyes, still crying softly, and walked out from under Cedra's roots. Wyo stayed close by watching – wisely not reaching out to her just yet. He perceived that more was about to happen.

She continued to walk a few more steps and stood looking out over the lush fields and the land of Cordaya Valley and the hill she had climbed up moments before. As she pondered over the letter, she didn't notice that her father was racing up the hill behind her. She was so deeply engrossed in her thoughts, that she didn't even feel the rumbling vibrations under the ground, as he ran and ran toward her. Some of the oil from Cedra's roots had spilled out of the pool below and flowed down the hill unto R.T.'s roots. He immediately recognized it as the *'oil of healing'* and knew it could have only been released through Cedra's roots by the presence of one of her seedlings!

As he ran, he didn't know yet which seedling was up there. Once he reached the top he ran past Cedra's roots and grabbed the seedling from behind – laughing and crying at the same time. Aya caught her breath and looked up to see who was holding her so tightly! Immediately she recognized her father! She clung to him and began to weep with joy. After several moments, he stopped to look at her as he held her up in his massive branch arms.

He then recognized which one of his seedlings he was holding as he shouted, "Aya! Aya! You found us, you've come home!" Through her uncontrollable tears she cried out, "Yes Father, I've come home, home at last!"

As they hugged again, the entire community of trees, having heard the loud voice of R.T., came tearing up the hill and gathered around them. Other bushes and animals that had survived the storm also came up the hill shouting out - "Who is it, who has come?"

Then they saw her; Aya, being cradled in the large arms of her father. They all stood still and quietly watched, letting them have their moment. Wyo flew over to the animals and stood with them.

The Music of the Wind began to drift through the clouds and into the atmosphere around them. Aya, still in her father's arms, closed her eyes, trying to take in what had just happened. Her heart of painful longings to come home, were being healed as she heard the music and swung around in her father's arms. The bark of her tree continued to drink in the healing oil, as it traveled up her trunk and into her branches and foliage. The forest was alive with excitement as her father finally set her down. All of the trees in the surrounding area began to blow and rustle in the wind - each one breathing into her being. She almost fell over as she felt their strength go into her. Wyo began to fly in a circle above her in the air. He had known, ever since they stayed at the old run down house, that they had entered Cordaya Valley – but he couldn't tell her. There were some things she had to find out for herself.

Wyo continued to fly full circle above them again and again. Aya looked up at her father and he reached down to pick her up once again. The depth of joy caused them both to weep for several more minutes. Many other tears were falling into the ground all around them. Some of the trees and animals were remembering the storm. Some were remembering their loved ones having been swept away. Others were crying with joy and hope that one day, they too would find some of their family members. Aya's healing of her past continued through R.T.'s strong embrace. His heart was full of joy - knowing that one of his seedlings was alive. If one lives, so will the others. They are strong, he thought to himself. He pulled Aya closer, holding her tightly in his engulfing embrace. With hope igniting in his heart, he remembered Cedra's last words echoing into the wind before she died . . .  *"They will all live!"*

Chapter X

# Cordaya Valley

## Father & Daughter

ach day since Aya had arrived, all kinds of trees, bushes
and animals came to visit with her under Cedra's massive
roots – which had become Aya's favorite resting place.
Aya and her father spent several weeks together. He listened as she
shared the stories of what she had experienced on her journey to find
home. She also told him about the letter she found within Cedra's
roots. He knew about Cedra's deformed branch and the design of
the lock. But he didn't know about the letter. He wept as he read it.
A few more tears ran down his face. "We were very close. When we
stood together, we were like one tree." He smiled then as Aya looked
at him with concern. "Don't worry little one, this letter brings me
comfort. The tears will subside."

During the next few days, he took his young seedling around to
the various lands and forests, introducing her to several of the families. Then he showed her some of the areas in the land that had been
rebuilt and restored. As the Overseer Tree of Cordaya Valley, R.T.
had pulled the community together after the Great Storm. Aya was
proud of her father. He was one of the few Elite Overseer Trees who
didn't need the permission of the Soil of the Earth to release his
roots. He was able to come and go at will and adjust his height when
needed.

Today was going to be even more special for Aya. Her father
was going to share about the history of Etainia, her family and the
Ancient Ones. On top of that – Wyo, who had found his mother,

also found out he had a younger brother and Aya was going to meet him today! *If only my brothers and sisters could be here with me,* she thought. There was no time to linger on any of those thoughts because R.T. was calling out to her from the hill below. When she heard his voice, she came out from under Cedra's roots.

"Yes, Father?"

By then, R.T. stood in front of her and lifted her up to sit on his gigantic tree branch shoulder. "Let's walk over to Wyo's Tree House and meet his little brother."

"Oh yes!" she replied as she held onto R.T. with her strong branch arms.

Before long they were at the tall Tree House that Wyo's family had built. R.T. placed Aya on the ground and stood up again to visit with Wyo's mother, Seono. Almost immediately Wyo flew down to the ground, with another little owl clinging to his back! As Wyo landed he told his younger brother to jump off. The little fluffy owl did as his big brother told him and looked up at Aya with saucer like brown eyes, that had golden flecks in them.

"Aya, this is my little brother, Eno. Eno this is my best friend, Aya." said Wyo.

Aya bent over and held out one of her branch hands. Eno looked at his brother who nodded. Eno then turned back toward Aya and held out his one of his wings and they touched. They both smiled at each other.

"I'm so glad to meet you Eno," said Aya.

The little owl quickly jumped under one of Wyo's wings and hid his face.

"He's a little shy. But wait till he gets to know you!" said Wyo.

Aya laughed and stood up. "Oh I don't mind. I'm just happy to meet him. He certainly has a kind look on his face!" Hearing that, Eno popped his head back out and looked up at Aya with a big grin on his face.

"Looks like you won him over Aya, just like you did me," said Wyo.

Eno was sitting on one of Wyo's claw feet, holding on so he wouldn't fall off as Wyo walked over to give Aya a big hug.

"He's quite a character!" said Aya watching Eno holding on for dear life.

They visited for a while longer and then heard R.T. clear his throat, indicating that it was time to leave.

Aya looked up and shouted, "Hello Seono! Wyo's little brother is amazing!" Seono leaned over her tree house railing to look at Aya. "Thank you Aya!" she replied, "I must say, he was quite a surprise, but he is such a delight! And so happy to meet his big brother!"

"I'll bet!" said Aya as her father picked her up again, preparing to go back to Cedra's roots.

They all waved their goodbyes to one another as Wyo called out, "See you in the morning Aya."

## The History of Etainia & The Curse

Aya enjoyed looking out over the beautiful valley as she sat on her father's shoulder branch while he walked through the forest. They were nearing the area where the Soil of the Earth had opened up to encase Cedra's Oil. R.T. had named it *The Healing Pool*. The healing oil mysteriously hadn't soaked into the ground and was around four feet deep. R.T. sat down on the bank near it. He bent his left knee branch and lifted Aya down from his shoulder and set her on his knee, so she could face him. It was quite a sight to see this huge Overseer Tree, with many battle scars all over his body and limbs, gently placing his daughter on his knee, so he could talk to her, face to face. Aya lovingly looked up at her father, waiting for him to speak.

"Aya," he began. "You've seen most of the land in Cordaya

Valley and have learned a lot over these last few weeks. But now, I have many other important facts and hidden secrets to share with you. It may take a few days."

Aya nodded, "I'll listen very closely father."

"Long ago many Ancient Trees had sojourned to Etainia from an Island named Gruaknoka. Over time, it became a cursed land – doomed to slowly dissolve into the sea. It is now underwater. No one here knows who cursed it or why it was cursed. Perhaps the Secrets of the Earth will reveal those truths one day. In the meantime it's important that you know these things, even if you don't know all the answers right now."

Aya thought about what he said. "Yes father, I think I understand. Willow once told me that I would hear and experience many things that wouldn't make sense to me. But that I should still pay attention to how each experience or information fits into my life. So, even though I don't understand everything about the land under the sea and the Ancient Trees, I should still listen and not discard the information. Because one day, it might fit into one of the Timely seasons of my life."

R.T. smiled, impressed at the wisdom of one so young, and proud that she was his daughter. *A true leader*, he thought to himself. "Yes Aya," he said, "that's right."

Aya smiled, waiting to hear more as her father continued.

"After it was cursed, the soil of Gruaknoka began to slowly break apart. Day by day the land dissolved, seeping into the Sea of Darkness."

Aya looked at her father. "Is that the only sea that exists in Etainia?"

"No. There are several other seas that are not dark."

Aya looked relieved as her father continued.

"The Ancient Trees had to always be on guard and keep moving themselves and their seedlings away from the edge of the Dark

Sea. But the Sea kept coming after them. It was relentless in its mission to destroy. Little by little it inched toward them until one terrible night, when the Ancient Ones had fallen into an exhausted asleep, the Sea rushed in with it's mighty waves and snatched away every one of their seedlings into its darkness."

"But father!" said Aya, "how did that happen?"

R.T. looked at her shocked face and tried to explain. "We believe it's because the seedlings little roots were tender and small - unable to grab the deeper part of the soil.  So they were uprooted swiftly. The Ancient Ones had continuously moved away from the Sea for several days, trying to get to higher ground. But there was very little land left for them to hold on to. They had gathered all of their seedings into a small circle. Then, in an effort to protect their seedlings, the parents formed another larger circle around them and dug their long roots into the ground. They didn't realize how weak and tired they were! Soon they fell into a deep exhausted sleep. When the tremendous force of the waves rushed in, the Sea easily pulled at the seedlings tiny roots and whisked them away. The seedlings probably tried to grab unto their parents, but the waves of the Dark Sea were too powerful for them."

### Tears

"Immediately the Ancient Ones woke up and saw what happened, but it was too late. They frantically waved and rustled their branches into the air, crying out into the Wind for help. In their agony, they all to cried out in unison . . . male and female alike. This painful crying went on for days. In the meantime, they didn't notice that the Sea was taking advantage of their grief by pulling away sections of land from under their roots, until hardly any land was left for the Ancient Ones to hold unto – now their lives were threatened."

Aya had tears in her eyes as she listened to her father. "It's kind of like what happened to our family. We were whisked away too," she said sadly.

R.T. looked at her tears and nodded. He wanted to comfort her, but knew he must finish telling her this part of the history. It would be needed – for the journey that she would soon take.

"I know this is difficult Aya, but there's more that you need to hear," he said.

Aya wiped the tears from her face. "Yes father, you can tell me," she said in a voice that was stronger than her years.

R.T. looked away and continued. "An interesting and strange thing happened. Hundreds of Giant Plabeian Pelicans began flying over them. Four of them would land at one time. Immediately the Ancient Ones discerned that the Giant Pelicans were not enemies. They also saw that the Pelicans had huge mouths, large enough for a tree to fit in each one. So one by one the Ancient Ones began to climb in each of the Pelican's mouths. Right after than, hundreds of extremely tall and agile Sea Horses, called the Shuanni, came racing across the top of the Dark Sea, shouting out and commanding the Ancient Ones to prepare to climb on before the sea overtook them! Each Sea Horse was able to carry two trees on it's back. Some of the older Ancient Trees fell and couldn't get back up. There was so much commotion, mixed in with the grief of losing their children that they were left behind. Several of the weaker trees simply gave up. Then, just as the Dark Sea was pulling back, preparing to send it's last devouring wave – Pelicans and Sea Horses took off! One group flying in the air and the other group riding through the water! Several trees looked back and watched as the land of Gruaknoka disappeared under the Dark Sea. The Giant Plabeian Pelicans and the Shuanni Sea Horses carried the Ancient Trees far and deep into a new unclaimed land. As the Ancient Tree's roots touched the soil, they fell down, weeping."

Aya touched her father's face so he would look at her and asked, "Did they cry because they lost their children?"

R.T. took her hand in both of his." Yes Aya, that was one reason. But they also cried because they had been given another chance to start over. They knew that the Plabeian Pelicans and Shuanni Sea Horses were sent to save them. That gave them hope. The Ancient Ones knew, without a doubt, that they were destined to establish the land that they were on – as their land, naming it Etainia.

"I guess it's like what I felt after I read mother's letter to me," said Aya.

"What was it you felt Aya?" asked R.T.

"Well, I felt that even in death, mother was still giving life. And now, after hearing what you said, I think that the Ancient Ones were determined to find life again, even though the little seedlings died. That's what I felt."

Again, R.T. was astonished at Aya's ability to perceive into the Unseen World.

"Yes, it's something like that. You are very wise Aya." R.T. looked up into the sky saying, "It can be sad - this thing we call death, but life will always immerge, if we look for it."

Aya sighed, "I'm finding out it's not always fun to be wise, is it father?"

R.T. smiled as he shook his head side to side.

"Where did the Pelicans and Sea Horses go after they brought the Ancient Ones to Etainia?" she asked.

"No one really knows Aya, they disappeared as quickly as they came. What we do know is that all of the Ancient male and female trees of that time were honorable, with noble causes. Once they recovered from the trauma and loss, they gathered together to discuss what to do next – agreeing to split up in order to claim all of the undiscovered lands and waters in Etainia."

*The Travelers*

"Several male and female trees of each species traveled to different territories. Once they claimed a certain area, they named it and then appointed an Overseer Tree to guide and protect the land and those who came to live on it. Soon animals, bushes, and trees began to come, desiring to settle on some of the territories – the land began to flourish and grow. Soon, the Ancient Overseers were the ones who ruled all of Etainia. And they did it with nobility and integrity. Although Etainia had it's usual problems, there was peace throughout the land."

R.T. looked up as the sun went down, lifting Aya off his knee and setting her on the ground. "I've given you a lot of information in a short amount of time Aya. Let's get you off to bed."

Aya tugged at his arm as he placed her on the ground saying, "But father, I'm really interested! I want to know more!"

R.T. grinned and stood up to stretch. "Well, I'm glad, but I'm getting kind of tired too. I'll tell you the rest tomorrow afternoon. I promise."

Aya waited for him to pick her up and put her on his shoulder. As he did she quietly said, "All right father, I'll be patient."

He walked back to Cedra's roots and knelt down as he watched Aya go underneath.

"Why don't you spend the morning exploring some other areas of Cordaya Valley with Wyo and his little brother Eno?"

Aya yawned. "Yes, I'd like that, but don't forget, you promised to finish telling me the stories about the Ancient Ones!"

He chuckled, "Don't worry. I'll pick you up in the afternoon and tell you the rest of the history."

Satisfied, Aya turned over and fell asleep.

As he stood back up he leaned against one of Cedra's huge roots and gazed upon his daughter in her restful state. "Rest now little one," he said as he turned and walked back down the hill.

## The Legacy

Aya woke up excited! ! After hearing all that her father had shared she now had a brand new perspective on her life. She was amazed at the many incredible events that took place, even before she was born. *Oh yes, I'm going to see Wyo again today!* She quickly rose and headed out toward his tree house.

Wyo was just as excited as she was to get together. The sun had barely risen as they both went on their way to explore many other communities in the valley. She laughed and cried as she met new animals, trees and bushes. Several of them shared about the losses they had experienced in the Great Storm and yet were still grateful that she was able to return home to R.T. and Cordaya Valley. She was surprised that many of them had already heard some of the stories about her travels to find Cordaya Valley.

Before long, it was noon - and as wonderful as it was visiting with several of the smaller communities, Aya was anxious to hear the rest of the stories about the Ancient Ones and her family lineage. It was early afternoon when Aya left Wyo at his tree house and returned to Cedra's roots to meet her father. While walking, she pondered over the vast amount of information her father had been revealing to her, hoping she could remember it all.

Soon R.T. came up hill. "Come on little one. Let's take a walk." He gently placed Aya on his left shoulder and began walking into another area of Cordaya Valley.

"Let's see," he said, "where did I leave off?"

Aya affectionately patted his shoulder. "You know father - The Ancient Ones ruled over Etainia."

"Oh yes," he said somberly while remembering. "When the Ancient Ones ruled over Etainia, there was peace for many years. Over time, many of the Ancient Overseers died of old age or were destroyed by the elements. Then, new leadership came into the land. But several of the new leaders hadn't been properly trained and they weren't as watchful as the Ancient Ones. As a result strange and evil trees began to invade some of the territories in Etainia and overtake territories – often making prisoners out of the trees and creatures that lived in them."

Soon R.T. came upon a stream and stood watching the running water for a while. "It only takes a few to destroy something, when it's not protected." Then he sat down on the edge of the bank and once again placed Aya on his knee. "Of course," he continued, "it only takes a few to build something back up. It's important to learn lessons from whatever good or evil things happen and then work together!"

Aya looked up at him. "Like Cordaya Valley?"

"Yes," he replied, "like Cordaya Valley."

Aya remembered something and her eyes lit up as she spoke it out.

"I met a tree once named Xeraino. It had all kinds of birds on it. It burned one of my branches to teach me a lesson. See?" Aya held up her burnt tree branch and waved it back and forth front of her father's face.

He looked it over and said, "That tree wasn't evil. That tree was a warning tree. He appears to seedlings when they are young and need direction. You must have been starting out on a journey."

"Yes," Aya said, "Wyo and I had just left the Land of Valorous." R.T. looked tenderly at his little wise seedling.

"And did you learn a lesson from Xeraino?" he asked.

"Oh yes father, but I haven't had to use the singed branch yet," she replied.

"You will," he said. "Probably sooner than you think."

Aya looked at him with a questioning expression on her face.

"You see Aya, you were born into the Royal Tree Family of Ancient Cedar Trees."

Aya's eyes grew large and her mouth fell open. R.T. reached over and gently closed it as he continued.

"My name, R.T. stands for Royal Tree. I was instructed as a young seedling to travel to the north side of Etainia. I wasn't sure which land would accept me. When I saw your mother Cedra, I immediately fell in love. I deeply hoped that my Destiny Land would be in Cordaya Valley and that Cedra and I would be together. The moment I saw her I wanted her as my companion and the mother of my seedlings. I found out later that she was waiting for me. How she knew we were to be connected and bear seedlings together, I don't know. Evidently, the Soil of the Earth and the Sun of Splendor agreed because they sealed our unity of oneness and positions in Cordaya Valley." Aya once again felt tears well up in her eyes as she listened to the beautiful story of her parents and how they met.

R.T. placed his large branch hands on her small, yet strong shoulders. "Aya," he said, looking directly into her clear blue eyes. "You have Ancient Royal Ancestors from both your mother's heritage and mine. Because of this, many evil forces attempted to destroy Cordaya Valley and prevent your births. The evil is relentless and will continually try to destroy you and your siblings – because of the powerful future that resides in each one of you. They want to keep you from fulfilling your purposes and destinies. They will go after your friends if needed - to get to you. But I am confident in you. You know how to persevere. You don't give up easily. You proved that on your journey to find Cordaya Valley. You learned how to be patient and how to trust when you fell into the ditch. In the Battle at the Snap-Dragon Flower Field you faced fear and gave of yourself, without expecting anything back. You learned how to take counsel through Willow. Aya, you are as ready as you can be for another journey you will need to take."

Aya looked down at Cordaya Valley. She was sad, but not totally surprised that he was sending her on another journey. Over the past few weeks, he had been intensely teaching her and sharing many hidden secrets. Yesterday and now today, he was revealing an even fuller picture of her family's background and ancestry. Somehow she knew that there was more for her to do. She felt ready.

"I can't go with you Aya," he said. "I must remain here and continue building up and protecting Cordaya Valley. Other lands and Overseers also depend on me. Although this land is smaller than some, Cordaya Valley has the richest and most fertile soil in Etainia. Over a thousand species of noble and honorable trees and seedlings now live here – many of the seedlings will soon begin their journey to search for their Destiny Land, just as your mother and I once did. Aya, tomorrow I will be sending you off to search for your brothers and sisters. Time has spoken to me. You must prepare to leave now. Things will happen very quickly in the morning before I send you off."

Aya jumped up quickly and stood on her father's knee, holding out her branch arms so he would lift her up. "Oh father, I'm honored to do this, not only for you and mother, but also for myself." R.T. lifted her up and she began planting kisses all over his face. Relieved that Aya received the news so well, he hugged her. "I'll make sure you are well equipped. You won't be traveling alone. Wyo will go with you. His mother agreed to send him." Aya started kissing her father's face all over again in happiness with the news of her friend joining her on this honorable and important quest.

As the Dawn began to envelope them, R.T. stood up. "Let's get you back to Cedra. You'll need a good nights rest." He set her up on his shoulder and began to walk up the hill toward Cedra's massive roots.

"I'm very excited father, I hope I can get to sleep!" she said as her father kissed her goodnight and placed her under Cedra's roots.

"Don't worry little one, sleep will come quickly and prepare you for the day." He stood outside for a moment, next to Cedra's roots, watching over his strong little seedling as she fell into a restful sleep.

# Chapter XI

# The Misty Vision, The Oil, & The Proclamation.

"Wake up, wake up Aya!!!" Aya opened sleepy eyes to see Eno flapping his wings with Wyo standing nearby.

She laughed and laughed. "Boy, are you two related or what? Wyo was always flapping his wings at me!"

Wyo chuckled, "Yes, and I usually had to wake you up too!!!" Fully awake, Aya sat up and visited with Wyo and his little brother for several moments. Soon they heard chattering outside of Cedra's roots. As they came out they saw several animals, trees, and bushes gathering. They were all standing in a half circle in front of Cedra. The morning sun was barely peeking out.

"Good Morning Aya!" a group of squirrels shouted out to her. Several baby rabbits hopped over to look at her and then scampered away as she moved toward them. R.T. came toward Aya with a gentle but serious look on his face. "Time has arrived little one. We must move now."

He lifted her up, placing her in a standing position on a large seven-foot boulder that was several feet away from him. He adjusted his height to a lower level for the occasion that was about to happen. She looked to her left and noticed that oil was beginning to slowly drip down Cedra's roots. The group behind her was still standing. She looked up at her father and her heart began to race in anticipation. She felt very proud to be his seedling. He was so majestic standing before her. *Gosh,* she thought, *that's my father . . . my father.*

"Good Morning everyone!" said R.T. "As you all know, we're sending Aya on a quest to search for her brothers and sisters. Time has spoken. I've invited those of you who are mature in Wisdom, young and old, to witness this event and give her your support. During the Great Storm Aya was not able to complete the declaration of her name into the atmosphere or to see her Misty Vision. Before we send her off, this must take place. I want everyone to now keep silent." Everyone immediately stopped moving around and became very still.

R.T. stood several feet away from Aya as he opened up her Naming Scroll. His voice reverberated into the forest as he spoke. "5th born female seedling . . . your name is Aya – Leader to Many!"

He handed the Scroll to Aya who repeated what her father had said, *"I am Aya, the 5th born seedling. My name means Leader to Many!"*

Once she spoke out her name, the sound of her voice penetrated into the elements that surrounded her and traveled up into the atmosphere. As she opened her Scroll a red transparent Misty Vision appeared before her, waving in the air. In the vision Aya caught a glimpse of her future. First she saw herself on a journey, and then she saw herself standing strong and tall, with full branches. She saw flecks of red and gold on her roots. In the vision she saw herself leading many other tree seedlings. Several animals were with her. Her deformed branch was no longer deformed. It was shaped like a staff, camouflaged with lush foliage. The community let out a loud sound of exclamation. Although they weren't allowed to see everything that Aya saw - their thoughts came into agreement with what they did see.

## Colors Speak

Colors of red and gold then began to wisp around the Misty Vision Scroll. Out of the Colors came musical sounds, ever so gently. The Colors then whispered, "Aya. Speak Now." Aya knew how to respond and what words to say.

"I know my name. I hear the music. I see the vision. I now decree that I will go into my future with honor, truth, courage, kindness and love."

This time, instead of the roar of a storm approaching the valley, there was a roar of excitement from the close-knit group standing behind her. Shouts of joy rang into the air. Two of the elder trees came forward and lifted her up, as hundreds of trusted bushes, trees, animals and flowers gathered around her - shouting and singing!

R.T. watched from a distance, knowing that this affirmation and agreement was necessary for Aya *and* for the community. He allowed it to go on for several more minutes and then called out, "Everyone! Look over here!"

They stopped and looked at R.T. who simply said, "Time has arrived."

They all said their joyful and tearful goodbyes to Aya and Wyo, and then quickly disbursed to their homes. Eno, who had been privileged to stand with his brother, reached up to hug him goodbye and swiftly flew home with his mother Seono.

The two elder trees gently placed Aya back onto the boulder in front of her father, who nodded at them as they turned to leave. Soon it was very still and very quiet. Aya looked to her right and saw a colorful bird fly over and settle on a tree several feet away from her. "It's the Toucan Seer!" she gasped.

R.T. looked at Wyo, who then flew over to sit on the boulder near Aya.

"Aya, walk with me now to the Pool of Oil," said R.T. Wyo and the Toucan Seer stayed where they were as Aya walked with her father toward the pool. As they stood in front of it R.T. spoke. "This pool holds the Oil of Healing that was released from Cedra when you came back home and walked under her roots. Step into the center of the Oil now."

Aya stepped in and stood in the middle of the Pool of Oil. Immediately it began to seep into her roots. The Sun of Splendor broke through the clouds and shone his Amber light over her. She let her head drop head back. She closed her eyes, basking in the warmth of the Amber Rays of Light, as the Oil traveled upward into her trunk, strengthening her. When the efficient amount of time had passed, R.T. called her to come out.

"You won't always see the Oil on the outside of you. But when needed, the Oil will release itself to travel throughout your entire body and replenish your strength."

She followed R.T. back up the small hill toward Cedra. Dripping with Oil, Aya was already feeling strengthened and fortified.

R.T. lifted Aya back up onto the boulder. Wyo quickly flew over and settled on her right branch shoulder. They both looked at R.T. expectantly.

"Squeegie, you can come out now." R.T. said.

Running out from behind a bush near the Toucan Seer, came Squeegie, the rambunctious squirrel who had scampered through Cedra's and R.T. branches before the seedlings were born. Aya remembered him from her youth.

As he jumped into her arms she shouted, "Squeegie!"

R.T. smiled. "Yes, we're sending Squeegie with you. He's grown into a very wise and inventive squirrel and will be a great help to you." As Squeegie climbed up and sat on her left shoulder, R.T. handed Aya a map and her small pouch that still had her other treasures in it.

"The Neoflight birds and others who have traveled through some of the areas of Etainia, gathered together with me and we formed a map. Not all of the lands are shown on it yet. But at least it will give you an idea of where you are at times. There are still many unknown lands yet to be found in and around Etainia. As you discover some of them – and you surely will – make notes on the map inside. Now hide it."

"Yes father," said Aya. She put the map into the pouch and hid it within one of her branches. "Who are the Neoflight Birds, will I see them?"

"They are small white birds with green eyes and short golden beaks. Their black and white feathers are like silk. They are Messenger birds – owned by no one. They come and go as they see fit. They are birds of integrity and work for good, not evil. If they come to you, stop whatever you are doing and listen to every word they have to say."

Aya was amazed at this information. "I will father. I will listen very carefully."

"Another thing that is extremely important. You must come back within a year, even if you have found no one. Do you understand?"

Aya looked at him, "No! I don't understand. I'm going on this journey to find my siblings. How can I come back without them?"

Her father looked at her sternly, "Aya, you must do as I say. You don't know how Time will weave itself into your journey. Many hidden truths and hidden lies are out there. Trust what I say. Once you leave the borders of Cordaya Valley, word will spread quickly about your quest. Be watchful and listen to the signs! Many traps will be set by unseen enemies."

Aya took to heart what her father was saying. "All right father, I'll do as you say, even through I don't understand the reasoning behind it."

He briefly smiled and continued, "Don't worry, you'll also discover many friends that will help you." He looked at the three of them as they stood on the huge boulder, listening intently to his instructions. There was Aya, standing tall and straight with Squeegie sitting on left shoulder and Wyo on her right. It took every ounce of strength within R.T. not to hold her tight and keep her at home.

The Toucan Seer flew into the air and circled over the three travelers, speaking a loud, strong proclamation over Aya:

"The staff you saw in your vision will assist you. Look for the flowers to bloom. The Blue Renegade Butterflies will guide you. Listen to their colors speak. There will be Stones that cry out to you, heed their warnings. Rest, even when you think you don't need it. Come home when Time speaks to you. You will know. Go now Aya, Leader of Many. Move into your future and bring others into theirs."

As a red Feather floated down, Aya reached out her hand to catch it. The moment the Feather touched her branch hand; the color red reminded Aya of the vision and the Courage and Strength that she already had found within herself. The Feather, having fulfilled its purpose within Aya's mind, found its way back to the Toucan Seer – who sat in a nearby tree.

After this moment transpired R.T. spoke. "Aya, never forget where you come from. I seal all of the words and proclamations that have been imparted into your life since you arrived in Cordaya Valley. I now send you on a journey into known and unknown lands with your two loyal companions, to find your siblings and bring them home."

He reached over and embraced Aya, holding her tight.

"I love you father," she said.

"I love you too Aya."

They stood embracing each other for a moment before he lifted her up and set her on the ground. Squeegie jumped down, run-ahead of her as Wyo flew past him. Then, they both stopped ...enly and stared back at Aya, excitedly waiting to begin their ...rney.

Aya turned abruptly away from her father, knowing that if she didn't, she would break down and cry. She caught up with Wyo and Squeegie. The three of them walked through Cedra's roots and began going down the same hill that Aya had climbed up on, when she came back home. As they walked Aya looked straight ahead and said to Wyo, "Should I turn back and wave to my father? Would that be O.K.? I don't want him to think I'm being childish."

Wyo, who was once again perched on her shoulder said, "He won't think that Aya."

Feeling very vulnerable, R.T. watched the three of them walking under Cedra's roots; hoping Aya would turn and wave to him. When she did, his heart leapt as he waved back.

"He waved back Wyo, I think he was happy that I waved to him," Aya said as she turned once again toward the direction they were walking.

"I have no doubt about that," said Wyo.

R.T. continued to watch Aya. Suddenly he felt terribly alone. Aya had been home for such a short while and here he was, sending her off to places that even he had never gone to before.

"It's so hard to let her go," he said out loud.

Still sitting in the tree across the way, was the Toucan Seer. "Yes R.T.," she said in a quiet, yet firm voice. "But Aya is strong and this is the way it must be done."

When the last top of Aya's branches had disappeared over the hill, R.T. took a deep breath, closed his eyes and said, "I know."